THE LAST FLEET

FOG OF WAR

THE LAST FLEET
BOOK 3

JOSHUA TREE

PROLOGUE

The fleet headquarters was housed in the oldest habitat in the solar system, which had been expanded innumerable times since its founding three hundred years ago as a tiny research station. It looked like the ugly twin of its sister habitat, Remus, the seat of the nearly omnipotent Jupiter Bank. Where Remus gleamed and was surrounded by a luminous shell from which Duroglass starscrapers protruded from the upper end cap like the spines of a hedgehog, Romulus was a marred cocoon. Around its central axis rotated a pot-bellied cylinder, littered with replicas and mismatched modules that had been added over the centuries. Between them, the barrels of powerful guns jutted into space. Dozens of openings in this dark dragon's lair served the endless stream of coming and going shuttles that frequented between the hundreds of ships of Marquandt's fleets and headquarters.

It took Nancy less than half an hour to get from the docks to the Fleet Admiral's quarters. She was excited but determined to be professional. After all, this was just an errand, and she worked daily with the highest-ranking officials in the Star Empire, many of whom she even had to transfer. However, she had never felt particularly comfortable around fleet personnel. She was uncomfortable with the whole microcosm of the military, perhaps because she had never been part of it and viewed it like some sort of violent black box.

When she arrived in front of the unadorned steel bulkhead, where a holosign announced that 'Fleet Admiral Dain Marquandt, High Lord' resided there, she straightened and put her index finger on the bell symbol of the control panel. Sometimes she wished her husband, Timothy, could see her in all that she did every day and who she met. In weak moments, she disliked her job because all the high-level personalities made her nervous; in others, she was proud of how far she had come from a lowly office worker.

The bulkhead moved upward into its socket, and she stepped into the anteroom of the quarters, where two assistants sat at minimalist desks. One seemed engrossed in a VR environment, whispering instructions to himself so fast she couldn't understand a word.

The other, a young fellow in a commander's tailored uniform, greeted her with a noncommittal smile and held out his hand.

"Nancy...?"

"Just Nancy," she interrupted him with a wink, trying to shake off some of her nervousness. She knew this assignment was highly unusual for her master and that she was a pawn in their chess game. A simple errand, and yet it made her nervous not knowing why her move was important, what strategy it belonged to.

"Of course," the commander said, pointing to the nearest door, which had an old-fashioned handle and was

The last Fleet

painted in a wooden look. "The Admiral is already waiting for you."

"Thank you." She had regained her demeanor and gave him a businesslike nod. Just another day at work.

That impression immediately shattered as she entered Marquandt's quarters. He was seated on an uncomfortable-looking sofa, along with Chief of Staff Albius and Senate Vice President Darian Bonjarewski, a close associate of the late Varilla Usatami.

"Nancy," Marquandt greeted them with a humorless smile, gesturing to his other guests. "I'm sure you already know Marius and Darian."

She was briefly surprised when he called them both by their first names in her presence, but didn't let on and nodded politely. The Admiral from Wall Sector Delta was one of the few members of the Admiral's Council she had never met in person. He looked more gaunt than in the feeds, and his hair was grayer. She was aware that he was not exactly considered the most affable and approachable of admirals, but his narrow mouth with the corners of his mouth pulled down seemed to express even more seriousness. In her eyes, he looked like someone with a heavy burden on his shoulders, the weight of which had robbed him of the ability to smile. The sparse furnishings also matched this. The was no luxury to be seen, except for all the space there was in the quarters. There wasn't even a window with a view of Jupiter, although he certainly would have been entitled to it in his position.

"Of course. Admiral, Vice President," she greeted the two guests and shook their hands one by one. Marquandt made no move to offer her his hand, instead gesturing to an empty seat.

"Please, sit down."

She wanted to protest, to say that she had only two

3

sentences to say and turn on her heel again, but the commanding manner with which he spoke had already made her body obey.

"So," Marquandt continued, folding his hands in his lap. When he spoke, there was no mockery in his voice. More like curiosity. "What can I do for the secretary of the honorable First Secretary of State?"

"Lord Darishma sent me to deliver a personal message to you." Nancy felt her hands grow clammy, but forced herself to keep them very still in her lap. The very thought of the words she had come here to speak made her nervous.

"Well?" Marquandt raised one of his mottled gray eyebrows, which formed thin lines under his high forehead. He unfolded his hands. "I'm all ears."

"I... I don't mean to be rude." She swallowed and avoided looking toward the chief of staff and the vice president who had taken over the official duties of his murdered superiors. "But the words are for you alone, Admiral."

"Unfortunately, there's no way to ask these two gentlemen to leave." Marquandt did not sound as if he particularly regretted this circumstance. "Our schedules are extremely tight, I think you understand."

"Of course," Nancy returned automatically, not knowing what to do.

"I don't suppose these are highly confidential matters. Your decision. But make it quickly, because as I'm sure you've been following in the feeds, there's a lot of work to do."

She took a deep breath, then decided to get it over with, "The First Secretary sends word that he knows, and so does the Network."

The last Fleet

If Marquandt was surprised by the words, he didn't let on. He merely raised a brow and looked to his guests.

"The Network?" he asked, but Albius and Bonjarewski merely shook their heads.

The older admiral grumbled, "Darishma must think he's particularly clever. He's just trying to drive you crazy."

"He knows?" asked Bonjarewski, sounding alarmed.

Nancy wanted to get up and leave, but she somehow sensed that wasn't possible. At an audience like this, you didn't just leave, you were dismissed.

"Of course he does." Marquandt waved it off. "Makuba was a vulnerability we were aware of, and since Rogoshin's passing we've been expecting it. This doesn't change anything."

"What if this reference to an ominous *Network* is not a bluff?" the parliamentary speaker wanted to know. He was a small man with a paunch, which was tantamount to a statement given today's possibilities for genetic optimization. His face was that of a haggard bureaucrat with no joy in life.

"It is irrelevant. What is happening now cannot be stopped."

"That still leaves Darishma, that lowborn son of a bitch," Admiral Albius cut in again.

At the disrespectful mention of her boss, Nancy winced inwardly. Bonjarewski scowled at the derogatory mention in reference to Darishma's standing. He was a commoner.

I'm still here! she thought.

"Yes. He can become a problem. He's clever and well-connected." Marquandt put his fingertips together and seemed lost in thought.

"We'll get him to make mistakes," Albius suggested,

tapping his wrist terminal. "A headless opponent is no longer an opponent."

Opponent? The uneasy feeling in Nancy's stomach area grew more oppressive. These men should not be saying all this in front of her. She should have been long gone by now. Behind her, the door opened and closed again, but she did not turn to look. Instead, she tried not to move at all, so as not to attract anyone's attention, even though she was sitting right in the middle.

It became quiet for a moment, and the three men looked in her direction with different expressions. Marquandt's mouth twisted disapprovingly, Albius looked impatient, and Bonjarewski swallowed.

Nancy was about to ask if she could leave when she felt a fine tugging on her neck that became a sharp pain, as if from a cut, only deeper and more prolonged.

Reflexively, she jerked her hands up and felt the area, only to feel a fine wire pulling tighter and tighter, cutting off her air. Her eyes began to swell, along with her entire head. She wanted to protest, to call for help, but she could not get out more than a gasp while hands that were far too strong took her life.

A cleaning bot on six legs climbed up her and extended a suction proboscis to suck the blood that ran from her throat. The cold casualness of the machine was horrifying.

"This is cruel," Marquandt complained.

"It's necessary. If she doesn't show up again, the son of a bitch will get nervous and make a mistake. That's all we need," the chief of staff objected, turning away from her.

Nancy could barely see, hearing the men only as if through water. Their voices blurred together. But she didn't want to listen, wanted to think of Timothy in her last moments.

"It would have been quicker. But this is how it is now. Is Congress assembled and prepared?"

"Yes. Most of the senators and lords have already arrived."

"This doesn't change anything. We will proceed."

1
JANUS

"Still nothing, Dorothy?" asked Janus for the third time now of his second secretary, who had filled in for Nancy in her absence in the outer office.

"Sorry, my lord."

"Stand by." With that, he disconnected and pulled his jacket off the chair. He needed to speak with the Emperor, since the Navy could confirm whether Nancy's ship had docked at the Romulus habitat hours ago but was still in the docks. He trusted the pilot, Lieutenant Greer - even after she had assured him that her guest had not reported back. His other contacts on Romulus could not help him either. It was as if his assistant had been swallowed up by the station.

He postponed the thought of contacting Marquandt's office and asking about her whereabouts until later. The best thing to do now was not to make a fuss and keep things quiet. If he overreacted and Nancy reappeared, he would just look foolish and play into Marquandt's hands.

Fortunately, the Emperor was currently in his dressing room between appointments with Zara Vance, the head of the New York Arc Police, and Sirius Falkland, who was organizing the funeral service for Usatami. He passed by the guardsmen and two-tiered security areas before encountering Haeron II among his massive closets.

"I've never liked brocade," he said, giving Janus a friendly nod. "All that frivolity for the cameras, yet the fabric is heavy and scratchy. Shouldn't a modern ruler wear a suit?"

"It's all about representation, Your Majesty. The people like the distinction, the grandeur, even desire it." Janus folded his hands behind his back, as he was always wont to do to contain impatience and fidgeting.

"The people want to make a reality show out of the monarchy. That's the way it's always been."

"And the monarchy is profiting from it."

"With itchy necks and tense shoulders," the Emperor grumbled, closing the brooch that held the red and gold cloak. He looked at Janus and sighed. "So, what can I do for you, my dear?"

"It's about Marquandt."

"Of course. By now, do you have the evidence so I can have him removed?"

"No. Not directly."

The ruler's gaze became searching. "But you know something."

"Yes," he admitted with a sigh, "I know that Marquandt bribed a high-ranking IIA agent to cover tracks for him in the fleet archives. I know he's in cahoots with a man named Dimitri Rogoshin from Warfield and making dalliances with Yokatami. It all has something to do with the Seed Traverse, probably with Yokatami's own Seed World."

The last Fleet

"If you know all this, why don't you have any proof?"

"My source has informed me but has not given me the data."

"Why not?"

"The price was too high."

The Emperor eyed him and finally nodded. "I understand. I trust you to make the right decisions. That is why you are my First Secretary of State."

"In that case, Your Majesty, I have a request," Janus said.

"Ah." Haeron II smiled, but there was no joy in it. Not since Magnus's death. "So, we come to the reason for your visit."

"It is obvious that Marquandt is playing some secret game, and Andal's destruction must have something to do with it. If he would go that far, I do not know where his limit is," Janus said. "He has the largest force in the system right now."

"Any force in the Star Empire is *my* force, Janus." The Emperor sat down on a gold-trimmed stool and began to put on his gold-trimmed boots. "Even a busy fleet admiral knows that." he said.

"That is correct, but the Wall Sector units are extremely conspiratorial, as you know. And a major combat unit committing a crime like the one in Andal with him is another matter entirely. Every officer down to the recruit will know that they tied their fate closely to that of their commander when the order was given to isolate the system and leave them all to die. We must not make the mistake of underestimating our enemies."

"Enemies? Are we there already?"

"I must fear the worst." Janus straightened his shoulders and held his master's gaze. "That is my job."

"Even if Marquandt is blinded by too much ambition,

he is still in Sol. That system is a fortress, and even five Wall Fleets - dangerous though they are - could not take Terra. We would crush him and his followers, and he knows it." Haeron II paused, and his expression reflected no pleasure at this notion. "And," he added, "the soldiers under his command know that, too. To flee from the Never and pay a high price for it is one thing. To attack the heart of the Star Empire and commit treason is quite another."

"You are right about that, Your Majesty," Janus agreed with him. "At the same time, we should not underestimate Marquandt. He has been moving funds and ships for the last few years, and he may know more about the Orb than we do, which would be a crime in itself. If Gavin Andal is correct in his accusations, and he looks considerably more credible and loyal at the moment, then we are dealing with someone who has been playing a game in the shadows for months, perhaps years. Can we really afford to underestimate an admiral like that?"

"As you know, I abhor rhetorical questions," the Emperor returned, not unkindly. "But you are right. We should not be naive. So, what do you propose?"

"Your plan so far is a good one, Your Majesty. Marquandt will be given the title of commander of the Home Fleet and will be forced to stay close to you. We will have him watched and narrow his breathing space, isolate him from his eyes and ears. It is well within your power to assign him his staff officers and administrators, even though he will see it as an affront. If we mix in some IIA agents handpicked by Juao, chances are we'll catch on should Marquandt make contact with anyone who raises questions."

"I hear a but in there."

The last Fleet

Janus sighed. "Yes. I am concerned about the funeral service for Usatami."

"Because you weren't at the planning meeting for the flight path," the Emperor surmised, nodding thoughtfully. "I understand that. I've already decided that you're going to set it."

"I beg your pardon?" he asked, taken aback, forgetting his manners in his surprise. "Please excuse me, Your Majesty. But..."

"What is it, my dear Janus? Are you surprised that I trust you? That would hurt me a little."

"No, it's just ..." The tesponsibility. "Thank you, master."

Haeron II stood up and waved it off. Then he stepped in front of the mirror and checked the fit of his formal uniform, with its starched shoulders and brocade coat that made it look even broader.

"What do you think?"

"Very stately, Your Majesty."

"What do you really think?" the Emperor prompted, giving him an expectant look over the mirror.

"You look like a Christmas tree. The Senate and the audience will love it."

"Ha!" the ruler of mankind laughed loudly, smirking before turning to Janus and patting him on the shoulder. "Here he is at last, the one I made my right-hand man. Christmas tree! A tree could not itch any more than this dreadful ornament from a thousand years ago. I feel like I am attending a costume party every time, where I am the only one who's followed the dress guidelines, and then I look silly."

"With the difference that everyone who sees you would wish they were wearing the same thing," Janus pointed out.

13

"If only they knew," Haeron II sighed and turned to leave. Janus stepped up beside him and together they walked through the vast office to the door. Behind them, Terra shone like a sparkling blue jewel. "One more thing."

"Anything you wish, Your Majesty."

"Elayne. I think she's taken off for the civilian sectors again."

"Because of Peraia?" asked Janus anxiously.

"I cannot see why else. I do not want to send agents or my guardsmen after her again. She has only just left her chambers."

"Elayne is extremely clever, Your Majesty. She will not put herself in danger recklessly."

"That may be true, but you know there have been sporadic happenings in the last twenty-four hours," Haeron II reminded him, and his brows furrowed into a worried expression. "I know she is no longer a child, and that these protesters aren't many, but I'm still worried. I would rather she not be alone at this time."

Janus thought of Nancy and a heaviness settled in his stomach.

"You are right, Your Majesty. I will take care of it."

"Good, she probably loves you more than me anyway." The Emperor laughed without pleasure and patted him on the shoulder. "Bring her here afterwards, will you?"

"She will not accompany you to the Senate?" asked Janus in surprise.

"No." Haeron II shook his head and paused before the heavy double door. To the two guardsmen of his bodyguard, who were about to take the handles with their hands, he signaled with a wave to pause. They obediently bowed their heads. "She will remain here. Elayne is my last remaining heir now, and I do not think we should travel anywhere together anymore. The risk is just too great."

"I understand."

"Bring her here. If she spent half as much time preparing to take office as she spends inflicting pain on herself searching for Peraia, I would sleep considerably more soundly," Haeron II found.

"I will find her, Your Majesty."

"Good, select my pilot and security team and bring the flight path when we leave. Five hours."

"Of course."

In the anteroom, Janus bid farewell to the Emperor, who apparently had an appointment to speak with his assistants, as they did at least once every day. Sometimes he felt infinitely sorry for the man, watching him struggle to be someone who was approachable and not completely withdrawn. Of course, this was not possible, and he had to fail because no one could see the human Haeron II who was behind the Emperor. He was a walking projection screen who worked solely through his office, and how difficult that might be Janus could not even imagine. At the same time, his master was not immune to what he himself feared most - losing touch with that part of his empire that *truly* comprised it, beyond all the war machinery and institutions that had created a perfect cogwheel of interlocking rule and control - its inhabitants. This had been demonstrated not least by the use of the orbital defense platform with which Janus's enemies had orchestrated to get rid of him - and he did not know who else but Marquandt was behind it -. In order to protect his First Secretary of State, Haeron II had agreed to melt half a block to glass. Because he could do it and had been of the opinion that he had to.

That the commander in charge of the platform was now sitting in a holding cell awaiting execution for exceeding his operational authority and wantonly destroying half the interstate was far from justice. Those lost would not be brought back by any of this.

"Dorothy," he called to his secretary.

"My lord?"

"Put together a team of undercover guardsmen for me. I need to get out of the Imperial sector and look for someone. As inconspicuously as possible, please." He pondered. "And prepare my special wardrobe."

"Are you expecting trouble, my lord?"

"I always expect trouble." He disconnected and turned back toward his own private quarters. His office was only five minutes away and in close proximity - a decidedly more private place with all the eyes and ears always on him. But he was expected to prepare to depart for Saturn, so he gave his shadows what they were waiting for. It was probably the safest thing to do at the moment.

His guard of ten guardsmen accompanied him as he left the emperor's area, making sure that the corridors in front of him emptied quickly. Outside his quarters, which were directly opposite in the main corridor, the artery of the *Rubov* orbital ring, he asked his bodyguards to wait for him until it was time to leave. Once inside, he found his form-fitting body armor already on his bed, a two-millimeter-thin second skin of mono-bonded nanite fabric, over which he pulled one of his civilian coverings - a jacket of synthetic leather with tasteful but boring digi colors and a pair of denim pants.

He then left his quarters through the secret exit behind the bookcase and, using imperial codes, ordered the computer system to continue displaying his vital signs as if he never left. Through the narrow tunnel, past the many hoses and cables that rushed and gurgled, he reached the ladder. He climbed down three levels until he finally reached the offices of the orbital administration

The last Fleet

through another secret door in the restrooms of the residents' registration department. Because of the late hour, no second glances were given to him by the few bureaucrats still at work. Just a normal bore who had finished work and left his suit in the office.

His bodyguards - in this case rather aides - were waiting for him at the elevators. They wore various civilian clothes and were of different statures: slim, stocky, tall, short, bald, curly haired, older, younger. They belonged to the guardsmen specializing in undercover operations, who could blend into any crowd because they did not look at first (or second) glance like the heavily armored fighting machines they were.

"My lord," they greeted him one by one as they were in the multidirectional elevator and on their way to the civilian sector. One of the guardsmen had turned off the car's surveillance sensors.

"Good evening, gentlemen." He shook their hands one by one. Unusual for a nobleman toward his soldiers, but not for Janus. Since they did not seem surprised, but had the beginnings of smiles on their lips, he assumed they had worked with him before. He could not recognize any of them, so they were apparently doing their job very well.

"Trigger, Maxwell, Charly, Deezer," one of them, Maxwell, introduced them. Aliases.

"Sunaj," Janus said. "For this mission."

"Backwards. Clever," Charly, the short and squat one, remarked wryly. He looked like a dwarf with a big appetite. Nothing about him radiated the danger he was. Like any elite guard in the Emperor's personal guard, however, he was more cyborg than human and capable of killing an entire company of unmodified soldiers.

"The Emperor's daughter has gone to the civilian

17

sector. Some of you have almost certainly been involved in her protection at some point."

"Yes, my lord," confirmed Deezer, a tall, bear-like guardsman with a full beard and wild curls, both of which violated any usual regulations. "We all have. She usually goes to the data brokers with the same Reface mask every time, because she's built up a network of contacts over the years."

"Is that so?" asked Janus in surprise.

"She's obsessed with finding her missing sister." Deezer shrugged his rounded shoulders. "Trying to reconstruct the entire period before her the last jump out of *Artemis*."

"We never caught everything, but enough," interjected Maxwell, who was of normal height, had a sprinkling of gray hairs at the temples, and an average figure - at least under the too-big civilian clothes. "With her implanted tracker, we can find her quickly, but even without it, it wouldn't be particularly difficult."

"That sounds reassuring," Janus felt relieved, for he did not have much time. The ship would be leaving in five hours, and he still had to determine the flight path. Although he would be able to do that ad hoc, after all, it was just a matter of making sure no one else knew the route they would take to Saturn. "Now then, lead me to it."

Maxwell nodded and turned the surveillance sensors back on. Because he had instructed the control computer using an Imperial priority code, automatic heuristics in the *Rubov*'s system covered all tracks.

When they finally reached the eastern civilian sector in Section H, affectionately called 'Hellgate' by its two million inhabitants, Janus stepped out onto the wide street of the main corridor. His companions disappeared into the stream of passersby faster than he could look. Then he was alone among many.

The main corridor was officially named 'St. Archibald Tunnel' and ran parallel to the central corridor, the artery of the orbital ring, which was over one hundred thousand miles long. While high-speed vactrams raced through it, things were much quieter here in the Archibald Tunnel. Lined with multi-story apartment block facades, electric carts and grid bikes cruised the road, controlled by their own version of Gridlink. To the right and left of the moderate traffic, civilians pushed their way across the sidewalks under the already dimmed light of the fluorescent tube high above on the ceiling. Since the *Rubov* followed a fixed day-night cycle, adapted to Terra's cycle, it was already evening here. Many residents found themselves in the small cafes and snack bars that flooded the first floor augmented reality with exuberant billboards and flashing lights. Janus instructed his neural computer to activate advertising filters, and a street full of irritating sensory impressions became one that could have come from the 22nd century.

As he let the impression of so many people in a confined space wash over him, he took a deep breath and waited for his discomfort to subside. His position at court meant that he rarely got to be around crowds, and New York had shown him that he did not miss it a bit. But he loved Elayne almost like his own daughter and had no regrets about being here. She had a hot-blooded disposition, and her father did well not to let guardsmen bring her back.

The signal from her implanted tracker showed him that she was a mile to the east, to the left of the Archibald Tunnel, so probably in a building.

He made his way along the sidewalk with brisk steps,

passing ramen restaurants, soy food snack bars and cocktail bars whose changing olfactory impressions made his head spin. Sometimes it smelled sweet, sometimes sour, then savory and of an almost incomprehensible number of different spices, of which he probably did not even know half.

The passersby were a motley assortment. Some looked worn out and were obviously on their way home after a long day at work. Others came in small groups, laughing and joking boisterously with rosy cheeks and glazed eyes, only to head for the nearest pub. When they disappeared through the entrance, a dense barrage of sounds from booming music, laughter and clinking glasses blew onto the sidewalks.

How good they have it, Janus thought, not without wistfulness. Their world did not revolve around intrigue, doomed fleets, shady admirals playing dangerous games in the shadows, and lasers vaporizing entire street blocks of innocent people. Ignorance could be such a blessing, a luxury that would forever be denied him. The 'price of power' the Emperor had warned him about when he had asked Janus to become his right-hand man back during a sightseeing flight of Neptune's cloud refineries. Five years had passed and it seemed to him like an eternity, but at the same time like it was just yesterday. And how right his master had been after all.

"Careful, my lord," he suddenly heard a voice in his head. No identity was shown to him, only that it was an authorized user with an imperial seal. So, one of his men.

"What is it?" he asked over transducer.

"I'm two hundred yards ahead of you and something is brewing here. Two men have hacked a car and put themselves on the roof. They're setting up a holo-projector."

The last Fleet

"Mental cases?"

"Maybe." The guardsman sounded unconvinced. "Better change sides of the street."

Janus obeyed and crossed the street. The vehicles connected to Gridlink gently slowed or gracefully drove around him with their electronic swarm awareness.

After a hundred yards on the other sidewalk, the stream of people suddenly became increasingly more dense. First it was nearly impossible not to brush shoulders with the crowd, and then there was hardly any getting through.

As he stood on his tiptoes, he saw two men in neat clothes and brightly colored hair standing on the roof of a car. Above them, visible to everyone, rotated a four-sided holocube showing the destroyed Arc de Triomphe of Paris, just after the attack a few days ago. Then it disappeared, showing footage of Imperial Army soldiers flooding through the city gates into the interior. Janus did not know if it was due to post-processing of the camera data, but in their full-body armor with red visors, they looked like sinister demons. They drove civilians back to their homes, roughly yanking others into the street to secure them and round them up. Others who resisted were roughly beaten down with shock launchers and loaded onto trucks. One shot showed a soldier shooting a woman in the chest as she grabbed her jacket pocket. As she plunged, dying, into an alley, her hand came loose from her pocket and held the photo of two children in it. The camera - apparently hidden - zoomed in on the image and then it froze.

"Paris was just the beginning! Eight thousand dead!" shouted one of the two men with Terra's accent-free English. His voice was carried by an amplifier far above the crowd that had unwillingly formed because there was no way through.

"We're worth nothing to them up there," the other continued. "We're just the cheap labor that slaves and grovels so they can live their extravagant, excessive lives. Just pawns in their chess game. They blind you with censorship! But we won't close our eyes to the truth any longer!"

The image on the holocube changed, and the four rotating sides now showed a different scene.

New York. The thought ran through Janus like a lightning bolt, and nausea rose in him as the smell of burnt flesh mixed with vaporized asphalt hit his nostrils again. All the death came back to his memory in one fell swoop and he felt dizzy.

He bumped into someone behind him and muttered an apology, but apparently the woman had no eyes - or ears - for him at all.

Janus wanted to turn away, but instead he stared transfixed, like the hundreds of passersby, at the horrific images apparently taken from a balcony on one of the middle floors.

The rattle of automatic weapons popped as a brute staccato from the speakers, and the shaky recording showed dozens of muzzle flashes to the right and left of the interstate. The shooters could not be seen, but they were well spaced, aiming from half-open windows. On the road, he spotted three vehicles - one of which had been his. He watched the sparks from impacting projectiles that were conspicuously focused on them.

Then it happened. A glaring laser beam the diameter of a slender skyscraper pierced the cloud cover and streaked across the interstate farther ahead, from where

The last Fleet

shots were also fired. Screams bounced off the facades of apartment blocks, building to a crescendo of horror as passersby on the boulevards ran for their lives in panic. But the fiery beam from orbit did not let up, gliding mercilessly across the facades where the attackers were, vaporizing balconies, windows and walls, bursting fugitives on the ground in the heat where they came too close to the beam. The beam moved in a small arc and then across the interstate to the other side. Only now, in this shot, could Janus see how unerringly it was aiming at his motorcade. The betrayal was unmistakable.

Just as his stomach was about to lose the battle against his nausea, he was grabbed from behind and pulled back. Before he realized what was going on, he slipped unwittingly through a door and stood in a bar. One of the guardsmen - Maxwell - let go of him and patted his clothes briefly.

"We need to keep moving," the bodyguard reminded him, gesturing for him to follow.

Janus' head and stomach were still churning as he followed Maxwell past the kitchen to the back exit, where there were stairs leading to the second floor and a long hallway.

"We'll bypass the cluster outside," the guardsman informed him via transducer, keeping several steps ahead of him as if they did not belong together.

A single, lightly dressed woman with smeared makeup approached them, but did not dignify them with a second glance.

"Rebels," Janus replied. "So close to the Imperial sector."

"They are becoming more brash, my lord. But it doesn't matter, the security forces are on their way and will disperse them shortly. Look at the tracker on the Princess."

Janus did so and frowned. Only when he looked to see which building Elayne had gone into did he understand the urgent concern in the guardsman's voice and quickened his steps.

INTERLUDE
ELAYNE

Elayne resisted the urge to scratch her chin as she stepped into the reception area of the 'Dark Caesar'. Reface masks were an amazing development in recent years, hard to outwit and expensive to procure, severely limiting their user base. But they were still a second skin, a sophisticated polymer layer subject to basic physical laws. Its useful illusion of a foreign face did not work when scratched, which would interrupt circuits in the network of fine nanonic circuits. A single flash twitching from her chin to her cheek would be enough in a place like this to make her disappear into a dark hole. At least until the Imperial Guard followed her hard to jam tracker signal and incinerated everything around her.

Hard to jam, not impossible, she reminded herself. After all, she herself had already experimented with the best White Noise generators in the Science Corps and had spent considerably more time out here than her father or Janus could know. She did not want to hide it entirely, because that would only make them more suspicious - the last thing she needed now that she was so close to her goal.

At the reception desk, she deposited the emerald-colored key card. The young woman looked like a dainty little doll in a costume, but Elayne was not fooled by her appearance. She had spent too much time in Hellgate in recent years for that. Here, everything was a facade, much like in the Imperial Sector. Behind it all, it was similar as well; games in the shadows, deceptions, and trading of information, favor, and desire. Everything had a price tag that was only readable if you knew the language.

"Heron is already waiting for you, Miss Burnett," the fake receptionist purred, gallantly gesturing with one arm toward the doorway into the club area.

At the mention of her contact's name, she had to restrain herself from rolling her eyes. Instead, she smiled noncommittally and walked past the counter through the darkness between the walls. From the outside it looked like darkness, but when walking through it, it appeared like an immaterial veil. Her neural computer warned her of active military scanners and target acquisition aimed at her. It calmed down again, however, when she reached the other side and immersed herself in the loud thump of electronic dance music that filled the club.

The Dark Caesar was one of those establishments of which there were several in Hellgate, yet it was unique. Everything was a bit awkward, just enough to make you feel uncomfortable and yet somehow intrigued. The music a little too loud, but not yet painful - the artificial smells of rain-kissed autumn leaves and a touch of burnt rubber confusing the mix, and the lights alternately glaring and dull, so that no eye could get accustomed to the conditions. A night at this place was like a drug trip without substance, too overwhelming to remember details the next day and at the same time reserved: it was never too crowded, the receptionist and a restrictive invitation system with days of advance registration made sure of that.

"He's waiting upstairs in the VIP area," said someone next to her, a dwarf who just reached her chin. He wore a tailored suit, and his temple was plastered with various data jacks from which cables disappeared into his collar.

"Thanks," she replied over the loud music, leaving him at the door.

Once she had circled the dance floor, past the seating areas where guests with built-in mutes went about their conversations (and business) undisturbed, she reached the VIP area, which was quite old-fashioned with a raised mezzanine and silver railings. The entrance, a staircase, was blocked off with a red cord, which was pulled aside by the two doormen in suits as she approached.

"Miss Burnett," the one on her left said with a subtle grin. She shuddered as she realized that it must be Heron himself speaking from this man's mouth. "Welcome."

She merely nodded and swallowed as she made her way up the stairs. The soundproofing in the elevated area was amazing. Although there were no walls, nothing could be heard of the music from the large dance floor except a distant bass thump. Instead, relaxing lounge music sounded from invisible speakers, just loud enough that conversations from the luxurious open seating areas did not filter through to the neighbors, but not so loud that one had to raise one's voice.

Heron, surrounded by two beauties in unseemly, revealing cocktail dresses, sat on one of the sofas and was talking to an older man in a pinstriped suit. Without pausing, his eyes twitched briefly to her and a smile flitted across his lips, as if he had two faces that could do two things at once.

The infamous information broker, who enjoyed a

reputation on the *Rubov* as an all-knowing man, was tall and lean as a beanpole with a face that resembled a skull with sunken cheeks and deep eye sockets. His raven-black hair, matchstick-length with a neat side parting, made him look even paler than he actually was. His suit of digi colors displayed a complex pattern of checkered red and black.

He was not notorious for inconspicuousness or understatement, which usually gave his craft a rather short lifespan. The fact that he still existed spoke to his power in Hellgate. And his connections.

Heron gestured a gracious wave, whereupon his guest gave a hint of a bow and then withdrew.

"Ah, my dear Jessica," he finally greeted her with outstretched arms and shooed away his two attendants, the sight of whom brought a blush to Elayne's cheeks. It was fortunate she was wearing a Reface mask. "Have a seat, please."

"Thank you," she said, taking a seat next to him an arm's length away.

"Second visit in two weeks already. Do you have something nice for me? Or do you hope I have something nice for *you*?", Heron inquired, smiling his charming, bright-white smile that did not reach his eyes.

Not that she had ever seen an honest expression of joy in his gaze during their previous meetings. Still, something was different this time. He seemed more tense. Hungrier.

"Both, I think," she replied, looking around at the other groups of people sitting around them. She did not recognize anyone, but that hardly surprised her. The group of people she would recognize and cared about would never come here without the protection of a Reface mask, and those who had no access to that kind of technology basically did not matter and were no threat to her.

The last Fleet

"Aaah," Heron cooed, licking his lips greedily. Like a snake. Or a vampire that had licked blood. "My gift first!"

Elayne did not engage. Jessica Brunett was many things, but not naive. "I've been coming here for five years, several times a year. You have made more money off me than you deserve. First it's my turn."

"But my dear Jessica. I gave you everything you were looking for, did I not? Engine fabrication data, secret flight paths of former Science Corps ships, even the crew list of a ship that has not been around for over two decades." Heron made a disappointed face and put his spider-like hands on his chest as if it had affected him greatly. His theatrics almost had an artful quality to them, they were so artificial.

"I get it," she countered, waving it off. There was no time to waste. "The final data package, I need it now."

"Now? Why the impatience?"

"I'm not impatient." Elayne pretended to step impatiently from one foot to the other. "Maybe I'll come back tomorrow. I have an important appointment."

"But you haven't given me my surprise yet," he said, placing his skinny fingers together. "I would like very much to have it."

"Why the impatience?" she asked laconically.

"Aha." He chortled like an innocent boy, which he certainly was not. Finally, he pulled a simple sheet of paper from his lapel and handed it to her with two fingers. When she tried to reach for it, he pressed them together and prevented her from doing so.

She gave him a questioning look.

"I hope your surprise consists of the codes I asked you for?" he asked with the same fake smile from the beginning, but this time his eyes, deep in their sockets, fixed on her like a prey animal.

Elayne pulled out the note with a jerk. It was folded once. On the inside was a single name: *Shirin Farad*. She read the name a few times and handed the note back to him. "You're certain?"

Now her counterpart seemed truly struck. "Don't insult me in my house, dear."

"Fine." She did not respond to his play, releasing the transmission from her wrist terminal via neural computer. His gaze became absent for a moment, then his smile widened.

"I like that surprise."

"I hope mine is also satisfactory," she replied, hardened enough to evoke pride for herself. After struggling to keep herself from nervously smoothing down her dress, which she was not even wearing, she stood up. She liked being Jessica Burnett. At first, she had thought it was because she felt like she was escaping from her constrained daily life. Of course, she knew that her father was keeping an eye on her, that there were some bodyguards here at the club, or at least outside, shadowing her. But that did not matter to her. If it was to be the price for her little freedom, it was fine with her.

"Why don't you stay for a drink?" suggested Heron, beckoning one of his waitresses. "What will you have?"

"I can't stay. I was not lying when I said I had another appointment just now," she replied, shaking her head.

"But we have reason to celebrate!" He took two glasses of Antibes champagne from his employee's tray and handed one to her. Golden bubbles rose in the crystal glass and burst apart at the surface into a fine rain.

Elayne tensed all at once. He had never asked her to stay longer, and he was not a man of small talk once he had what he needed. Someone like him did not reach such heights by wasting his time on trivia. To buy time to think, she took a glass and toasted him briefly. She pretended to sip the expensive drink, but looked around the club for something that might be different: someone looking in her direction, dancing particularly listlessly, sitting at the bar and looking around.

"What are you going to do now? You are on some puzzle, am I right?" asked Heron in a chatty tone, as if he had all the time in the world. Someone like him had everything: money, connections, power. But never enough time.

"I'm going with '*none-of-your-business*.'"

His grin turned wolfish. "Spoken like one of us."

"What is this?" she asked, straight-faced. "Why are you stalling?"

Again, she looked around the club, but everything still seemed normal - as normal as a large hall with overflowing sensory input and too many people could possibly be.

"It's all good," he replied, spreading his arms like Jesus on the cross. "You're among friends here. Relax. Enjoy the time. At the end of a marathon, you have to give yourself the break you've earned, too."

It's not 'all good', she thought, and her fingers began to tingle.

"I'm going," Elayne said firmly, putting down the glass and about to turn toward the stairway exit when suddenly the lights went out.

2

JANUS

When they returned to the street ten minutes later, station security was just arriving with squad cars disgorging dozens of officers. Two Riotbots - clunky, ten-foot-tall spiders with bulky legs - walked behind them with terrifying elegance, ready to disperse the crowd.

"This is station security," a humorless voice rang out over the loudspeakers. "This is an unauthorized assembly. Clear the area immediately. This is your final warning."

Janus, who was already behind the officers with Maxwell, stopped for a moment and watched as the security guards with cortical disruptors and duroglass shields rushed the dispersing crowd and abruptly began to pummel them. At first, he thought it was sheer brutality, but then he realized they were forming a wedge to allow the riotbots in the middle to get to the vehicle where the two men with the holocube were standing. They were trying to get to the Riotbots.

"They can't just ..." he started and was about to run toward the vehicle nearest him with the station security logo when someone held him back by the arm. The grip was as hard as iron.

"My lord," Maxwell whispered. "We need to..."

"This commander here is exceeding his authority. He's just beating..."

"My lord," the Imperial Guardsman repeated. "The princess has gone to the Dark Caesar, and Trigger has made a disturbing report."

Janus wheeled around to face him. His anger turned to concern.

"Invitros."

"Invitros? Here?"

Maxwell nodded.

"Go!" Janus did not wait, but ran up Archibald after his bodyguard, who was much faster than he was. They attracted little attention as everything on the street now sought to get away from the security forces behind them. Many tried to get into the stores, hoping to sit out the situation there, but he saw countless shaking or knocking on doors in vain. As he walked by, he could see through the windows that the patrons inside were also unable to get outside and were in turn pounding their fists against the glass.

"Something's not right here," he said over transducers to his team. It got louder on the street as fleeing passersby also noticed that something was different than it should be. Some ran from door to door, only to find that none could be opened and there was no escape. Though security guards were busy attacking the crowd behind them, the street had become a violent river of people for which there was no overflow, only the way forward.

"Our guys at Dark Caesar say the doors aren't opening either," Trigger reported over the transducer network. "There's something going on here."

"Something's happening up front, too," Charly interjected. "Another meeting. Two guys with speakers."

Janus heard it already.

"The lies stink to high heaven. One thousand four hundred dead!" shouted a voice over loudspeakers on a large electric bus two hundred yards ahead. To the right and left of it, people suddenly came running out of the houses. Exceptionally large people. They formed a wall against which the fleeing civilians surged. Shouts were raised, protests and curses, but the chain of giants held firm and pushed them back.

Janus spun around and saw the security forces at about the same distance seem to realize that something was brewing behind them as well. The Riotbots, easily recognizable even at that distance, came running in their direction. The vibrations of their powerful metal feet continued through the street to his bones.

"My lord, we should..."

Janus saw it for himself. The entrance to the Dark Caesar was less than a hundred yards ahead of them, tinted double doors of duroglass with inconspicuous lettering above.

"Go!" he ordered, "We're getting the princess out, by any means necessary. Maxwell, you stay with me." As he watched Trigger reach out near the club and blast lurid muzzle flashes from the barrels of his implant weapons, he plugged into the local security network with his priority code, which relayed his signal without delay to the Imperial Guard barracks, to which he sent a distress call with his position ...

A dull *whump!* sounded and suddenly all was dark except for the muzzle flash in front of them and the glint of myriad glass shards in the flickering light. Maxwell yanked him aside and onto the hard floor. Janus groaned in shock. His neural computer was no longer responding, even his nanocephalon was offline. His eyes, though enhanced with natural residual light amplification that did not rely on electronic circuitry, could no longer access any residual light from the environment, and so he was trapped in darkness.

"EMP!" whispered Maxwell beside him.

At first there was an eerie silence, then the first people began to scream in panic and fear spread like wildfire.

"I can't see anything."

"Neither can I," the guardsman replied, his calm voice contrasting sharply with his frightening words.

"Guardsman, we need to get to the Princess. NOW!"

"Understood, my lord."

Janus felt a hand groping along his chest, then clawing into his jacket to pull him along behind him. To their left was the facade. He could feel it with his left hand. It felt cold like the worry for the princess that spread through his guts like liquid ice.

Among all the eerie clamor of lost men and women in the nothingness of darkness, he heard other, worse things: the trampling of heavy boots, unnaturally steady and coordinated. Choppy shouts of security officers yelling orders.

When the first light finally reached his eyes, it only made things worse: a single red signal flare came hissing loose from a pistol and flew leisurely upward toward the failed light tube. As if in slow motion, it climbed up and seemed to make everything around it stand still for a breath. Janus saw the outlines of people crouched on the ground, standing spread out on the street as if frozen in mid-motion. Two Riotbots, close by, stood slumped uselessly, smaller and distinctly less impressive.

And there were large figures, twenty or thirty, running

The last Fleet

in two squads to where Janus was also headed with Maxwell: the Dark Caesar. There was no mistaking that they were Invitros. Hulking giants, eight feet tall, developed and bred many decades ago for the heaviest physical labor. In the red light of the signal flare, they were no more than shadows in black battle armor with shaved skulls.

And in their hands, they carried weapons that soon began to fire with deafening rattles. The muzzle flashes formed large, glaring flowers of fire, short-lived sources of light in staccato that made every movement around seem choppy. A figure at the entrance, who had just wheeled around to join them, became riddled with bullets and fell back.

"Chemical weapons," commented Maxwell, who had crouched down with him. Growling, he added, "That was Trigger."

"We need to get in there and get the Princess out," Janus calmly brought out as old reflexes took over that had lain dormant as distant memories in him for five years.

"Understood, my lord." The guardsman stood up again and walked slowly ahead, pulling him aside behind an electric cart and waiting until the hit squad from Invitros had disappeared into the Dark Caesar's foyer. Then they emerged again and began to run in the fading red glow of the signal flare that clung to the useless fluorescent tube above them, illuminating the chaos that had been reignited all over again with the first shot. To make the mess perfect, police officers were now also walking among the groups of civilians, working their way toward the remaining Invitros who were standing guard at the entrances to the houses from which they had come.

Only to be mowed down in a flurry of their chemical weapons. Whoever had planned this was well prepared, knew the procedures and response times of the security forces.

I know who did this, Janus thought, clenching his hands into fists as he followed Maxwell to Dark Caesar. *Marquandt. And Albius.* Only the Grand Admiral had enough contacts and access rights to smuggle a unit of Invitro terrorists into the *Rubov*. That was what Mirage had warned him about. The traitor must have known that in his anxious state about Nancy, he would go in search of Elayne himself, so close to the departure of the Emperor's flagship.

Maxwell pressed himself next to the destroyed entrance and peered inside. Then, with a quick wave, he motioned Janus to stop and wait. The Invitros further ahead were busy getting rid of the security forces, and that gave them a short window of opportunity to get into Dark Caesar. Without a second thought, he slipped into the reception area right behind the guardsman, where it was even darker than in the diffuse twilight on the street.

Most of the invitros had already disappeared through the entrance to the left of the counter, above which hung a woman who seemed to be staring in their direction with a hole in her forehead and a broken expression. Two had apparently stayed behind and were just turning in her direction, positioning themselves to guard the escape route.

Maxwell did the only thing he could and began sprinting, and Janus followed suit. While the guardsman was hardly the most lethal weapon in the Star Empire without his numerous military combat implants, his limbs were still composite and carbotanium, his artificial muscles trained to support close to four hundred pounds of body weight. This made him significantly faster than Janus, and

The last Fleet

he had already reached the first invitro while Janus was still halfway there.

The guardsman dropped the last two yards, escaping two volleys that crashed into the marble floor behind him. His kinetic momentum caused him to slide feet-first and sweep the giant on the left off his feet. As he did so, he jerked his hands up and grabbed the old-fashioned 22nd century gunpowder rifle and jerked it around to shoot the second Invitro. Then he leapt aside and narrowly escaped the bullets, which shredded the facade behind the counter at his back.

Maxwell escaped the return fire by rolling backward, but in doing so crashed into the frame of the club's doorway, through which the thunder of weapon fire reached them in the foyer. The Invitro emitted a grunt and pulled the trigger, only to find that the guardsman had tricked him. Instead of staggering, he slid around the frame and let himself fall. His volley hit the clone in the leg and sent him crashing to the ground.

Meanwhile Janus was ready for him, and kicked him in the temple with a twisting kick.

Powerless, the mountain of muscle collapsed, and Janus snatched the old-fashioned assault rifle from his slackening fingers. It was heavy and cold, the shoulder pad seemed to promise a heavy recoil.

Maxwell looked in his direction, face barely visible in the twilight from the few red glows that shone through the entrance to them.

"Into hell, my lord," he said, and his lips parted into a pugnacious grin before he ran into the doorway to the club area, into the infernal chaos of weapon fire, death screams, and ruined furnishings.

Janus could feel the tingling sensation he thought he had long forgotten. Every one of his senses seemed to be at the limit of their capabilities, and adrenaline pulsed to the tips of his hair. He sank every thought into a black hole he pictured in his mind, as he had learned to do. Lord Janus Darishma faded into the background. He faded and slowly disappeared until only his old self remained, without enhancements, without the superhuman speed, but with the same focus and clarity.

Zenith returned.

Gun at the ready, he followed Maxwell, his torso slightly turned and bent forward to provide a smaller attack surface, his knees partly bent and his steps slanted forward. Narrowing his eyes, he entered the club area where flares had already been lit. The natural residual light amplification, coupled with his analytical calm, turned the chaos into a coherent situation with participants and things he automatically categorized into dangerous and non-dangerous.

Non-dangerous were the many corpses on the floor, unnaturally contorted figures lying motionless in spreading pools of blood that shimmered like molten basalt in the glow of the magnesium flares. They hung over the bar and covered the dance floor, their chests riddled, or in some, their faces half shredded. Because they had stood in the way. The Invitros were obviously aiming for the VIP area at the other end, at the foot of which two bouncers were currently fighting with the intruders.

A skeletal figure behind them yelled over the din: "STOP IT! THAT WASN'T THE DEAL, YOU FUCKERS!"

One of the attackers shot him in the head.

Janus used what little time he had left behind the enemy, who apparently had not noticed the noise in which those left behind had died. He ran on the balls of his feet to the right along the edge of the dance floor to the bar, where he dove for cover and leaned back against the clad steel. Maxwell had made his way to the left and disappeared behind one of the seating areas.

The noise of battle was slowly dying down, but he still ventured a glance around the corner, searching for Elayne under the glassy stares of the dead. It was clear to him that she was not stupid enough to come here without a mask, not that she could have even taken a step out of the imperial sector as a princess without being recognized and provoking a crowd. But he knew the look in her eyes almost as well as he knew the look in his own children's eyes. Instead, he saw the bodies of Deezer and Charly among four badly battered Invitros.

He did not spot her, so he moved on to phase two of the plan: Since she had not gotten past him, either there had to be a back way out, or she was hiding somewhere. Either option meant he had some work to do.

"You killed him, you moron," one of the Invitros boomed his powerful growling bass.

"The boss wanted it that way. To keep him from talking."

"And how's he going to tell us where the damned princess is now, you fucking moron?"

"Hey, don't talk to me like that," the scolded man complained, dragging his feet.

Janus aimed his rifle and began firing. He had trained with chemical weapons - he had trained with *all* weapons - but it had been a long time. Still, it startled him that the old habits and reflexes had been only the crook of a finger away. After all this time. He might no longer possess his augments, but he still had his great talent from back then.

Headshots, Zenith, he heard Mirage say in his mind. And then he began.

Two shots.

The first two heads he hit from behind, just below the skull. They were the two who had been discussing at the foot of the stairs as they ran up. They clattered forward silently.

Janus did not wait, taking advantage of the momentary confusion among the sixteen remaining attackers, who were startled and looking around for the shooter.

Aim. Fire. Aim. Fire.

He then hit the two closest to him on the side of the temple and through one eye, which burst like a depth charge filled with viscous slime. Their bodies slid to the floor like wet bags. He imagined that the floor rumbled slightly from their weight.

He quickly retreated as the others returned fire at him. Projectiles slammed into the corner of the counter like a hail of meteors. Ricochets whistled through the air, filling the area with dust and steel shards.

No one spoke a word; they simply acted, presumably with hand signals, or as a well-rehearsed team. Professional.

That changed when there were two shots and then another.

Maxwell. Crossfire.

Janus remained crouched and moved to the wall where the waist-high counter door was. There he wheeled around and put the rifle to his shoulder.

A shadow came around the corner and Janus would have fired reflexively out of fear. But he was Zenith. So he watched the body sail by and fall limply to the ground. Those who had thrown it, trying to figure out if the shooter was still around the corner, came next. One dove sideways through his field of vision and failed to pull the trigger as his head caught the next bullet, through the top

The last Fleet

row of teeth into the larynx, and through the C1 and C2 vertebrae.

The other bent over the counter, and Janus saw the movement too late. In the past, it would have looked different. The angle was not perfect for the Invitro, but it was enough to graze his shoulder. Pain stabbed him like fire from the wound to his chest and neck.

Ignoring it, he jerked his rifle up and fired a volley into the hulking, hairless face. Then he switched his gun hand to the right and pulled open the small door with the hand of his wounded arm to crawl behind the counter. On all fours, he took cover, and when he looked up, he was looking directly into the eyes of the heiress to the throne. Tiny short-circuits flashed on her cheeks like thunderstorms observed from orbit.

"Elayne," he said, the words nearly swallowed by the rattle of guns on the dance floor. That he was not allowed to address the princess by her first name did not occur to him at that moment. Zenith did not care about clumsy etiquette.

"Janus?" she asked in surprise. Her eyes were wide, moist and reddened. Her hands trembled as she touched him, as if she could not believe he was the same First Secretary of State who usually spoke with calm words, wore expensive suits, and fit the image of a bureaucrat through and through.

"I'll walk you out," he promised in a familiar tone, and she nodded. At that moment she was not the Princess, but a frightened girl who had never in her life seen two people do violence to each other. "Do you trust me?"

"N-naturally, Janus, but..."

"Elayne," he hissed. "Do you trust me?"

She blinked and nodded quickly.

That would have to do. He grabbed her, yanked her to

her feet, and held the barrel of his assault rifle against her temple, which required some contorting.

"Janus!" said Elayne, her voice rough with shock. "What's that got to..."

"We all calm down now, or your target is dead," he shouted, scanning the situation. Ten attackers still. Six were holed up by the seating areas, four just shot up from the counter directly in front of him and took aim, walking carefully backward. Two stood upstairs in the VIP area among the bodies and laid into him.

"Easy, little normie," one of them called out. His voice sounded like an out-of-control bass. "Don't have to die here if you behave. But we're not leaving here without her."

"I'm aware of that."

"Imperial Guard, huh?"

Janus did not answer. "I want my partner. Then we'll retreat and you can have her."

"Ha," the Invitro laughed boomingly. "So much for your loyalty."

Janus did not correct him.

"Maxwell? Come here," he bellowed so loudly that Elayne winced beside him.

The Marine stepped out from behind his half-tattered cover of the seating area on the other side, aimed suspiciously at the Invitros who were following him closely, and sprinted to join him behind the counter. His training was evident in the way he stayed in front of the low swinging door and crouched behind it.

"Plan?" he asked quietly.

"We'll see," Janus replied without taking his eyes off the mutants.

"Well, get a move on," said the Invitro, who had

fought hard for his VIP access. Beside him, the tattered furniture looked like toys.

"Tell your meatheads to back off," Janus demanded in a loud voice.

"You have twenty seconds to get your scrawny asses out of here."

"We can take them down," he heard Maxwell hiss.

Brave, but wrong, Janus thought. *Two gunners in elevated positions, the rest using the breather to fan out and improve their firing angles. They're good. Widely spread targets, worse for us. But we have cover, they don't. All the sitting corners are visible. So they're about to make a mistake. Maxwell sees it differently and prefers to keep his distance.*

"No," he said.

"We're stuck here. They know that too," the guardsman reminded him.

"Yep." Very quietly, he whispered to Elayne, "When I say now, you drop. I hope you've been as conscientious about planning your trips as you have about everything else."

"Well?" boomed one of the Invitros. "Time's almost up."

"I'm getting paid to make sure the Princess is brought out alive. Plan B is pretty clearly defined, though," the obvious leader boomed from the VIP area. How apt.

"Plan B, then," Janus decided, extending his rifle and pulling the trigger, sending one of the muscle monsters to the ground. "Now!"

Elayne dropped, and he did the same. Not a second too soon, as the countertop was shredded to pieces in automatic fire moments later. A dense shower of splinters rained down on them and the bottles that had been whole on the shelf disintegrated into a flurry of shards.

"Ever escape from here before?" he shouted over the din.

"No, but there are maintenance shafts that run in the wall behind the counter door," she gasped, pulling her head in to shield herself from the shrapnel. Janus would have been appalled to see the bloody streaks on her velvety cheeks.

The grenade was not long in coming. He heard the click of the pin during a brief pause in the fire, dropped the rifle and jumped from his crouch to the other side of the counter. The small explosive device was nothing more than a shadow, flying toward them in a high arc, well aimed. Janus tensed, yelled "COVER FIRE!" and then leapt up to fish it out of the air.

Maxwell reacted quickly, forcing the opponents into cover. Still, he earned the next grazing shot in the same shoulder, two fingers down.

He nevertheless got a hold on the grenade and threw it at the wall in a direct line behind Maxwell, where it detonated with a deafening bang, kicking up dust and smoke in a gritty cloud.

"GO!" he yelled at Elayne over the ringing in his ears and shoved her ungently toward the counter door before her catatonia could turn to shock.

From the other side he heard the rattle of an assault rifle. So, Maxwell had survived. Good.

Screaming, the Princess pushed the door away from her with outstretched arms and rushed into the open area beyond, right past the guardsman crouched next to the badly battered corner of the counter, providing them with cover fire. Still, bullets whistled closer to Janus' head than he would have liked.

"Damn good catch!" roared Maxwell over the thunder of his gun. "Didn't know you had it in you!"

"A-league," he replied without pausing. Out of the corner of his eye, he saw that the elite soldier's entire left side was covered in blood. Apparently, the blast had gotten him after all. The fact that he was still able to fight at all was probably thanks to all the metal he was made of.

"What?"

"Baseball," Janus replied, breathing a sigh of relief as they dove into the smoke that brought them some cover. What truly encouraged him, however, was the gaping hole in the wall paneling, which, as suspected, was made of expensive but not particularly sturdy digipanels that could change light, color, and pattern-when they had power.

He did not need to prod Elayne, as she nimbly scrambled into the open maintenance tunnel and disappeared inside.

Janus followed her and grunted when he felt two short bites. One in his left thigh, the other in his right arm.

"Maxwell!" he shouted as soon as he had scrambled after the princess. With narrowed eyes, he tried to penetrate the only slowly dissipating smoke. At that very moment, the guardsman was hit several times in a row in the chest, twitching like a puppet on unsteady strings. Janus would have been frozen in shock by his death. But Zenith was functional.

"Quickly," he ordered Elayne, who immediately began crawling through the narrow shaft. Janus blanked out the pain in his shoulder, leg and arm, felt the pinpricks where he touched the cold composite of the walls. Still, he crawled on, swallowing the pained noises that rose from his throat.

Beyond the first bend, he collided with something soft in the darkness.

"What is it?" he hissed.

"I need to catch my breath," Elayne gasped, sniffling.

"The clones are too big for the shafts." And so am I, for that matter. "But if they hear us ..."

As if to punctuate his words, bullets crashed through the wall behind them. All at once, the Princess no longer needed a break and started moving again. In complete darkness, they continued on. Straight ahead and to the right, at some point to the left and again to the right, until he lost his orientation. The darkness seemed to become more pervasive, heavier with time, and to join forces with the eerie silence that formed an unpleasant contrast to the loud chaos of the carnage.

Eventually they collided again, but he did not complain. His body took control and he lay flat on his stomach before he could even consciously think about it.

"Janus," Elayne whispered. "Are you okay?"

"Just need a short rest."

As his exhaustion, accelerated by his blood loss, which his bionic platelet factories valiantly contained, faded, so did his old self.

"Did you get hit?"

"Yes," he admitted, groaning. "Nothing a simple Medidoc cannot fix. I think we can catch our breath for a minute."

"When do you think the power will come back on?"

"The Guard knows we're here. Our trackers are military standard, they should still be working. So I'm sure there are already Imperial Guardsmen swarming outside," he assured her. "And they have more of a ... more of a reputation for cleaning up thoroughly."

"As soon as there's no more danger, the technicians will come and replace the relays at the central distribution nodes." Elayne sounded as if she was trying to bolster her confidence. Not a bad idea.

The last Fleet

"Where did you learn to fight like that, Janus?" She asked.

"Rifleman at Hadron's annual midsummer fair," he replied. That was no lie, even if she would never know the whole truth. *Must* never know, for he loved Elayne almost as he loved his own children and had undoubtedly spent more time with her over the past five years.

"Sure," she mumbled. A voice in the void that gave structure to the immaterial. The structure disappeared for a while until there was a rustling in the wall. Water, maybe coolant, he guessed. "Janus?"

"Yes?"

"What's now?"

"We wait," he decided, though the thought drove him crazy. It would take time to free them, and time was something the Emperor didn't have. Haeron II would already be informed that his first secretary of state and his daughter were alive, but would still be terribly worried since he would not be able to delay the departure for Congress any longer. What kind of danger was his master in?

Worst of all was the fact that Janus could do absolutely nothing for him.

INTERLUDE
HAERON II

"This is outrageous!" raged Haeron II, glaring at the colonel with the most withering look he was capable of. Apparently it was enough to make the seasoned officer slump in his chair. "An attack by damned mutants here in Sol? On *my* Rubov? And in close proximity to the Imperial Sector, to top it all off?"

"Your Majesty, we don't know how these terrorist elements managed to bypass our security systems and infiltrate ..."

"Of course we know!" he snapped at the man, pounding the table with his right fist. His powerful signet ring produced a bang that made his counterpart wince. "Someone with authority and connections planted them!"

"That is regrettably to be assumed, Your Majesty. But the situation is under control. Most of the attackers have been shot and several have been taken into custody," Colonel Bazagan endeavored to paint a somewhat more positive picture. "And your daughter and the First Secretary are safe."

"I can see the vital signs myself," growled Haeron II,

and his anger fueled by unending concern faded all at once. What remained was exhaustion and the basic grief that had not left him since the news of Magnus' death and had become something like the background noise of his days.

"We are currently busy trying to find them in the network of maintenance tunnels," Bazagan continued, apparently misinterpreting his silence as a momentary lull before the next storm. "Due to the influence of magnetic fields and power lines in the walls, it's not easy to correctly target their signal, but we're making great progress and will have them out within the next thirty minutes."

"See to it." Haeron II got a call from his assistant Brian for the third time now. He ignored it and stood up. The colonel immediately went up like a jackknife. "My daughter and Lord Darishma will be brought directly here to my chambers, in one piece. You are responsible for this, Colonel."

"Of course, Your Majesty." Bazagan saluted formally and stomped out of the office.

Haeron II watched him go and waited until the two guardsmen in their powered armor had closed the double doors again before calling Brian back.

"I know I'm late," he grumbled.

"To make it on time, we have to leave in fifteen minutes, Your Majesty," his assistant reminded him.

As Emperor, I should be able to get around the jump ban in Sol, he thought, yet he knew his hands were tied once again. Paris had shown him once again that while he *could* do whatever he wanted, there was always a high price to pay.

"We'll take the *Majestic*," he decided, "I'll be there in ten minutes. Contact the Chief of Staff, I want him to accompany me."

The last Fleet

"Your Majesty?"

"You heard me." He disconnected and left his chambers on a direct route to the Imperial docks, which were five levels below and directly accessible via his private elevators. There were always six special frigates docked there at any given time, kept ready for launch around the clock. It had been Janus' idea to choose one to fly him to Saturn only at the last minute. How he wished his friend were here. But that would mean his daughter would not be taken care of, so he preferred it this way. Her safety was much more important to him than his own.

Still, he was not naive. An attack by terrorists in the *Rubov* was downright impossible without inside help and the smuggling of dozens of mutants with chemical weapons, not to mention an EMP bomb. This could only mean that someone at the highest levels had pushed buttons, filled pockets, and stalled reports. Janus had reported to him that there might have been some strange interaction between Albius, Marquandt and Usatami, which in itself was hard to believe. Usatami seemed to have nothing to do with the two officers, and the admirals were considered rivals and were anything but friendly to each other. So, either Janus was off the mark and chasing a mirage, or the three were hiding something and Gavin Andal's accusations were true. Then Dain Marquandt would be the highest form of traitor and they would have to bring forward their plan to get him out of the way. For example, after his arrival at the Saturn Congress, when all the cameras of the Star Empire were turned on. A traitor was best executed for all to see.

To do that, of course, he first had to get safely to Saturn, because Marquandt would also know that this danger existed. Especially after the failed attempt to kidnap his daughter. Or to murder her?

He shuddered.

But Marquandt was poorly connected in the Sol system. To infiltrate with a task force of rebel mutants required the highest security clearances and powers - all of which were held by his chief of staff, Grand Admiral Marius Albius. If he was one of the conspirators and the one who had infiltrated the enemies, he best kept him close until the time came - as life insurance in case his subordinates were up to something stupid.

The emperor clenched his hands into fists and forced himself to take a calm breath.

"Major," he said to the commanding officer of his guard, who was standing in the elevator with him and four of his elite guardsmen. "Double the guard on board. I want a full company of two hundred and fifty soldiers."

"That's the full complement of readiness," the officer replied over the helmet speakers of his Titan Motorized Armor. Beside him, Haeron II felt like a gnome. "So, no problem. I've relayed the order. You will be aboard in ten minutes."

"Very good."

As they reached the docks and he and his six armored bodyguards walked down the long dock hall with its elaborate decorations and carvings in gold and platinum, he saw the Chief of Staff just stepping out of one of the east elevators and with him a handful of aides, who were undoubtedly bodyguards in disguise. A common procedure for members of the Council of Admiralty.

"Marius," Haeron II greeted the older man seemingly lightheartedly as they met and marched toward passageway 'C' across the marble, beyond which was the *Majestic*'s airlock.

"Your Majesty," Albius replied. "Your assistant told me to accompany you?"

The last Fleet

"Quite so. I'm afraid your entourage will have to stay here, though. I have increased my guard, so we need every square foot of space on board." He made a wave, which the major repeated, whereupon the chief of staff's entourage dispersed even without his order. The only sign that Albius was uncomfortable remained a brief twitch of the corners of his mouth, but Haeron II did not miss it.

"Your Majesty, forgive my asking, but isn't it unwise to take me away from the ongoing investigation into the attempted kidnapping of your daughter? This should be a top priority, and I have personally taken up the matter due to its seriousness."

The rumble of massive footsteps could be heard in the background, and they both turned to see the Imperial Guardsmen coming out of one of the doors as an orderly line of two, like Greek gods in shining armor, and walking at a run through Dock C to disappear into the *Majestic*. Only when they were gone did the Emperor reply.

"How do you know it was a kidnapping and not an assassination?" he asked his chief of staff, piercing him with his gaze.

"A guess, Your Majesty." Albius' jaws began to grind as he wondered, no doubt, how deep in trouble he was and how much Haeron II really knew. If this man was not guilty, nobody was. And now he was beginning to realize that he was no longer Chief of Staff, but Life Insurance.

"Of course." He gave the major a wave, whereupon he turned on a high-frequency radio signal blocker. The Guard knew him well.

"Then at least let me inform my second-in-command that he needs to take over the investigation," Albius suggested, but Haeron II shook his head.

"No need, I'll have him replaced. My Guard will take care of the matter, and once Elayne and Janus are safe, my

First Secretary of State will take the reins. You are in agreement, I'm sure?"

"Of course, Your Majesty." Albius bowed his head like a cow before slaughter.

"Good, then it is settled. Come now. We have a fifteen-hour flight ahead of us." Per transducer, he addressed the major, "Continue to block all signals until we are underway. Talk to the pilots. As soon as we notice anything suspicious along our route, lift the signal block."

"Your Majesty?" the commander asked in confusion as they boarded in outward silence, bowing to the guardsmen who passed them.

"Albius is a traitor. If he and his conspirators have it in for me as well as my daughter, they will try something. This flight is secret, but if we assume the worst, they have an informant on board. In that case, they must know that their leader is with us and an attack would mean his death. So if he can send out signals, he will order them to call off the attack to protect his life. Traitors want power they don't have, and you only get that if you are still breathing. It makes them predictable."

"I understand, your majesty. A wise suggestion."

"A necessary one."

3

GAVIN

They spent the first few jumps licking their wounds. Gavin spent most of his time on the Medidoc after the mysterious woman, who introduced herself to them as Mirage, replenished her supply of Smartnites. Dodger and Hellcat barely visited, as they had their hands full helping Bambam fix the Lady. There was still a lot to do, and much was improvised out of necessity, but at least their ship was flying, and the primary systems were working flawlessly.

After three hours and six jumps, they were in the Dagger system on their way to Sol, and Sphinx informed him that the treatment was complete but that he would have to take it easy for a few more days.

"I don't think that's going to happen," he said, grumbling as he released the straps and began to float. Pulling himself along the handholds still hurt his shoulder, but no longer felt like he had a handful of thumbtacks stuck in his muscle. By only ever jumping, charging the jump thrusters and jumping again, there was no opportunity for thrust and thus gravity, which was rather disruptive to wound healing. Blood flow needed direction to function normally, but that was not an option if they were ever going to catch up with Akwa Marquandt. So it was up to his Smartnites to help the body do its job.

On his way to the mess hall, he radioed the rest of the crew. "Hey, guys. Back up and running. Meeting in the mess hall in 10 minutes."

To his surprise, they didn't argue. Since their escape from Yokatami's Seed World, they seemed somewhat more mellow, more streamlined. He blamed it on the terror that their brief time there had given them all. They almost died as mediums for an Orb through violating their brain somehow. Agonizingly, until blood and brain matter would have spurted from their eyes and ears. Plus the helplessness as ostensibly well-treated prisoners, like fattened pigs to be subjected to no stress just before slaughter and to be nice and round and fat when the time came.

He had never felt so helpless and humiliated. They still didn't have answers as to what exactly had been going on, and that seemed to have awakened a kind of silent agreement among the crew that they now had to pull together.

Once in the mess hall, he prepared the holoprojector and set it on the table. Then he plugged into the cockpit systems via neural computer and merged with the virtual view of the command and control elements.

They hung motionless in the vacuum at the farthest point of the Dagger system, just off the bow wave of its heliosphere. Out here, the inner system was no more than a distant glow in the sea of stars, barely distinguishable from points farther away. Even the outer system's space control was still so far away that their signals would not arrive until they had long since jumped again. Pirates used

The last Fleet

this type of transit, and it would make them suspicious, but they had no choice. Either Akwa Marquandt did exactly as they did - and why not, she was cloaked after all - in which case they would have to do the same to arrive in Sol at least shortly after her. Or else, for some reason, the traitor flew on official business, in which case they would catch up with her that way. He did not believe that, however.

The *42-QLUE* was two thousand clicks to port, at exactly the same distance as after each jump. Whoever this Mirage was, Gavin had never seen more precise jump navigation. He sent her a quick message.

"You're doing better?" Hellcat inquired as she floated in.

Gavin unlatched himself from the cockpit and eyed her. Her orange technician jumpsuit was stained and looked puffed up in zero gravity, as if it had been pumped full of air. She herself looked worn and tired, but she seemed back to her old self, combative and blazing like wildfire.

"What?" she asked, catching herself on the table before magnetizing her boots and landing on the metal deck like a statue with a loud clonk.

"It's good to see you again," he replied with a smile, already expecting her to hurl an insult at him. But she merely nodded.

"Likewise. I haven't even thanked you yet."

"For what?" He knew, but waved it off.

"A body check in overalls against the leg of a red samurai?" She smirked. "You'd have to have pretty damn big balls for that, or you just don't value them very much."

"It was worth it to me," he said. *To save you.*

Their gazes lingered on each other, somehow gentle and yet like fire and water, surging back and forth like elemental tides in an attempt to find a point where they didn't have to snuff each other out. They were still learning, he knew that, but what really touched him was the realization that they both sensed this willingness to learn in each other. Something that would have been unimaginable just days ago.

"You..." she started as Bambam came floating in.

"Hey, guys." the mechanic said good-humoredly, unknowingly destroying whatever it was that had just been created. He was like the needle for their balloon - or rather the nail.

"Why so chipper?" asked Hellcat. "Did you fix the transformer?"

"Yep. This Kepal here," Bambam landed between them with his boots activated, grinning as he pointed both thumbs at himself, "is a goddamn genius! Railguns?" He formed a pistol with his right hand and pulled the trigger. "Bam. Rockets?" Another imaginary shot. "Bam. Port side molecular bond generators?"

"Bam?" asked Gavin, nodding appreciatively. "Good job. Where's Dodger?"

"Pooping, I think. Tried to hold it off until we got thrust again, but I think the snake already had its little head out, the way it's been looking for the last half hour."

Gavin wrinkled his nose.

"Not yet such disrespectful language near His Most Serene Majesty," Hellcat scolded her comrade in an artificially piqued voice.

"Hey, that wasn't bad at all," Gavin found, nodding appreciatively. "I could make a real lady with manners out of you yet."

She stuck her tongue out at him.

"Is that an invitation?" he asked, grinning.

"Only in your wet dreams."

The last Fleet

"You know you're in my wet dreams?" Gavin acted surprised.

"Ah, there she is," Bambam said as Dodger joined them with her massive frame. She looked content. "So, did you poop?"

"Yep." The mutant said. "Had a coffee beforehand, that always helps."

Gavin closed his eyes in resignation. "Can we get off the brown topic now? What's wrong with you guys?"

Dodger and Bambam looked at him uncomprehendingly. Even as he shook his head and spread his arms in a desperate attempt for them to come to their senses.

"We're talking about the fate of humanity here, and you're talking about your bowel movements like we're on a class trip."

"I've been constipated," Dodger said.

"It's a serious thing," Bambam stated.

"Not everyone can pull a nougat stick out of their behind on command...," Hellcat put in.

"You guys are so..." Gavin interrupted himself as he realized what she was alluding to. "Hey! We wouldn't have found the sergeant and Masha without that transmitter!"

"I get it, Captain Brownie." She began to giggle. The sound was so strange on her, so girly, that he couldn't think of a retort.

"Captain Brownie." Dodger tilted her head as if she were moving the title back and forth.

"No!" said Gavin indignantly. "No, no, no!"

"I like that."

"Should we call the Sergeant in for a briefing?" asked Hellcat, nipping his next protest right in the bud. She still couldn't help a grin, and he threw his hands in the air in resignation. Let them have their fun. If he was the outlet for their relief at being alive, then it was probably a captain's responsibility not to nip the spark of hope and relief in the bud by acting humorless. If it had to be at his expense, then so be it.

"Yes, and Masha, too."

"The civilian?" asked Hellcat in surprise.

"She was separated from her children and kidnapped, locked in a steel container for days, then prepared in a secret Yokatami facility to have her brain fried trying to communicate with a creepy alien. Besides, she brought us that thing." Gavin pointed to the eerie sphere stored in the oven. Memories of how three of those had flown out of the Ushuaia with no apparent propulsion in his home system and turned the battle into a disaster made him shiver. Fortunately, the drone, if it was one, seemed to be inactive at the moment. "I think she deserves her place here as much as any of us."

They all nodded in turn. Hellcat gave him a slightly longer look that could mean anything.

"He said that's valuable," Bambam quoted the Arcturian, grinning. "I like that little one. Never thought I'd want a notrious thief on my hands."

"Notorious," Gavin corrected him, winking sugary sweet as the mechanic's brows drew together.

"Now he's starting to joke around."

The Master Sergeant and Masha came floating in to join them. The Arcturian looked like a ravenous gnome next to the bulky elite Marine who, along with Dodger, seemed to fill the entire room.

"My lord."

"Sergeant, Masha." Gavin gave them both a friendly nod. "I wanted you along when we discussed our course of action. It's just under twelve hours to Sol, twenty-four jumps, just under one hundred and forty light years. I had agreed with Mirage that we would take a few hours to lick

The last Fleet

our wounds. Now we should prepare for what comes next."

To his relief, there were no more bad jokes. Dodger seemed as equanimous as ever, Hellcat nodded thoughtfully, her gaze fixed on the distance, and even Bambam gave him an expectant look. Sullen as ever, but expectant.

Beside him, the air flickered as Mirage's hologram formed. It flickered a few times and formed interference fractals until the connection was stable and it looked almost lifelike.

"Mirage," he said, bowing his head respectfully because he didn't know how to act toward her. Whatever she was exactly, and whoever she worked for, she should not actually exist, and the fact that she was standing next to him after all - or at least flying next to them - reassured and worried him at the same time. She was a black box that had returned from the dead and apparently had abilities - and a ship - that impressed even him. Yet he had made it his mission when he started cadet school that it should always be the other way around, if possible.

"Hello," she replied curtly. "What is this about?"

"We need to discuss our strategy."

"Good."

"Can I ask questions first?" asked Dodger, looking in his direction.

"Sure."

"I mean to her." The mutant nodded at Mirage's live image.

"A good questioner is already half answered."

Dodger frowned as she pondered her answer with obvious effort.

"Nietzsche," Gavin volunteered. "That was a quote."

"Yep."

Now it was his turn to be irritated. Something seemed

to be going on between the two women, because they looked into each other's eyes for a long time.

"Are you a 'robot'?" asked Dodger finally with a serious expression. "Saw you weren't bleeding. And Bambam hooked you up to our reactor through the voltage transformer."

Gavin felt a chill run down his spine. Cautiously, he turned to Mirage, as if at any moment the hologram might turn into flesh and blood - or circuitry and metal - and attack him.

"Sometimes people don't want to hear the truth because they don't want their illusions shattered," Mirage replied with another quote.

Again, Dodger took her time in answering. Then she said thoughtfully, "Beliefs are more dangerous enemies of truth than lies."

The corners of the hologram's mouth moved upward. Very slightly, barely noticeable. Gavin looked to the mutant as if seeing her for the first time.

"No," Mirage finally replied to Dodger's earlier question.

"Are you one of the good guys?", Bambam threw a question of his own into the ring.

"Such a subjective categorization of deterministic events depends on the observer and his limited field of vision. I saved all of your lives. Him," she pointed to Gavin, "even twice. From your perspective, that probably qualifies me for the good category."

Her tone possessed little inflection, but he thought he detected a hint of mockery in her voice.

"Can we trust you?" asked Hellcat.

"No," Mirage replied impassively. After silence fell, and only the gurgle of the air conditioner between two power spikes filled the mess hall like a mechanical hiccup, she added, "But we have the same goal: Akwa Marquandt's stealth ship and uncovering the conspiracy going on on Yokatami's Seed World."

The Master Sergeant barely stirred noticeably. Gavin looked in his direction and noticed the Marine's questioning look.

"Go ahead, Sergeant," he prompted him.

"With your permission, Lord Captain?"

Gavin gave him a wave and he looked to Mirage with a serious expression.

"What team are you playing for?"

"Not for your opponents," she remained vague, and now Gavin realized how cleverly she had answered so far. She could not be accused of a lack of honesty up to this point, and what had seemed like an affront a moment ago had merely paved the way for the question that would have eventually come anyway. The look on the Marine's face revealed that he, too, had understood.

"All right, let's move on to the most important part," Gavin suggested. "Akwa Marquandt's ship is obviously a *Triumph*-class vessel, so it has about as much engine power as we do. Better weaponry, weaker armor. At least if it were a normal frigate of the same class. But we know that's not the case."

"It's the same scumbag that kicked our asses in Andal and S1-Ruhr, am I right?" asked Bambam resignedly.

"Almost blew our asses off," Gavin corrected him, not without pride.

"What makes you so sure?" asked Hellcat.

"We shot a couple of their spikes off, and the forward heat shield was damaged when we jumped out of CX-2's atmosphere. I could see both of those damages in that hangar. They didn't even have two days to make the repairs and whatever they did was obviously related to cloaking capability."

"One of the engines was also damaged," Mirage said. "I could see it on one of the displays in the control center. Three of the four engines were operational, one of them only fifty percent. So were the jump engines."

"Exactly. That's why we know Marquandt can't jump faster than we can. So their biggest trump card is out of play," Gavin explained, starting the holoprojector built into the table. On starships, space was always used sparingly, and it had been established early on that the mess hall was well suited as a meeting room. After all, this was where the Botcha source was located.

"It's still cloaked," Bambam pointed out. "What greater advantage would she need."

"Time. She could have everything done by the time we get there and can warn the authorities."

"Or a sister ship," Mirage agreed with him coolly.

"See? It could be worse. Besides, she," he pointed to the hologram beside him without looking at her, "confirmed that the cloaking field is based on some magnetic effect. And magnetic fields can be disrupted."

"Theoretically," the mechanic objected.

"Theoretically. But we still have time to figure something out." Gavin now pointed to the hologram in front of him, which showed a three-dimensional representation of the Sol system. "We'll have to surface outside of space flight control and its defenses, and in Sol, as we all know, jumps are forbidden and punishable by immediate destruction. We will have to do it anyway if we are to protect the Saturn Congress and the Aurora habitat."

"Akwa Marquandt will jump right into Saturn's vicinity because it doesn't have the problem of possible detection," Mirage picked up his thread. "Even deflections of the interferometers will not provide target bearings."

"So what's the plan?" asked Hellcat, looking at them both in turn. "You guys seem to have one, don't you?"

"I suggest we jump directly into the restricted area of Aurora Station."

"Exactly," Gavin agreed. "And then... wait, what?"

"We jump into Aurora's temporary exclusion zone," the stranger repeated.

"They'll shoot at us."

"Yes. But they will also put all ships into combat mode and call for reinforcements because they smell treason. A Navy ship with valid transponder codes - well forged, by the way - entering the tightest security area of all without authorization. Not just flying in, but jumping in."

"They might think that's a navigational error, too," Bambam opined, rubbing his unshaven chin thoughtfully.

"Yes."

"For that matter, the restricted area is large, but tiny in terms of jump navigation. Jumping into it, over several light years accurately, is about the same as trying to land on a Botcha cup during a parachute jump," Gavin said, shaking his head decisively. "I'm sorry, but that's simply impossible. Sphinx?"

"That assessment is correct. The probability of a successful calculation for that is ..."

"I'll take over navigation," Mirage cut the AI off. "I'll send you the appropriate data for your on-board computer."

"Okay, let's put aside the fact that that's impossible," he said, clasping his hands. "I'm someone who doesn't like the word *impossible*, and I've already done some things that had an extremely low probability of success. What then?"

"We warn them about the stealth ship. The important agencies know about your message."

"My message? It made it to the Emperor?" he asked in surprise.

"Yes."

"But Marquandt was already on his way to Sol when I left Earth. He is likely to use his influence. The First Secretary of State believes you, High Lord, so all the message has to do is get to him."

"Sounds easier than it is." Gavin thought about alternatives, but found none. Even if they showed up at the edge of the outer solar system in the transit areas, it would still take hours to get to Saturn. But hours in that case equaled half an eternity, during which Akwa Marquandt could do what she planned with the help of her father.

"No, it doesn't sound easy. It sounds like there's no alternative. Grand Admiral Marius Albius is also in cahoots with Marquandt. Not just Usatami," Mirage said casually.

"The emperor's chief of staff?" asked Gavin incredulously.

"Yes. He tried to assassinate the First Secretary of State - with the help of an orbital laser. Janus Darishma was just bringing to light covert dealings of Albius, Marquandt and Usatami and connecting the dots. But not only that, he was on his way to Newark."

"To Newark?" asked Hellcat. "What's that?"

"Is north of New York. There is a sealed-off planning center there for flights of the Emperor's ships. It's not connected to the dataverse or the grid to prevent anyone from accessing the Emperor's travel routes."

"So Akwa Marquandt's plan is not a quick fix, that's

The last Fleet

to be expected," Gavin commented, unsure of what she was getting at.

Mirage seemed to notice. Her hologram crossed its arms in front of its chest. "We have to expect that the fleet will not react as you expect. Especially since the majority of mobile naval units in the system are provided by Marquandt's wall fleet."

"I have a question," Hellcat spoke up after a long silence, and all eyes turned to her. "It's always like that with you guys, isn't it?"

Gavin reflexively wanted to ask who she meant by you, but he had a hunch when he saw the blazing anger in her eyes, so he remained silent.

"On Arcturus, thousands of people are being kidnapped, families torn apart. Fucking Cerberus is a hub for human traffickers. Out in the Seed Traverse, privileged assholes are conspiring with bloody aliens to sacrifice the abductees so they can extract knowledge from an Orb," she listed each point, eyes blazing with anger. "And what are you thinking about? About saving the Emperor, under whose fucking gaze this all happened. Why don't we even talk about flying to Cerberus and fucking blowing it up? We know where it is, we could stop the human trafficking."

"Young lady," Mirage said, and Gavin was sure Hellcat would have jumped on her and strangled her if she weren't just made of photons. "When a lion is standing on your chest, all you see are his claws. You could trim them, but then he'd shred you with his other claws. I'd rather have his head right now so he can't use them."

INTERLUDE
MIRAGE

"What's your impression?" the Voice inquired.

"Capable, but disparate. Like talented kids with too many hormones buzzing in their heads. I like the Invitro."

"Are they going to be a problem? Or useful?"

"Both," Mirage replied. She sat in the pilot's seat of the *42-QLUE*, watching the web of stars through the windshield. Their twinkling possessed a depth, infinity, that was more a feeling than real understanding. Even to her. Out here, everything was just the light of distant suns, and all the problems and conflicts were no more than sound and smoke in a sea of silence.

"Explain."

"They are competent and have a strong will to win, coupled with a willingness to take great risks," she explained. "But they come from two different ends of society and two different ends of early learned introjects."

"It will come to conflict," the Voice concluded.

"They are in perpetual conflict, but they are welded together by the necessity of impossible situations they have gotten into so far without a chance to catch their breath. The Invitro is driving on sight and wants stability. The mechanic carries some hatred for the Navy that runs so deep he's probably had to bury it for a long time, and the blonde rebel is just that: a rebel. And she's a rebel by the skin of her teeth. Young Andal has her respect, but she doesn't know how to deal with it because he is everything she should hate. This conflict hasn't broken out yet because they keep saving each other's lives."

"But it will erupt."

"Yes."

"Then you have to make sure it doesn't happen while you still need them."

"I'm not a psychologist."

"No, you're much more. We need them in Sol. Once you reach your target, they can do whatever they want," the Voice said.

"I need current data on ship movements out of Sol," Mirage changed the subject. "Deus can calculate the exact exit points, but needs the final vectors of all the starships at least fifteen minutes before our final jump."

"You'll get those."

"Good."

"Mirage. This may be our only chance that we've waited so long for."

"I understand what's at stake." She hesitated.

"There's something else."

"Yes. Zenith."

"He's alive. There has been no other attempted attack on him," the Voice revealed to her. "But there was an attempted kidnapping of Princess Elayne from the *Rubov* that he was involved in."

"Involved?"

"It seems he tried to rescue her. Successfully. Right

now, task forces are trying to recover them both. But they are alive."

"Understood," Mirage said with trained indifference.

"Remember your objective," the Voice cautioned her, "That's the only thing that matters now."

4

GAVIN

Gavin dreamed of an alien that had neural cables instead of fingers, which it tried to connect to all his orifices. To keep it in a peaceful mood, he invited it to breakfast, and baked a loaf of bread especially for the occasion using his mother's recipe. As the alien sat with its wriggling neural cables at his breakfast table, which apparently had no table legs, Gavin tasted his baked product, only to discover that he had forgotten the salt. Even as he frantically pondered whether that might be an advantage, because the alien guest with enthusiasm for connection might be allergic to it, he started awake from his sleep.

Blinking against fatigue and confusion, he was startled when the buzzer squealed over his cabin door. A glance at his chronometer told him it was middle of the night shipboard time.

"Open," he muttered after unbuckling his seat belt and floating to a sitting position.

As the door slid upward into its socket with a hiss, Hellcat appeared out of the corridor into the entrance. "Can I come in?"

"Uh, sure," Gavin said, watching her come in with magnetic boots clicking and looking around. "The captain's cabin was supposed to be Roger's. I wanted it, but I never said it."

Roger? he thought, wondering who she could mean. However, since she seemed to have something on her mind, he didn't interrupt her.

"I got the ship. Sure, with Dodger's and Bambam's help and a lot of others from the underground," she continued, stroking the faux wood of the small desk next to the wet room. "I thought it was my right after everything. But we couldn't have flown this thing without Roger. We couldn't have gotten out of the system without the codes that Bambam snatched from a contact in the Navy. And without Dodger, we wouldn't have gotten the stash at the port. So, I let Roger have the cabin."

"Your pilot," Gavin said. It felt like a memory from another life, when he'd shot Lizzy's killer. He searched for guilt inside himself, but found nothing but grief over Lizzy's death and anger that another man had snuffed out her life with the crook of his finger. Just like that.

"Yes."

"Were you..."

"No." Hellcat shook her head and turned to him. By now Gavin was hovering over his bed, one foot hooked in the restraining loop on the mattress. "I hate everything you stand for."

"Uh, okay." The words hit him harder than he wanted to admit.

"I hate the favoritism at birth. I hate the oppression of all those who weren't born with a golden spoon up their ass and keep the Star Empire alive as a working mass. I hate that my mother was considered a second-class human being. I hate that you were never shown how normal people have to live and work, in fourteen-hour shifts on mining asteroids, in the vacuum docks. I hate that people like you don't even know that third- and fourth-degree injuries leading to disability are not covered by citizens' insurance because occupational risks are excluded. Supposedly because of appropriate bonuses and personal responsibility."

Gavin blinked in surprise. He actually hadn't known that.

"I hate that you not only tolerate but secretly control and direct Assai smuggling to profit from it, while addicts are imprisoned all over the Star Empire only to be offered Navy or Army recruitment as a way out to pad the ranks," Hellcat continued without taking her eyes off him. With each angry sentence, she took a step closer. "But most of all, I hate that I can't hate you."

"Thanks, I guess?"

"Shut up," she snapped at him. Their knees were almost touching now. She smelled like mint. With her wild eyes she seemed to look straight into his soul like an untamed animal. They contrasted sharply with her soft skin, her full mouth, always slightly tense, now merely full and soft, as if something had loosened. Her hair framed the elfin face like a cloud of gold and silver in the dim cabin light. "I hate that you're different than I wanted to see you. I hate your willingness to sacrifice. I hate your loyalty. I hate your honesty, and I hate that you saved my life."

"You started it," he said softly.

"I hate that you saw me defenseless," she whispered right in front of his face. Her breath warmed him. "And I hate that you didn't take advantage of it. That you had compassion and made me feel safe, even though I told you something that only Dodger and Bambam know about me."

"I think you have too much hate in you."

"Shut up," she hissed, "I'm not done yet. I hate that you're none of the things I've hated so far. I know who the enemy is, have always imagined him to be like you, and yet you are completely different. But most of all, I hate that I trust you."

Gavin considered her words, though it was difficult when confronted with her beauty and almost magnetic presence so close in front of him. *She's afraid to trust me.*

Her eyes still blazed, but the fire in them burned hotter and steadier now as she seemed to probe the depths of his soul. It was as if she was asking him an unspoken question, with her hand on a door that had never been opened. Behind it was everything Hellcat did not show because it made her human and vulnerable, and Gavin could feel it terrifying her as it emerged.

"I hate it," she whispered, "that I can't hate you. Don't want to hate you."

Gavin didn't let go of her gaze, opening to the deep blue of her eyes that said so much more than words ever could. Then he said softly, "I see you, Hallewell Hatami."

When their lips touched, it happened silent and gentle, warm and moist like the touch of a late summer breeze on naked skin. An intimate affection, primal and indescribable, made way after being held back too long. Their tongues found each other first hesitantly, then they loosened and became demanding. Fireworks of sensation exploded in Gavin's chest, spreading as tingles from the crown of his head to the tips of his toes as he grabbed her by the shoulders and pulled her against him. Her hands clutched gently but firmly at his curls, and her arms wrapped around his neck in the process, warm and strong.

The last Fleet

Time narrowed to the present, words became feelings that transcended their meaning, expanding far beyond themselves and allowing the universe to expand into true infinity in the intimate merging of two souls that needed no space or time at all.

All was here and now as all else faded away.

5

JANUS

When the rescuers extricated them from the wall, Janus was barely conscious. His Smartnites had worked wonders to keep him from bleeding to death, but in the end, it had been over four hours before the first lights had gotten through to them. Vague impressions of Elayne's face, huge figures in powered armor, blue lights everywhere, and dead bodies being carried away in black bags accompanied him like a fever dream. He saw destruction, heard screams and wails, heard barked orders and the trampling of boots on the ground.

Then a strange face bent over him, wanting his consent for something, until another voice spoke - Elayne, sounding somehow imperious.

Then he faded out of consciousness.

When he woke up again, he felt like he had slept long and deep. Free of pain. Not even tension.

"You're awake!"

He was lying on a medidoc in a white room with dim lights. Elayne beside him in a chair where she had apparently dozed off.

"Princess," he said formally, looking around. He was in the Emperor's private medical quarters in his chambers.

"I don't want you to ever call me that again, Janus," she replied with mock sternness. "That's an order, if you must."

He nodded and raised his hands scrutinizingly, turning them in front of his face as if they weren't his own.

"We've swapped out your entire Smartnite supply and replaced them with Deltaware," she explained. "I'll bet Father didn't know you still had Beta nanites in you."

"There's been no reason to ask for the latest generation so far."

"You're too modest. Your position doesn't just come with duties, you do realize that, don't you?" Elayne gave him a smile full of sympathy and put a hand on his arm after he lowered it again. "Thank you, Janus. If it wasn't for you, I would be... I don't even want to think about where I would have been taken by those monsters."

"I'm glad we made it." He cringed. "Your father! Has he taken off yet?"

"Yes. Four hours ago."

"Oh, no!" Janus tried to get up, but she held him back. "What is it?"

"He's in danger. I believe that Albius..."

"The Chief of Staff is aboard the *Majestic* with him."

"He took Albius with him?"

Elayne nodded and frowned. "Yes, why?"

Janus thought about it. The idea was perhaps not a bad one. Albius was in cahoots with Marquandt. The laser attack had been a strong suspicion, the Invitros' operation in Hellgate downright proof.

"Nothing. It's okay. What about the attackers? Were the authorities able to find out anything?" he steered the

The last Fleet

conversation in a new direction so as not to worry her too much.

"Colonel Bazagan says that they are members of some criminal organization from the Border Worlds. Vaults, I think," Elayne said. "Does that mean anything to you?"

"Vaults and Bone Eaters. They're two former gangs that have merged into a syndicate that controls Assai smuggling from the Border Worlds. Possibly even most of the entire trade in the drug in the Star Kingdom."

Marquandt.

"Is my father in danger, Janus?"

"Yes." He couldn't bring himself to lie to her. "But not acutely. I think he's made a smart move."

"Is it Marquandt? There are rumors about the lost battle in the border systems," she said with a worried expression.

"And where are these rumors coming from? Not from the Imperial sector, I take it?"

Elayne shook her head. "I know what you're going to say. But here in this gilded cage, it's like an echo chamber. I only ever get to hear what I'm supposed to hear and not what there really is to hear. But Heron, I mean the informant I've been in contact with…" She paused and seemed to be thinking about something that, judging by the expression on her face, was not pleasant. "He knew an amazing amount. Things I've never heard of in my life. And don't tell me now that I can't trust him because he's a criminal."

"He's well-informed," he surprised her. Of course, he knew Heron before he was First Secretary of State, but he knew him after, too.

"You know him?"

"Of course. In my position, I'm not paid to choose your father's wardrobe, but to direct the Star Empire in its day-to-day affairs. It's like an elephant, and elements like Heron or the Broker are like the parasites on our skin. We can't get rid of them, so we might as well use them to inform us of what's happening behind our backs."

Elayne eyed him with a whole new set of eyes. Apparently she was adjusting the image she had had of him so far.

"Did you know..."

"Of your visits?" he asked. "Yes, and no. You have done pretty well for yourself. Where did you learn that?"

"From Peraia," she said, without hesitation.

Janus frowned, then nodded. "I see."

"Sometimes you really puzzle me."

"What do you mean?"

"Anyone else would have said something like: When she disappeared, you were only a few years old! How could she have taught you anything then? But you did not. You think it over and then you understand. It's always like that. It's almost as if you're peering into my head, or have had the same experiences I have." Elayne eyed him inquiringly. "And then there's this super agent thing."

The creases in his brow deepened.

"Janus." She slid forward in her chair, her sleek one-piece reinforced polyamide creaking on the seat cushion. "In Dark Caesar, you were... different. You were shooting that old rifle like a VR action hero. How do you know how to do all that? And then the grenade. Baseball?"

"You're deflecting," he said, clearing his throat. "You were clearly following Peraia's tracks. Tracks that no one has found in over twenty years."

"That no one wanted to find," she corrected him, and her expression darkened like the blue sky just before a thunderstorm. "If I could figure out what she did, a couple of agents could have done it."

Janus didn't answer right away, and her eyes narrowed to narrow slits.

"You know something."

"No," he returned, shaking his head. "I promise you I don't. But I've been First Secretary of the Star Empire long enough to know where the sore spots of our society are."

Elayne gestured for him to continue. For her young age, the graceful wave looked rather stately.

"We are not a democracy as in the old days of the Solar Union. We have bought order and security through authority and control. That is an open secret. In my opinion, it was necessary in order to give humanity a future where it would not tear each other apart and fall into cosmic oblivion," he explained. "There are several prices to pay for that. One of them is that nobody likes to deliver bad news because no body is backed up. No separation of powers, no real legal security, even though they probably didn't teach you that at the academy."

"That goes for bad news, too," she surmised, sighing. With the casual grace of a princess, she brushed a golden curl from her face and stared into her open hands. "If anyone knew anything, they kept it to themselves and destroyed the evidence so they would not end up being blamed for the death of the heir to the throne."

Janus did not answer, but his silence was answer enough for her.

"I was afraid of something like that. It's so damned unfair." She glanced up at him like a caught child. "Sorry."

He waved it off. "You put the puzzle together, I take it?"

"Yes. I got a name from Heron after I completely reconstructed Peraiah's path. To a point where I lost her."

"Where?"

"In the Dust system."

"She was with your uncle?"

"So it seems. Yes." Elayne nodded. "But I don't understand why she didn't jump to Orb territory from there. Why the detour via Artemis in the Wall Sectors?"

"I don't know."

"I can trust you, can't I, Janus?" Her gaze turned serious.

"With your life," he assured her of the truth. Since he could see her struggling, he added in a lowered voice, "My parents died in Republican insurgent fire during the McMaster dynasty. I know the consequences chaos can have and how close it has brought us to the abyss. Your father has always been an example to me of responsible use of power, with all his self-doubt and open ears to critical opinion. His children are much more than that. Both Peraia and Magnus were as kind-hearted as one could wish for in a ruler and blessed with wisdom and empathy. You, dear Elayne, combine the best of them in you. You are one of the reasons why I still fill my position with the same conviction as on the first day."

Elayne was too empathetic to ruin this moment with a flippant retort just to make him feel good. Instead, she nodded slowly.

"Shirin Farad," she finally said, after the regular beeping of the luxurious medidoc had been the only sound to defy silence.

"That's the name Heron gave you, I assume?" He hated to speak that name, which sounded like a mockery of Emperor Haeron.

"Yes. Does it mean anything to you?"

"No," he replied truthfully. "But I would have the resources to find out." When her eyes grew wide, he made a placating gesture. "Through unofficial channels, don't worry."

"Would you do that for me?"

"You have a theory about Peraiah's disappearance, I take it?" he asked evasively. "A well-founded one?"

"Yes," she said in a chest tone of conviction. "Her ship, the Persephone, she had assembled from individual components over two years with the help of her Imperial powers. No supplier to the New California orbital shipyards charged money for it, but she paid them anyway."

"So the parts wouldn't show up on the books."

Elayne nodded. "Officially, her ship was from the Styx series, and she was fastidious about making sure the Persephone's signature was also exactly that of a Styx prospector. But I was able to find a manufacturer for all eighteen primary systems who had exactly one write-off - officially as a defective part - on their books, within the same week twenty years ago. That very week, she was in Dust for the first time. Supposedly on a family visit to Uncle Jurgan, with whom she had always kept in good touch."

"And when she was back, she asked for command of a Styx Prospector to search for microbial life in the systems near the Tartarus Void, which has always been considered a possible origin of Never and has therefore often been a candidate for major research missions," Janus concluded, eyeing her appreciatively. "You figured all that out?"

"Oh, there's more. One of their crew members, Doctor Aloisius Shepherd, was still a prisoner on the Kolassi penal colony two weeks before they left. Guess who got him out by Imperial decree?"

"Peraia."

"That's right."

"What was he convicted of?"

"Unethical experimentation on higher life forms. He allegedly tried to network the brains of two people and connect them into one, allowing one to take over the other by means of a special neural computer," Elayne explained with a shudder.

"A sequestration nanonics," Janus said, startled. "That's..."

"Highly illegal, yes. He tried to defend himself by saying that one of the subjects was a brain-dead twin of the other and they would have participated in the experiment voluntarily, but the court decided the case rather quickly."

"Was he successful?"

"I could not find out. My sister must have seen something in him that she needed. But what's even more interesting is that she recruited two members for her mission who had worked in the Artemis system in high positions for the Science Corps until they transferred to her. Monica Heynes and Ruben Kardashenko. A xeno-biologist and a physicist. So far, so normal. But they have something in common. They were stationed in Trabantius, eighty years earlier, when the second Orb incident occurred there. They were junior doctors and part of the crew of a cruiser named *Wallonia*, which disappeared with several other ships at that time. However, they came back and..."

"The *Wallonia* was Grand Admiral Albius' first command, under the Union Navy," Janus said.

"And do you know who his first mate was?"

"Dain Marquandt."

Elayne's eyes grew wide. "How do you know that? Someone went to a lot of trouble to blur that part of his career well."

"It just makes sense."

If the Princess wanted to press him for further elaboration, she said nothing, leaving him free to say what he wanted to say.

"Was Varilla Usatami also on board?"

Now she blinked in complete confusion. "How..."

"A hunch. The three of them still keep in touch, you might say."

"She was aboard as a civilian representative of an assessment mission on behalf of Congress. At the time, she was a simple office assistant to a congressman whose name I've forgotten."

Janus tried to tie the information together. If he were still part of the Network, he probably would have known all this. However, the Voice also did not know about Marquandt's collaboration with Yokatami in the Seed Traverse. Or at least it had not occurred as significant. The fact that Albius had been in command of the only one of the missing ships that had returned was well known in the Navy. Janus himself had read through his report, which stated that they had pursued an enemy ship several jumps and then fallen back with reactor damage that had taken several weeks to repair. The ship had been badly battered and only three had survived. Supposedly four ordinary crewmembers, but that could not be true now, when in truth it had been Marquandt, Usatami, Heynes and Kardashenko. He could only explain that they had managed to cover up this fact at all by the fact that it had happened shortly before the fall of the Solar Union and the rise of McMaster. In the transition period, many things were lost that influential people liked to see lost.

"What are you getting at, Elayne?" he asked in a familiar fatherly tone. He didn't let on that it was a rhetorical question.

"I believe that Peraia found out something about the *Wallonia* that justified her obsession with the Orb. Later, she was able to recruit the two scientists for a secret mission. Those two must have known if the *Wallonia* saw more than just a few jumps into unknown territory. She must have seen a cause worth risking her life for and leaving everything behind." Pain shone from the Princess' eyes as she brought the last sentence through her lips. The fact that her big sister had left her alone without a word seemed to be a dagger in her heart to this day.

"That sounds plausible when I consider all the information you've gathered," Janus said thoughtfully.

"Wait - you believe me?"

"Yes. The conclusions are logical."

"But... I thought..."

"What did you think? That I'd ignore all this and say you were chasing a pipe dream? No." He shook his head and took her hand. "I can imagine how hard it's been for you, playing princess here at home, doing all the chores at court, even though you hate them and you can only think of one thing: your sister. Losing someone you love is one thing, but not knowing what happened to them, whether they might even be alive or in trouble – that is worse. You have seen your father in the last few days. He..."

"It's okay, Janus. This stays between us," she assured him with a seriousness that seemed far too set and wise for someone as young as she was. But she'd never really had a childhood, in truth.

"He's on the cusp of being a broken man. He thinks it's because of Magnus' death in battle."

"Or betrayal."

"Or betrayal." He waved it off. "But the process started much earlier, I think. Your father was not always such a

The last Fleet

melancholy man, Elayne. The burden of Peraia's disappearance weighs heavily on him."

"But he didn't do anything!" Suddenly she sounded like the young woman she was again. Hurt and stubborn. "He would have had all the resources to do it. The entire IIA, for example. Your agents could have done my work for the last five years in days."

"You have to understand him," he instinctively took the Emperor to task. "He is the leader of humanity. He must function, be strong for the Star Empire. The mere risk that any investigations might turn up something traceable to your house, or that they might come to nothing, and he might lose himself more and more in a spiral of doubt and self-reproach, could have had consequences for everyone."

Elayne sighed. All at once she seemed tired. In a whisper, she said, "I wish we could have just been a normal family. I barely got to know Mom. Peraia left us because she didn't seem to trust us enough to share what she found out. And now Magnus, my brother."

She started to cry, then began sobbing without restraint.

Janus grimaced and slid off the medidoc. He knelt in front of her and wrapped her in his arms.

"I'm sorry. Fate is bigger than all of us. It is always bigger than us. And it always reminds us of that to keep us humble," he said softly into her hair. "I have spent many years of my life running from this truth, fighting it. But in the end, it is a constant, it is as elemental as gravity and the passage of time. We have no control, however much we wish we were the center of the universe and could influence which direction it spins around us. Magnus was a good man, and we will remember him as such. But we cannot bring him back."

"I know that."

"But," he continued, breaking away from her and looking into her teary eyes. His voice became fierce. "We can make the traitor pay for his murder of your brother, and..."

When he faltered, her gaze became questioning. "What is it?"

"I believe he also murdered my assistant, Nancy." Janus took a deep breath and slumped back against the couch. He clenched his hands into fists in frustration. "I had sent her to Marquandt to give him a message. I wanted to draw him out, force him to make a mistake. When she didn't get back to me, I started to worry. Now I understand. It's exactly what he wanted, because he knew about your forays."

"What? How?"

"Heron. The fact that you went to see him so close to leaving for Saturn was certainly no accident."

"No. His message said he had the last piece of information I was looking for," she explained, confused. "But that it had an expiration date."

Janus expelled his breath in frustration. "He knew your father would send me to get you and I would do it because I was worried by Nancy's silence and the worry would transfer to you. So he almost took us both out."

"I don't understand. Who? Marquandt?" Elayne blinked in confusion and a few tears fell from her long lashes.

"Yes. But we're still alive. I have a favor to ask of you, Princess."

"What is it?"

"I need a ship from standby."

"From my father's standby?" she asked, "I don't think my father..."

The last Fleet

"I think Marquandt is planning to kill your father." Her eyes widened. She looked like a skittish horse about to bolt. "And you, too. You are safest here, but I need to see your father."

"Then send him a message over the quantcom."

"That's not possible because he is on the *Majestic*. You know the rules of engagement."

"What do you want us to do?" she asked belligerently.

"I'll take a direct route to Saturn and hope to get to the Aurora faster than he does. Then I'll persuade him to do something that is extremely bad politically and will happen at the worst possible time: He must have Marquandt terminated, even without the ultimate proof."

"No."

"But..."

"No, Janus. *We* are going to do it," she decided, and he knew the stubborn look that now lay in her eyes, alongside fear and determination, like an immovable law of nature.

6

GAVIN

When Gavin woke up, Hellcat was gone. He had slept for eight hours, and for the first time since Andal, he was not plagued by nightmares. No screaming people fleeing the Never raining from the sky like black death. No eerie shadows in the firmament blocking out the stars. No faces of his family looking at him reproachfully or forgivingly, dissipating like ghostly mists as soon as they tried to speak to him.

Although the pain still lay as a depressing heaviness in his stomach and in his bones, something inside him had loosened. Not the part of him that had been destroyed forever with the fall of his home and all the people he loved. But the worst wound, the one that had bled him dry day after day since they had escaped, was closed for now. Hellcat had turned out to be strong-willed, but warm-hearted when she let down her guard. Very different from the angry fury he had come to know her as. What he could see in her when they had made love was a warm-hearted but scarred person who had let him in to see her innermost being and know her.

"Sphinx?" he asked.

"Yes, Gavin?" the ship's AI replied over his cabin speakers.

"When did she leave?"

"Shortly after you fell asleep."

She doesn't want the others to know about this? he thought, and the thought gave him a twinge of hurt.

"Where are we currently?" Gavin could have checked for himself, but his neural computer was still in sleep mode, and he wanted to enjoy the relaxed rest a little longer. He knew what a precious commodity it would be in the hours ahead.

"We're jumping to Alpha Centauri in thirty minutes," Sphinx said in her pleasant mezzo-soprano.

"Then we'll be leaving soon," he muttered, sighing as he unbuckled himself and floated out of bed toward the washroom. "The plan is suicidal."

"I've come to that conclusion myself."

"Very reassuring. Don't tell me about our chances of survival."

"All right."

Gavin opened the door to the washroom, slipped inside, and wedged his feet under the designated hollows on the floor before turning on the purification system and receiving a spray of bacteria-enriched water from nozzles scattered throughout. It settled on his skin like a transparent film until he was completely covered by it. Then it was all blown down from above by a strong, pleasantly warm stream of air and disappeared into the suction holes of the floor.

"Have you communicated with the *42-QLUE*'s on-board computer?" he asked as he made his way to his uniform. Hellcat, Dodger and Bambam would hate it, but he was still a captain in the Imperial Navy and would proudly go into battle against the traitors.

"Yes. It is very impressive."

"Oh?"

"An artificial intelligence that is superior to my own abilities."

"Well, you are quite advanced in years," he followed up.

"That is correct. I have already been sent all the jump data and the exit point. The precision and speed of the calculations are extremely good," Sphinx said.

"I certainly hope so, because if they're not, it's not just us who have a problem, it's the entire Star Empire." Gavin brushed his teeth and checked that his insignia and badges were properly in place before leaving his cabin.

The corridor was quiet, and the lights were dimmed. Since they still had thirty minutes until the next-to-last jump, he shimmied to the door of the crew compartment where twelve crew members normally slept in their bunks. The control panel had no bell, so he asked Sphinx to make an appropriate sound on the other side.

It took a minute for Bambam to open for him.

"Hi, Captain."

"Can I come in?"

"Sure," the mechanic said, making room. The cramped compartment smelled almost like Gavin's bachelor apartment during his first year at cadet school. Dodger had just floated out of the washrooms like the ancient Greek Colossus.

"We're jumping to Alpha Centauri and then Sol soon," Gavin said. "I'm glad you're along for the ride."

They looked at him attentively, but said nothing.

"I realize it must be difficult for you guys. A dilemma, probably. Marquandt is trying to wipe out the entire top leadership of the Empire in one fell swoop. I'd be willing to bet that's like the wet dream of every Republican terr... *Underground fighter*."

They did not disagree.

"But I also know what you guys are made of. I've seen you stand up for each other and for those weaker than you are on the Seed World. Marquandt's betrayal is not a betrayal of the Star Empire, but of humanity. You saw it on Andal, and you saw it at the secret Yokatami facility. If we don't stop them, things will only get darker."

"We're with you, Captain," Dodger said casually.

"Yep," Bambam agreed with her. "This is some sick shit. Wouldn't mind seeing the Star Empire tear itself apart and clear the way for equality. But hell if I'm gonna let these sick fucks take the lead. The present is real dark, but what they're doing is a whole different ballgame, man."

So, what happens to us after we stop them? Gavin thought. *Am I going to be your enemy again?*

He was all too painfully aware that it was a partnership of convenience, and they had not had time to remember that they were supposed to be enemies. There was constantly a larger, direct threat, so the subject had never come up. But that would inevitably change. The only question was when.

Not today.

The two seemed to realize that something stood between them that he saw at that moment.

"I just wanted to say that we're going to make it. After everything that's been thrown at us the last few days, it has to be a walk in the park." Gavin grinned his best daredevil grin. "Besides, I'm the best damn pilot in the Star Empire."

"Don't worry," Dodger said. "We'll pull this off."

The last Fleet

"The bloody bastards have murdered everyone we cared about back home on Andal, and over a billion people with them." Bambam's look turned grim. "People we wanted to liberate. Let's kick their asses."

Gavin next went to the first officer's cabin where Hellcat was staying, but she did not answer. So instead, he continued on to the junior officers' quarters. The Master Sergeant and Masha looked a bit disheveled as they opened the door, as if they were making a last-minute appearance.

"We're getting ready," Gavin said. "You should be strapped into the acceleration seats in twenty minutes."

"Of course, my lord," the Sergeant replied.

"Let's say thirty minutes."

Masha smiled in the background while the Marine looked as if he had to swallow a handful of nails.

On the bridge, he found Hellcat. She was already strapped into her seat, going over system checks.

"Good morning," he greeted her.

"Good morning," she replied, throwing him a warm but fleeting smile before refocusing on her readouts.

"You're up early." Gavin strapped himself into the pilot's seat and started his neural computer's link to the bridge systems.

"I like the quiet. It's where I can think and make myself useful."

He took her statement as a hint, went "Mhm," and then went through the checklists as well. Bambam and Dodger must have worked through the night, because most of the systems were working admirably, albeit forty percent on the redundancies that were supposed to be replacements in case of failure. So there would not be too much margin, but he was getting used to that by now.

"Mirage?" he called to their escort ship, which hovered

five clicks away in interstellar space like a phantom stalking them in the darkness.

"I'm here."

"Everything is ready on our end. We have received your navigational data. My ship's AI is quite impressed." he said.

"The data is good."

"I went over the plan again. Are your calculations as accurate as far as EMP effects from nuclear weapons?"

"Yes. A long-range network of simultaneous detonations would have to disrupt the stealth ship's magnetic fields. It's a gamble in terms of range and suspected enemy position, but it's the best we've got."

"We know far too little about the cloaking device."

"We know one thing," Mirage returned coolly. "So, we use that one thing."

"That is if the Navy plays along. They will think we are crazy."

"No. Trafalgar was destroyed by cloaked Orb ships, and so was a fleet of Admiral Taggert's when they tried to retake Trafalgar. Few survived."

Gavin thought about her words and took a deep breath. "But some did survive."

"Yes, through the use of antimatter weapons. They were even able to destroy some of the alien ships."

"Then they will think that the Orb are attacking."

"Yes."

"We'll see. We'll be ready to jump to Alpha Centauri in five minutes."

"You don't trust her, do you?" asked Hellcat when the connection was broken.

"No," he said flatly.

"But our whole plan is based on their calculations. What if she just wants to get rid of us?"

"I think she needs us. And we need her. That's solid enough as a basis for cooperation, don't you think?"

"She's a living violation of the Turing Agreement. The woman is a fucking robot whether she answered the question from your chained dog negatively or not," she insisted, turning her seat to face him. There was genuine concern and barely concealed anger in her gaze. "This whole thing is a bad idea."

"Do you have last-minute anxiety?" he asked, immediately regretting the words.

"I think that's obvious. Apparently it's normal for you, putting your life in the hands of an unknown robot that we know nothing about," she replied with a frown and turned back to her consoles.

Gavin wanted to say something else, but felt that he would only meet with a brick wall.

7
JANUS

All attempts to dissuade Elayne from accompanying him failed. She was determined to help protect her father and save the Star Empire from traitors. Her youthful drive to perform supposed heroic deeds reminded him of his own days as a young man, which had led him to join the Network nearly a hundred years ago. How he wished now that he had had a cautionary voice at his side then, warning him of the consequences.

But the Princess was once again an example of the fact that the youth did not let the older generation talk them into the fluff in their heads anyway.

So they slipped into form-fitting Mongoose-type body armor and donned medium-weight hardened military armor over it, which was self-sufficient in an emergency and certified for use in a vacuum.

On the way to the Imperial docks, he contacted the captain of the current standby shift and informed them that they would be taking the *Invincible* and needed a hundred-man Imperial Guard on board. The rest of the crew was already part of the standby shift anyway, and part of a three-shift system that ensured each of the six ships was manned around the clock.

In the marble vestibule with the large circular airlocks leading into the mighty cruisers, he held Elayne back by the arm.

"Before we leave, I need something from you," he said gravely. In his armor, he felt clunky and awkward.

"Of course." Her gold-framed angelic face seemed alien in the powerful armor with hardened plates protecting her chest and shoulders.

"I need you to transfer temporary command authority to me."

"What do you mean?" she asked.

"As a member of the Imperial family, you are automatically the commander-in-chief on every ship and station in your father's absence."

"But you..."

"I have the highest political authority in the Star Empire, but no military directive authority whatsoever unless I am acting under direct orders from the Emperor," he explained. "But I need command so I can act quickly and efficiently."

Elayne hesitated, obviously confused that he was now broaching the subject.

"You've seen me in Dark Caesar. I know what I'm doing."

"Of course," she finally said, and transferred a temporary command code to him, bearing the Emperor's highest certification and seal, valid for a period of six hours.

"Thank you." He looked over at the elite guardsmen in the background walking by in Titan armor, and sent a direct message to their captain via transducer, whereupon the entire group swung around and came running to them. Elayne frowned.

The last Fleet

"Shouldn't they be coming with us?"

"Actually, yes," he said evasively, waiting until the soldiers were with them.

"Your highness, my lord," the captain greeted them respectfully, removing his helmet. He was a tough-looking man with thin lips and small eyes.

"Captain, please escort the Princess back to her chambers and double the guard," the instructed the Marine.

"WHAT?" cried Elayne indignantly, staring at him angrily.

"Her safety may be at risk. Make sure there are at least four bodyguards near her at all times," Janus continued, outwardly impassive.

"No. You will not, Captain!"

Janus sent the command code she had issued him herself, and although the Marine was outwardly impassive, the look from his eyes left no doubt that he was struggling.

"You have your orders, Captain."

"I'm sorry, Highness," the captain finally said in the direction of the princess. "Please accompany me."

"Janus! How could you? I trusted you!" She just spat out the words, and the disappointment and anger in her eyes hit him like a hammer.

"It's for your safety, Elayne. I would never forgive myself for putting you in danger, and your father would never forgive me either." He took a step toward her and grabbed her by the arms before she could wriggle away from him. "Listen to me. I'll keep the Quantcom receiver on, you can virtually plug into the systems as an observer, and we can talk. But you need to be safe until this is over. We do not know what the traitors are up to, but there's currently no safer place in the system than this."

"As safe as Hellgate was?" she shot back.

Janus didn't elaborate. "When this is over, I promise you that I will lobby your father to authorize a mission to find Peraia, and you can do further research with official IIA help. Under your supervision."

She wanted to elude him, and he let her, knowing that the captain would intervene too soon rather than too late and, if in doubt, amputate his arms. At her hands, however, he paused, turned her left wrist and placed a personal quantcom unit inside.

"Careful, my lord," the captain rumbled warningly.

Janus ignored him and closed her hand. "I'm sorry, Elayne. We'll stay in touch the whole time, I promise."

The Princess said nothing and regarded him with an angry glint in her eyes. Eventually, however, she nodded and her anger faded, at least a little.

Turning, he ran at a quick pace, aided by the artificial muscle strands in the mongoose armor synchronized with his own muscle fibers, to the *Invincible*'s airlock and into the central corridor.

Two Marines in uniform assumed posture without saluting.

"Cast off!" he ordered, and stepped into the multidirectional elevator that took him toward the bow, where the bridge was located. Satisfied, he noted that weightlessness had already set in when he reached it.

They had cast off.

The bridge was a large circular room in the heart of the cruiser with the commander's swiveling seat in the center and twenty crewmen at consoles all around, facing a display wall showing camera and other sensor data.

"First Secretary of State," the captain greeted him, a tall woman with sternly slicked-back hair and a piercing stare. Her uniform looked as if it had come freshly pressed and starched from the closet. "I'm Emilia Gianni."

"Captain." He nodded his thanks as she gestured to the empty seat next to her that was normally reserved for the Emperor.

"Where are you headed, if you don't mind me asking?"

"Saturn. I'm afraid there may be an attempt on the Emperor's life," he said flatly.

"Set course, full thrust. Priority request to space flight control," Gianni ordered even before he had spoken. Only then did she turn back to him, her expression serious and tense. "What are we up against?"

"I don't know, but I have a reasonable suspicion that Admiral Dain Marquandt is behind this." That the commander wasn't blindsided either spoke to her discipline and professionalism, or the news of Gavin Andal had already spread farther than it should have. Perhaps the Network was behind it.

"Understood, sir, flight time is twelve hours by direct route."

"Good, we're not making any detours. Inform space flight control of our destination."

"That will attract attention," the captain indicated.

"That's what I'm counting on. Attention we draw is not on the Emperor," he countered.

"I understand."

After they accelerated away from the orbital ring and Terra grew smaller behind them, he looked at the small Quantcom unit in his left hand. At the same moment, his neural computer showed an incoming connection. Relief was about to spread through him that Elayne had gotten over her disappointment so quickly, but he was shown an unknown sender.

"I have declined and continue to decline," he said through his transducer as the quantum connection was established.

"We respect that, Zenith," the Voice replied. "I have information for you."

"What's the price?"

"No price."

"There is always a price."

"Not this time. Mirage has found out something, and both our interests overlap in this case. There will be an attack on the Emperor."

"That doesn't surprise me."

"No. You're on your way to Saturn, I see, but you underestimate the danger. Captain Akwa Marquandt is in possession of a cloaked hybrid ship that is also headed for Saturn. She plans to destroy the Aurora habitat when the Emperor addresses Congress," the Voice explained.

"The same ship that went after Gavin Andal?" he asked with a shudder.

"Yes. It is equipped with Orb technology and cannot be detected. Mirage was able to figure out that the cloaking field is based on some unknown electromagnetic effect, so it could help to use EMPs."

"Why are you telling me this?" he asked. "You know what? Forget it. I know the information is going to cost me, but I'll play along. Aurora is the target? When?"

"We have reasonable grounds to believe that their ship is damaged and can only jump at normal transit intervals. Eleven hours from now. Approximately." You could hear in their voice how much they loathed that word. "Be careful, Zenith."

"What else did you find out? Where did this information come from? From the Seed Traverse, am I right?"

"Yes." The Voice left no doubt that they were not ready to say more. "Good luck."

Janus disconnected and pondered about the call. It worried him. Not just the nature of the call. The destruction of the Aurora habitat seemed so out of the realm of possibility that the very thought of it seemed outlandish. But a habitat was still a space station and only as secure as its defenses. A few well-aimed nuclear missiles were enough to destroy it; after all, it was not a space fortress, but a civilian facility. An attack would mean that much of the Navy leadership and the civilian government and senior civil service would die. A guillotine for the Star Empire. That he had not seen it immediately when Andal had reported the stealth ship made him angry with himself. He should have seen it. The second concern was for the Network itself. The Voice never shared information without expecting something in return. That they had done so after all could only mean that their quid pro quo consisted of something it expected him to do and needed for their plans. In keeping with the Network, they had to have a good data base to go that far.

But what did that mean for him? Was he supposed to behave differently than he actually would, just to thwart their plans? Or was that precisely what they were counting on?

8

GAVIN

As they were about to jump out of Alpha Centauri into Sol, Hellcat, Bambam and Dodger were with him on the bridge, sitting in their gimbaled seats. The Flynite injectors of the seatbacks were stuck in their veins, ready to flood them with the spacefarer nanites should dangerous acceleration forces occur. The mood was calm but tense.

The transit countdown was at two minutes and the *Lady Vengeance* was ready. They floated parallel to the *42-QLUE* far out, where space was colder and emptier than at the center. The glow of the two central stars was a distant glow behind which sparkled an angry red dot, Proxima Centauri.

"Everyone ready?" asked Gavin, unable to stand the tense silence any longer. The others merely mumbled something unintelligible, except for Dodger, who said, "Yep."

"This is going to be a walk in the park," he assured them. "Get in, do a little strafing and send off our warning, then we'll have a little nuclear weapons competition,

Akwa Marquandt's ship will have no camouflage left, get shot down, and we'll be the heroes of the Star Empire."

Hellcat turned his head toward him and raised a brow.

"Well, if you're heroes, you would have a lot more influence, and you would be able to... help your cause."

"Sure." She snorted, and he could understand her. If the three of them had felt that anything could be changed in the Star Empire with words and good will, they probably would not have gone underground voluntarily to risk their lives on a bloody path full of hardships. He understood their dilemma and he understood his. The three of them had grown on him as only people who had faced death alongside you could. And Hellcat... he did not know what exactly those feelings were that he felt toward her, but they were big and engaging and confused him like an addictive pain.

The countdown reached the final ten seconds and Gavin closed his eyes, one hand on the flightstick for manual control, the other clutched in the armrest.

Sphinx counted down the final seconds, loudly over the ship's internal speakers so the Master Sergeant and Masha could hear it, too.

Jump.

The transition from normal space to subspace happened without any noticeable loss of time. The event horizon ripped open, and the *Lady* disappeared into her subspace vacuole, only to be transferred back to normal space five light years away as if she had never been anywhere else.

"Targeting circuits!" shouted Hellcat immediately, as the automatic battle alert blared simultaneously. "Several hundred."

Gavin saw it. They had come out at the exact spot Mirage had calculated, two clicks from Aurora's habitat

The last Fleet

and thus dangerously close, but providing some protection from the many guns around them.

Aurora spun its circles around gigantic Saturn with its endless clouds of gas in the middle of the vast rings. Like a dark cocoon in an inverted cone shape, it moved slightly faster in its orbit than the ice particles of the rings, which the habitat sucked in at its 'front' and split into water and oxygen to literally breathe life into Saturn's cone. The upper end cap of the three-mile-long behemoth from the early days of human expansion was made of Duroglas, under which were extensive gardens. It looked like green hair under a hood, while the lower termination cap resembled a red pimple. Around the base were rows of hangar openings through which, on normal days, the shuttles and private ferries of senators and lords frequented.

There was still traffic, but it was not even a dozen small spacecraft, presumably mourners arriving late for the ceremony. Of more concern to Gavin were Marquandt's five fleets, arranged around the station like a sphere of metal and weapons. In addition, there were over fifty automated defense platforms, fifty-yard-diameter spheres with fusion fire at their heart, railguns and laser cannons protruding from their surfaces like the spines of a hedgehog.

And they were all in a tizzy over them. Here and now, they were the center of the universe. A very violent universe.

"Twenty contacts," Hellcat reported. On the tactical screen, the missiles raced toward them as sobering red triangles. And they were coming from all sides.

"No contact with the *42-QLUE*," Bambam said in agitation.

Mirage? Where is she? The question flashed through Gavin's mind, but then he saw that there were only thirty seconds left before the missiles hit, and he blanked out everything but his ship and the flightstick.

"Hold on!" He accelerated them to 10g at maximum thrust and held on toward the habitat that loomed giantly before them. In its vicinity, they were no more than a fly buzzing an elephant.

"If Marquandt really is a traitor, he doesn't give a shit about...," Bambam put in, but was unable to speak as his jaws clenched. Gavin had raised to 12g and was racing straight at Aurora.

"He's on the habitat," he contradicted through the transducer. The other three could not answer him, but at least they could hear him.

He ignored the many incoming warnings and pushed them into a hard left turn at the last moment, putting them a few yards away from Aurora's hull. He stayed close to the station, just close enough that their plasma tail caused the composite to glow red, but the Congress radiators could still dissipate the heat. He dodged sensor systems and ledges, flying a tight spiral around the station.

Behind them, the missiles formed a dense swarm of much-too-fast celestial bodies with hissing flares of exhaust.

Three seconds before impact, their engines went out and they fell back powerless. They had come so close in an attempt to track the *Lady Vengeance* on her suicidal course, some of them bumped into each other like Mikado sticks. "They're not risking the Saturn Congress. No way!"

"We're still alive," Bambam admitted. "But where's that damned robot lady?"

"I don't know, but we've got to move fast now." Gavin cast a quick sideways glance at Hellcat, who was staring through the virtual window in front of them at the

The last Fleet

station, its pockmarked surface with its many windows and portholes racing past them. Her eyes twinkled longingly. "Hellcat? Don't even think about it!"

"Gavin, I'm receiving a priority message from Fleet Admiral Dain Marquandt that I cannot refuse..."

"Identify yourself!" a voice accustomed to command echoed through the bridge, and Gavin froze. Marquandt. The traitor.

"This is Lord Captain Gavin Andal aboard the *Lady Vengeance*," he replied before he could think about his words. He steered the Lady into a final right turn, slowing sharply as they approached the upper termination cap. Through the glass he saw hundreds of tiny figures in the man-made park - no doubt the mourners who had just been escorted to safety by their bodyguards out of concern for an attack.

There was a pause in the connection. Hellcat looked at him and almost imperceptibly shook her head.

"Power down your weapons systems and shut down your primary systems, Captain," Marquandt finally replied, and his voice was as cool and toneless as if Gavin were some mad ship leader and not the one who had survived and documented his betrayal. Before answering, he made sure to send his responses over unencrypted radio so that every ship and station nearby could hear them.

"We have evidence of an imminent attack on the Saturn Congress," he said, giving Hellcat a wave to send off the recordings Mirage had sent them of Akwa Marquandt's launch. "A stealth ship is planning to destroy Aurora when the Emperor arrives. I'm sending the relevant evidence as open data."

"Broadcast sent," Hellcat confirmed.

"As you can all see," he continued, but faltered when

he looked to her again and she had widened her eyes as if seeing a ghost. "What?"

"Jamming!" exclaimed Bambam. "They're shitting on us with jamming signals."

"What is it?" he repeated, startled, in Hellcat's direction.

"The file ... look at it for yourself. She sold us out."

"What are you talking about?" Gavin opened the video file, but it showed only white noise. *No! This cannot be!* Frantically, he ordered Sphinx to do a data analysis.

"The file was intact, but apparently overwrote itself when we jumped to Sol," the AI replied. "I didn't notice any file errors before, I apologize."

"Bloody heavens!" he swore, and slapped the armrest so hard that his left hand began to tingle painfully.

"She set us up," Hellcat growled. "I told you, goddamn it!"

The fleet's jamming signals scuttled any attempt to reestablish communications. There was nothing he could do but hover close above the termination dome and hope that the clearing of the park lasted long enough for them to jump away before they were branded terrorists and swept out of the universe.

"Charge jump nodes," he ordered hoarsely.

"What?"

"You heard me! We've got to get out of here."

"That takes..."

"I know how fucking long it takes, but we have no alternative. If we fly away like this, they'll shoot us right down. There's no escape!" Gavin let go of the flightstick, leaving Sphinx to hold her position. Mirage had betrayed them, and now the entire fleet believed they were at best madmen babbling about stealth ships, at worst deranged terrorists. But why? Why would Mirage save them first, only to have them run into the open here? It didn't make any sense.

The silence on the bridge was deafening.

No one tried to talk to them anymore, instead they were muzzled as the hundreds of Marquandt ships slowly approached, like a swarm of hornets about to pounce on a fly that had dared to invade their nest.

Minutes passed without a word spoken, and failure hanging over them like a storm cloud. Gavin had been so close, and again Marquandt had managed to get away. Now he was the crazed terrorist who had besmirched his family's name in the eyes of the assembled commanders.

It was nothing less than a disaster.

INTERLUDE
MIRAGE

The *42-QLUE* plunged out of subspace into the uppermost atmospheric layers of Jupiter like a black drop appearing from nowhere. The brown ammonia clouds that gave the gas giant its rather drab brown coloration lay far below it, moving with the direction of rotation. Hydrogen molecules and the occasional free helium buzzed around the bow, merely forming a real layer on the edge of Saturn's gravitational grip on the scanners. To human eyes, it would not even have been a flicker.

Mirage shut down all primary systems and directed all energy into the jump nodes. While the energy matrix cells charged, she looked at the data from the passive sensors.

The *Lady Vengeance* had appeared simultaneously at the designated location, and was currently heading toward Aurora in a mad maneuver to fly a spiral close to her hull. The young Andal was indeed a daredevil pilot, an obviously competent one at that.

"Twenty-five minutes," Deus said. "That's as fast as I can go, even with my optimization."

"It will have to do. Any sign so far?"

"No."

"Keep looking," Mirage urged the AI, staring at the telescope and interferometry data.

Saturn's rings pulsed with life in air-filled metallic bodies. Their passive systems picked up several thousand signals. About half of these were Navy signatures, forming a dense field around the Aurora habitat they seemed to protect like a jewel. The rest was industrial and bustling commerce in the rings. From there, much of the Sol system was supplied with water and oxygen, which the rings yielded in the form of ice more abundantly than humanity could consume in several million years. One of them was fed by Enceladus, the dark blue icy moon whose cryovolcanoes shot endless frozen water from its barely-present atmosphere where Saturn's gravitational pull forced the crystals into its orbit.

The moon itself was crisscrossed with dense networks of tunnels and ocean habitats, deep in the endless darkness. On its surface were extensive training centers for the Marines and Imperial Army, where soldiers practiced low-gravity combat.

Farther away, the larger asteroid stations were clustered on and in their regolith chunks, of which there were several hundred in the rings that had orbited Saturn for millions of years and had made Sol rich since space mining began. Seemingly inexhaustible supplies of platinum, gold, and silver were mined here and carried by freighters to refineries over Saturn's poles, from where the products were shipped along official transportation routes to population and economic centers around Jupiter, Mars, and Earth, only to be shipped as final products from the factories to remotely populated corners such as the fifty Neptune habitats, and Ceres and Pluto.

What interested Mirage, however, was only one thing:

an interferometer blip that indicated a transit but was not followed by a ship signature or transponder signal.

The minutes ticked by. The young Andal and his crew escaped the homing weapons of Marquandt's fleet, and he radioed out his message as she had expected. A bit more controlled and less angry than she would have thought a hotshot like him would be, but basically exactly as predicted, except that Marquandt stalled him with jamming signals before the captain could call him a traitor in front of everyone. The video file was sent and received by her as well; white noise. So the hidden cacodemon had run its program routine as planned.

"A new enemy on your list," Deus remarked.

"A useful idealist."

"A useful *idiot*, I think you meant to say."

"In my experience, the two are one and the same," Mirage returned.

A dozen Navy units began moving toward the *Lady Vengeance* with moderate thrust. Primarily they were corvettes, fast and maneuverable and by their sheer numbers quite capable of shooting down the frigate without any casualties of their own. But they were visibly hesitant because Marquandt and his staff could not estimate what someone whose family and entire homeland had been wiped out was capable of. She also assumed that Marquandt wanted as many officials and dignitaries on his side as possible, and for that to happen, they had to live, not be sucked out of a destroyed end cap into the vacuum.

"He's going to jump out of the system," the AI noted. "The Admiral is more cautious than you assumed."

"He seems to be proceeding quite prudently," Mirage countered. "If Andal escapes, I don't blame him."

"But he won't forget it. Not someone like him."

"That's his decision. It was the best way to get what we came here for. When he grows up, he'll understand."

"Or his crew will overthrow him. There will be conflict, as you predicted."

"We'll see."

The minutes ticked by, the distance between the corvettes and the *Lady Vengeance* continued to melt away. Ten minutes, then twenty.

Still nothing.

"Mirage," the Voice suddenly spoke up in her mind. "Our Quantcom bugs are reporting an extremely weak signal."

"Is it him?"

"We're assuming so. There are no registered or space control objects at the signal location. I've already sent the data to Deus."

"We're on our way. Only three more minutes until the jump nodes are fully charged," Mirage said, closing her spacesuit helmet.

"One more thing, Zenith is nearby."

"Zenith?" she asked, surprised. "Why?"

"He's looking for the Emperor. He put two and two together and he wants to stop Marquandt - both Marquandts," the Voice explained. "Is that going to be a problem?"

"No."

9

JANUS

Janus played the message from Gavin Andal over and over: "We have evidence of an imminent attack on the Saturn Congress. A stealth ship plans to destroy Aurora when the Emperor arrives. I'm sending the relevant evidence as open data."

The data was merely white noise. Why would the young high lord do that?

The fleet radio was surprisingly quiet. The many queries from commanders at fleet headquarters had long since died down since Marquandt had claimed fleet-wide that they were terrorists trying to confuse them. Why the alleged terrorists did not proceed to blow themselves up or make any effort to destroy Aurora's upper termination cap while the evacuation was still ongoing was apparently no longer questioned by anyone.

The good news was that the Emperor had not yet arrived. They themselves were still an hour away from the Congress, which was the center of the Sol system for the day. Janus had ordered Captain Gianni to go into drift flight and divert all power to the jump nodes as soon as the *Lady Vengeance* appeared, and to his relief the commander obeyed without comment.

"Can you tell me what exactly we're doing here, First Secretary?" she asked after fifteen minutes of Janus staring uninterrupted at the live tactical image of Saturn and its surroundings. At least it was almost live, if he ignored the fifty-second delay with which the data reached them. "Are we planning to leave the system?"

Her voice remained neutral, but he did not need to search her face to understand that she was worried he might take her and himself out of the picture while something was currently underway. Something that threatened the Congress and possibly the Emperor. Navy radio was full of commanders who did not know how to classify what was happening. The majority, however, did not seem to believe that it was really Gavin Andal who was in charge on the frigate that was currently threatening the Aurora like a poisonous leech that you couldn't remove without poisoning yourself.

"It is possible that..."

"Incoming Quantcom signal," someone from the bridge crew reported excitedly.

"Signal check!" ordered Gianni.

"Sixty million clicks ahead."

"Give me a signature check."

"Unfortunately not possible, Lord Captain, the signal strength is too low," apologized the bridge officer Janus had spotted somewhere to his left. He clenched his hands into fists nervously and forced himself to relax them again.

"Align bow telescopes, full magnification."

A holodisplay popped up in front of them, showing the starry panorama of the Milky Way with a fingernail-sized brown blob in the center - Saturn. The telescope zoomed in three times in quick succession until the image of a *Dominus*-class cruiser appeared on the display. The resolution wasn't the best at that distance, but the large lettering on the hull could be read with a little imagination: the *Majestic*. Besides, there were only six ships of that class in Navy service.

"That's the Emperor," Janus said, getting even more nervous. "But the *Majestic* should not be sending out any signals."

"No, it shouldn't," Captain Gianni agreed with him. "Lieutenant, is it a steady signal?"

"No, ma'am, it's already disappeared again. I suspect it is an AOD device."

Active on demand, Janus translated in his mind. Was it possible that... Albius!

"Jump to the *Majestic* immediately, Captain!"

"But sir, that's forbidden. I am required by Fleet Code to..."

"To hell with the Fleet Code," he snapped at her more harshly than he had intended, but the concern that clutched his heart all at once left no room for delay. He understood now what Marquandt's real plan was, and Gavin Andal had played right into his hands. "That's an order!"

"The jump nodes still need four minutes to fully charge."

"Shut down all non-essential systems to speed things up," Janus ordered impatiently.

"Sir, that could..."

"We could lose the *Emperor*!"

Now Gianni blinked uncertainly.

"Lock in on the *Majestic*. Directional beam!" he ordered loudly. He didn't want to cross the captain on her own ship, but they didn't have time.

"It's up, sir."

"Your Majesty, this is First Secretary Janus Darishma aboard the *Invincible*. You are under attack by a stealth ship in the service of Dain Marquandt!" He turned to Gianni: "Dain Marquandt is a traitor, but he is not the only one," he explained, and it suddenly dawned on him.

How had he not seen it? The attack on Trafalgar with cloaked Orb ships. Orb technology in Andal, a hybrid ship with stealth technology piloted by humans trying to kill Gavin Andal, the only witness to Marquandt's treachery. Then the funeral service for Usatami, which the Emperor could not remain absent from. Marquandt, in charge of protection, but fearing his arrest if his ruler believes the new High Lord of Andal. Attempting to capture or kill Elayne and Janus himself, Albius, who boarded with Haeron II as life insurance. "The Chief of Staff is working with him. This is a trap. The stealth ship Andal warned about is not targeting the Saturn Congress, it's targeting our master."

"I don't understand. This stealth ship really exists? And the Grand Admiral..."

"Yes."

"But that would be suicide," Gianni objected.

"I don't think he would volunteer to play the Trojan horse," Janus countered. "I think it's much more likely that Marquandt maneuvered him into that position, and he does not know about the implanted Quantcom transmitter."

"Implanted Quantcom transmitters? Such technology doesn't exist."

"Just like cloaked ships that aren't visible on radar or lidar," he returned, and she pursed her mouth.

"Jump ready in one minute!" someone from navigation reported.

The last Fleet

"Battle alert. Immediately after the jump, I want to see full combat readiness," Gianni ordered, tightening.

"Weapons signature!" the defense officer barked from his console. A moment later, they appeared: twelve missile signatures, less than four clicks from the *Majestic*.

"Too late," Janus breathed in horror.

"Identify attackers!" demanded Gianni, but he already knew what was coming next.

"No radar contacts. Lidar also negative."

The *Majestic*'s short-range defenses began pumping high-velocity munitions into space from two dozen Gatling guns. Their finger-thick tungsten projectiles licked at the missiles. Many of them exploded or turned into cold showers of debris, but two got through and exploded on the Carbin armor. The atomic explosions glowed so brightly for a moment that the cruiser disappeared behind them. But when the heat and radiation dissipated, the *Majestic* was still there, its hull unbroken, even though two dark craters on its upper surface did not bode well. The railguns began to fire, but blindly, and space was endless.

"How long until we can jump?" asked Janus.

"Twenty seconds."

It became the twenty longest seconds of his life.

Another salvo of missiles left the launch bays of the invisible ship, this time from a completely different position, five clicks behind the *Majestic*, which, in accordance with battle doctrine, had throttled back its speed to divert as much power as possible to hull magnetization and weapons systems.

The captain of the *Majestic* had made a mistake: He had acted according to the rulebook - a rulebook that did not include cloaking ships. And so his ship's plasma flare was down to one mile, creating space for the attacker to fire from the blind spot of the short-range defenses.

The *Majestic* turned frantically to get more Gatlings into firing position, but to no avail. This time six missiles got through, and the enemy had aimed well. In quick succession, three of them crashed into the craters struck earlier, where the three-foot-thick Carbin had been dented and burned. The cruiser seemed to inflate from within like a balloon and then burst along its midsection before breaking in half. Telescopic images showed exposed decks like after a bombing of a high-rise building, when suddenly all the apartments lay open with floors and ceilings torn away. The unmistakable silhouettes of dozens of crewmembers were torn into space where the nuclear hellfire had not turned them into fleeting clouds of gas.

As the *Invincible* jumped, the image of the poor souls aboard the *Majestic* burned into Janus' mind like a brand. His stomach churned at the thought that the Emperor might have just been assassinated.

They reappeared two clicks away from the two pieces of the cruiser. An excellent jump and yet worth nothing because they were too late. The *Majestic*'s debris was losing massive amounts of air and already lurching ominously through zero gravity. Hull fragments and splinters mingled with cables, furnishings and corpses that were repeatedly illuminated in the flicker of secondary explosions from the dying ship.

And somewhere out there was the cloaked enemy. Lurking like a black wildcat in the night, ready to bite their necks.

"Take us right to it!" Gianni ordered tensely. "Even if we can only do one thing, let's do it: play the target. Get shuttles ready to pick up survivors. And keep trying to make contact."

The last Fleet

"The *Majestic*'s transmitter is destroyed," someone reported.

And then the missiles reappeared. A whole swarm of them. Thirty-six of the guided missiles sped toward the remains of the Imperial cruiser, ignoring the *Invincible* in their path.

10

GAVIN

With growing impatience, Gavin watched the battle unfold eighty million clicks from Saturn. Fifty Navy ships were already flying at full thrust toward the explosions. He had known immediately that it had to be the Emperor's ship. Mirage had betrayed them, but Akwa Marquandt had lured them right into the trap, probably along with Mirage.

"Like hell, that bitch found the their flight plans!" snarled Hellcat in frustration. Her hands hung trembling over the controls on her armrests, as if she could only resist with the utmost willpower to finally fire on the Aurora habitat and everything she loathed about the Star Empire.

"You're right," Gavin admitted, clenching his hands into fists that hurt and his joints cracked. "The Emperor's ship was the target all along."

"Always thought no one knew his flight paths and the ships flew without active systems," Bambam commented, sounding anything but shocked. Why should he be? His biggest enemy had just been fired upon by a stealth ship and was on the verge of destruction. The Republicans might never have had a higher goal, even if it had always been considered unreachable.

"When can we jump, Sphinx?" he asked angrily.

"In two minutes," the AI reminded him, though the countdown was clearly visible on every display.

"You're not going to jump there, are you?" asked Hellcat, scowling at him.

"Of course! We've got to stop those bloody traitors!"

"We've got to save our own damn asses," she objected. "Don't you see that? The enemy is cloaked, and your emperor is fucked!"

"My emperor?" he snapped. Not hers, of course.

Hellcat ignored his comment. "Besides, there's another ship, just showed up. What do you think they'll do to us, huh?"

Gavin wanted to retort with something but stared at the tactics display. Sure enough, a second ship identical to the first had appeared, right next to the Emperor's, which was broken into two mostly destroyed halves that drifted away from each other. The debris was losing atmosphere from hundreds of geysers of various size, and more and more windows were bursting under the heat and built-up pressure inside. Those who were swept into the vacuum remained conscious for half a minute, maybe a minute, and died after two minutes. Those who made the mistake of reflexively inhaling had their lungs burst and died almost instantly.

When he saw the swarm of thirty-six missiles on the screen, he knew it was over.

"Ready to jump," Sphinx reported.

Gavin had long since had the target coordinates calculated.

"Jump!" he ordered, still hearing Hellcat's indignant

The last Fleet

"NO!" before the subspace vacuole formed and they disappeared from normal space, only to reappear eighty million clicks away as if they had never been anywhere else.

All the alarm sirens began to shrill.

"Update!" he yelled at the AI, and his pilot reflexes caused him to bring the *Lady* into a hard right turn and accelerate at 8g. His rage spurred him forward. Rage at Marquandt's murder of his family, his people, his homeland. Rage at the betrayal of the Emperor and humanity. Rage at their cruelty in pursuit of their depraved goals. But most of all, anger at himself for having been too blind in his desire for revenge to see how Marquandt and his daughter had outmaneuvered him. Too blind to question Mirage, if that had even been her name. He had grasped at the first straw just to get closer to his revenge, and had been coldly taken advantage of. In the end, he had even done his enemies a favor, because he had discredited himself in the eyes of the Navy with the action at Aurora, as Marquandt himself would not have been able to do. And now the Emperor had been assassinated before his eyes.

It was one huge disaster.

The missiles from Akwa's stealth ship raced through the defensive fire of the second ship, which had defied the jump ban in the Sol system. The high-velocity projectiles flooded space by the thousands in search of their diabolically fast targets and found rich pickings. But it was not enough. Twenty missiles were intercepted, exploding halfway or short of their target, but ten reached their destination. Eight flew at insane speeds into the tattered bow section of the Imperial cruiser. In rapid succession, they chased through the hull. This time, they were obviously not warheads, but kinetic projectiles that wreaked destruction with their force alone. They turned the dead ship into an expanding mess of debris and shrapnel in no time.

While the other two crashed into the stern section, Gavin opened a channel to the foreign ship, "This is Captain Gavin Andal aboard the *Lady Vengeance*. Whoever is listening to me: the enemy cloaking effect is based on magnetism. I repeat: The enemy cloaking effect is based on magnetism!"

"This is Janus Darishma," a foreign voice announced, echoing through the bridge. The First Secretary of State? "Thank you for the information. Stand by for survivor recovery."

"Understood, sir," Gavin replied automatically. "You should know that Akwa Marquandt is in command of that ship."

Darishma's ship, the *Invincible* - now that it had its transponders turned on - responded within seconds with a continuous burst of missiles that fanned out and blasted away in all directions of three-dimensional space. After a short time, the first ones exploded as short-lived flashes that expanded into balls of heat and hard radiation.

"Nukes," Bambam reported.

Gavin cursed as the first EMP waves of near detonations brought secondary systems to emergency shutdown.

"It's working!" the mechanic shouted, and Gavin saw it a short time later. A third ship appeared, five thousand clicks away on the other side of the debris cloud that had just been the front section of a cruiser.

It was Akwa's ship. The *Triumph*-class frigate, he didn't even need to look at the sensor data for that. Its hull flickered on the telescopic images, and the infrared data, just like the radar and lidar signatures, disappeared and reappeared before remaining constant.

The cloak had failed.

The last Fleet

Before he could give the order to fire, another ship appeared out of nowhere, but this time from subspace.

"It's the *42-QLUE*," Sphinx informed him with the composure of a computer program, and at that moment he would have preferred to delete her for that.

No navigator in the Star Empire was capable of doing what Mirage had done: the event horizon, elusive but measurable - was not a hundred yards above the *Triumph* frigate.

"Impossible," he whispered, rubbing his eyes.

"Either this bitch is luckier than an entire generation deserves, or she's..."

"A fucking robot?", Bambam completed her sentence.

Gavin watched as Mirage steered her ship into a swift sideways movement, away from the automatic defensive fire of Akwa Marquandt's melee cannons. But at close range, it was impossible even for her to dodge the projectiles, and they shredded the hull of her research vessel, tearing it open like sheet metal that flew into space in shreds shortly thereafter.

Only when the *42-QLUE* was under the frigate, no more than a cleaner fish under a shark, did it set upward before being completely destroyed.

"So much for that," Dodger remarked.

"High Lord Andal," Janus Darishma spoke up again, while orders could be heard in the background on his bridge.

"First Secretary?" Gavin watched on the tactics screen as the *Invincible* maneuvered around the debris field that blocked its direct field of fire on Marquandt's hybrid ship.

"I need your help," Darishma said in a strained voice. He sounded like someone who was just trying to process a trauma. "We've picked up two life signs heading your way. Could you recover them? We have six others on our side that we're taking care of, but we're running out of time. Even with breath packs, they only have a few minutes. The Emperor was on board, and if there's even the slightest chance that he's among the survivors, we must get to them."

"Of course," Gavin assured him, looking at the infrared signatures that were rapidly growing cooler.

"Thank you."

"Bambam, Dodger? Get ready, you're going out. Don't forget the safety lines," he ordered loudly, marking the two lifesigns on the sensor screen. When he heard no movement behind him, he turned around. Bambam and Dodger were still in their seats. "Didn't you hear me?"

"Sorry, Captain," the mutant said, turning to face him. "You can't really ask anything of us, but to save our arch-enemy? Nope. Certainly not that."

"A mutiny?" growled Gavin. "Now?"

"You put us in this shitty position," Bambam grumbled. "Would you blow up Congress because we care?"

"Of course not!"

"Of course not," the mechanic repeated his words. "That's what I thought."

"I didn't mean it that way. But we don't have time. There are people dying!" Gavin turned to Hellcat, who had remained conspicuously silent. She avoided his gaze. "Hellcat!"

"Our people are dying every day under the truncheons of Imperial policemen, the railguns of supposed pirate hunters, and discriminatory laws," she said in a quivering voice.

"I'm not going to let anyone out there die because you care more about your damn revenge. Bloody terrorists!" he raged, unbuckling his seatbelt with fingers trembling with anger and pushing off toward the tube that led to the central corridor. "Sphinx, transfer bridge rights to Hellcat."

"Done."

"Sergeant?" he called to the master sergeant over transducers. "Meet me at the lower airlock, we have comrades to rescue."

INTERLUDE
MIRAGE

The jump point was calculated to within one yard. Deus had done a good job, as expected. But even better was that Zenith had not needed a message from her first, but had got the idea to use nuclear weapons through Andal. Using them like 20th century depth charges, while not elegant, had clearly worked.

And now it was her turn.

At only a hundred yards from Akwa Marquandt's frigate, she was in no danger of being attacked by railguns or even missiles. Nevertheless, she reacted immediately and gave full thrust to the port thrusters to dive into a sideways motion.

Like a satellite, she flew parallel to the much larger ship, orbiting it at high speed as the *Triumph* frigate's short-range defenses began to fire. Thousands of tungsten projectiles plowed through the *42-QLUE* like hail through paper.

Mirage's *Reaper* suit had long since been sealed when she let go of the controls. Centrifugal forces pushed her against the starboard wall, where she made herself as small as possible and waited.

"You're sacrificing me," Deus stated.

"Is that a problem?" she replied through transducers. There had long been a vacuum around her, as much of the port side was tattered with shredded sealing foam that looked like the torn flesh of a large fish floating dead in the water.

"I would have preferred not to be destroyed,"

"You're just a copy. You will continue to exist." More holes appeared in the wall. The absence of any sound gave the impression that they were there from one moment to the next, for no apparent reason. Past the many major hull damages, she could make out the hull of the frigate, the Carbin plates welded together, bulging seams where damage had been repaired, and a strange blue pulsation reminiscent of Yokatami's Seed World. It ran over minute grooves in the hull and followed a regular pulse. She checked the fist-sized object on her belt and verified its integrity one last time. "See you soon, Deus."

Mirage pushed off with her boots as hard as she could and burst through a hull section nearly torn from the wall. The nanites of her *Reaper* suit hardened and absorbed the impact energy, dissipating it across its surface. Still, she staggered. Like a doll flung away, she flew through the vacuum toward the one-hundred-and-fifty-yard giant. Tracer rounds flashed around her repeatedly, and the frigate's extended gatlings glowed with a steady rhythm of deadly precision.

As she spun on multiple axes simultaneously, Mirage saw her surroundings as if from an out-of-control carousel. The pale hull above her, the blue pulsing. The *42-QLUE* that was nearing destruction, already riddled with thousands and thousands of projectiles. The bombardment did not let up, finally annihilating it completely until only cooling debris remained, none larger than a human. In the distance, more ship remnants glittered in the light of the distant sun, and somewhere beyond them were the *Invincible* and the *Lady Vengeance* - too far away to make out even with her eyes on full zoom. Before she collided with the hull of the *Triumph* frigate, she turned on her reflex boosters and surrendered to her body's intelligence. One hand swept forward and grabbed a spear-like appendage before she had formed a conscious thought.

The sudden anchor stopped her lurching, but the kinetic energy of her movement sent her crashing against the hull and caused her body to tremble. Her neural computer reported only superficial damage.

Once she stabilized, she blanked out the stars and the chaos of destruction. With magnetized boots and palms, she began crawling across the armor plates like an insect. She had stored the *Triumph*-class plans in her memory lacunae and had them played into her field of view as a live image so she could see her own position and progress.

So she moved toward the upper airlock, which was like a whale's blowhole on the top of the bow section. It took her a few seconds, during which Marquandt apparently reassessed her position. She was now up against a *Dominus*-class cruiser three times her size and an older, albeit heavily armored, Sphinx frigate. The latter would have been a near match for her; the cruiser probably would not even get a scratch.

So, she did the only thing she could do: Charge the jump nodes, hoping Zenith was busy picking up survivors. That was exactly what Mirage expected, anyway. The new Zenith was now extremely predictable in his newfound idealism.

The airlock was sealed, identifiable only by a circular gap in the hull. Normally it would be marked with white lettering and reflectors along the sides, but this was no normal ship. She ran her hand over the edge, scanning for electromagnetic fields. It took her an endless four minutes to find the right spot. Then she braced herself right and left against the composite with her magnetic boots and extended her monofilament blade. Even with it, it took her five minutes to cut a small hole in the mono-bonded Carbin.

Then the electrical wires and superconductor power cables were exposed. Mirage pulled the fist-sized data storage device from her hip and and activated the morphing universal connector, which formed tiny black filaments that searched like tentacles for a target. She provided it to them by placing the device on top of the exposed electronics.

A simple but highly effective cacodemon took care of controlling the airlock, keeping the on-board computer's firewalls and defensive heuristics busy, tying up its resources. The real work of the datastore was just beginning as the outer airlock door slid open.

Mirage pulled herself into the ship. White walls conformed to Navy regulations. She closed the bulkhead behind her and waited for the pressurization to complete and for her *Reaper* suit to report that she was in a breathable atmosphere. Then she removed the helmet, glad not to have inhaled any oxygen-enriched fluid. Keeping the rest of the suit on, she pressed herself against the wall next to the inner door until her torso and limbs stuck together like a snake's with the padded panels.

She had to wait another minute for the bulkhead to slide open.

"Where is she?" someone called out.

The last Fleet

Mirage activated her shock launcher before rolling to the side. For a split second, she saw a handful of sailors in black coveralls with *Inferno* rifles in their hands. Two of them were kneeling, three standing. Each aimed into the airlock. The barrels of their weapons followed her, but the speed her reflex boosters and artificial neural conduits gave her made them agonizingly slow.

She fired her pulse launcher, and the directed field effect burst the sailors' bodies like balloons of flesh and blood. All that was left of them were their magnetic boots, now stuck ownerless on the floor of the central corridor. Most of the blood had splattered against the opposite wall, forming a dense red pattern there, along with bone remains and other things that disgusted Mirage. The rest floated through the weightlessness as a red jumble of droplets.

Mirage wasted no time and ran into the corridor with her left arm extended in front of her. The disgusting bodily fluids slapped against her spacesuit, enveloping her in brilliant red. She wished the pulse launcher had not disintegrated nanites and clothing alike into particles before the stomach.

More soldiers confronted her, and more soldiers died. They were obviously not marines, but normal crew members. They were children pitted against a professional boxer. Mirage dodged their shots, answering them with bursts of fire from her Smartgun. Others she slashed with the monofilament blade, severing arms, legs and heads.

The last two targets were officers with handguns covering a third person, a woman with cropped dark hair, hard cheekbones and the nose of a hawk.

Akwa Marquandt.

Mirage's neural computer informed her that a scrambled radio signal was emanating from the fleet admiral's daughter. She shot the two officers in the head before they had even aimed at her. By the time she was about to give the captain a quick death as well, she was out of ammunition.

"Jammed?" growled Marquandt like a predator, firing an entire magazine from her pistol at them. Mirage moved with lightning speed in an erratic pattern, long before any conscious thought, and had cut her distance in half. Two hits in the torso had been absorbed by the *Reaper* suit as the nanites hardened. She ignored the system's integrity warning.

"Knife," she replied, raising her blood-dripping monofilament blade.

Marquandt's eyes twitched between the weapon and the corridor behind her.

"I'm going to kill you now," Mirage announced, taking a step toward her counterpart.

"You're not getting this ship," Marquandt returned, and the relaxed satisfaction in her voice was alarming.

"Deus?" she asked.

"Sequestration... not... self-destruct," the AI's voice sounded choppily from the ship's speakers. Apparently, the on-board computer's takeover process was not yet complete.

Marquandt took advantage of the brief moment and ran in the opposite direction. Mirage did not pursue her. If she took an escape pod, it would be Zenith who killed her. It did not matter to her. All that mattered was her target, and that was this ship.

She turned to the hole in the floor that led to the bridge and slipped through. The pilot's seat faced the center of the circular room, so all she had to do was throw herself in and buckle up. She deactivated her magnetic boots and activated the controls.

The last Fleet

"Deus, are you ready now?"

"I have infiltrated and taken over all systems," the AI replied.

"Good, I'm uploading the target coordinates now. As soon as the energy matrix cells are charged, you jump," Mirage ordered, seeing in the onboard system that the self-destruct sequence had stopped at thirty seconds.

"An escape pod has detached," Deus said. "Do you want me to shoot it down?"

"No, we need all power on the jump nodes. Every second counts."

11

GAVIN

Gavin ran to the lower airlock and met the Master Sergeant, who handed him one of the *Reaper* packs.

"Thanks." He clamped it to his chest and waited for the nanite mass to spread like mercury over his skin and solidify. The uncomfortable part went quickly: the last thing he did was take the mouthpiece, wait for the oxygen-saturated liquid to fill his lungs and the suit to close around his face and the top of his head. Next, he put on one of the tool belts that were magnetically attached to the wall.

Using electronic receptors on the front of his head, he looked to the Sergeant, who was also completely encased, and waited for the atmosphere to escape the airlock.

"Two survivors," he said. "We need to get them inside."

"Breathpacks?"

Gavin nodded and reached for one of the safety cables, which he attached to his belt with a carabiner. The other end he handed to the Master Sergeant. They each clipped another one into the wall next to the outer airlock.

As soon as the door control indicator showed a green light and it had gone dead silent, he opened the door and stared out into dark space. The *Invincible* lay like a dark cigar several clicks away at the edge of the debris cloud, which looked like glittering powdery snow. Stars twinkled like myriad glowing buttons in the void, dense and peaceful. Nothing hinted at the fact that they were in fact ultrahot fusion machines, hostile to life and incomprehensibly large.

And nothing served as a reminder that probably the greatest and worst crime in the relatively short history of the Star Empire had just been committed here.

His neural computer flashed the signatures of the two survivors into his field of vision, drifting motionless through the vacuum a click away. Only now did he strap one of the slender *Dragon*-type maneuvering units to his back and wait for the Master Sergeant to finish as well. As a Marine, his movements were routine and his use of the unit was second nature.

"Ready?"

"Ready, my lord."

They pushed off and headed for their targets with the aid of their *Dragons'* small impulse jets. As they did so, Gavin paid close attention to the safety cable at his back, which gradually uncoiled. After four hundred yards of gliding silently through the vacuum, accompanied by the echo of his own breathing, his journey stopped all at once and he was pulled back a bit.

"What the...?" He grabbed the cable attached just above his waist and turned around.

In the airlock, a square patch of light in the darkness with which the *Lady* almost merged, stood the silhouette

The last Fleet

of a bulky figure, holding the cables from him and the Master Sergeant.

"Dodger?" he asked over the radio. "What are you doing?"

"Sorry," she replied, tossing the severed ends of their only connection to the ship from her. They drifted through the weightlessness like lifeless snakes.

An icy chill spread through Gavin. It was the shadow of betrayal that settled over him, blocking out all light. For a moment it was as if he was sinking into a black hole, as if his boundaries were dissolving.

"You can't do this! You *cannot* do this!" No one answered, and the *Lady* quickly turned, the airlock already closing. "HELLCAT!"

He got no response. The *Lady Vengeance*, his ship, turned once around its own vertical axis, much more elegantly and quickly than such a large behemoth of metal should be able to do, and then accelerated with glowing drive nacelles. The plasma tail grew longer and longer, and after only a few seconds the frigate was out of sight.

"Masha," muttered the Master Sergeant beside him. Then he growled like a bear. "I knew this terrorist pack could not be trusted."

"We have allies to rescue," Gavin said tonelessly, turning back toward the signal sources. With practiced movements, he directed his *Dragon* unit to head straight for the survivors.

A hundred yards further and he slowed down to check the position of the Master Sergeant, who was just behind him.

The two figures were in orange pressure suits with breath packs in front of their mouths that covered their entire faces. Orange meant that they were emergency suits, which did not excel in longevity, but rather with a straightforward dressing procedure that could be accomplished in a matter of seconds. His concern for their lives was appropriately high.

A flexible cable extended from the *Dragon* unit, at the end of which was a powerful flashlight that swept over the two figures as the last gap between them closed.

The light reflected cold and white from the transparent breathing masks behind which the eyes were closed. Only now did he recognize the long hair that floated around both women's heads like halos.

Part of Gavin was disappointed that the Emperor was not among the survivors, but he pushed the feeling aside, ashamed of it. These peoples' lives were in danger.

He grabbed the one in front of him as he lightly collided with her, using the loose cable behind him to tie her to him. The Master Sergeant did the same beside him a moment later. Gavin ordered his neural computer to run a calculation and waited for the result.

Then he opened a channel to the *Invincible*.

"Lord Captain?" a female voice announced. "Lieutenant Gornadeh here."

"I'm afraid we are going to need an extraction."

"Already on the way, Lord Captain. The commander has already diverted one of our shuttles. It will be at your location in five minutes."

"Thank you, lieutenant." To the Master Sergeant, he radioed, "Five minutes."

"They won't survive five minutes," the Marine noted.

"No. But if we instruct our *Reaper*s to split up, it might work."

"Then it'll be close for us, too."

"Close, but we have a chance," Gavin countered. "I'm not going to order you to do it, Sergeant."

"Nor do you need to, my lord."

The last Fleet

After a final breath, he hugged the unconscious woman in front of him and wrapped his legs around her as well. Only then did he use the neural computer to instruct the *Reaper* suit to expand onto the second body. The nanites left their hard state and flowed over his arms and over the body of his charge. Thus, Gavin's protection from the vacuum thinned out, forming tiny pores and causing difficulty maintaining temperature and pressure. The latter was already beginning to drop, albeit very slowly, and the temperature was also gradually reducing.

"Did it work?" he asked the Master Sergeant.

"It's getting colder, and I feel like a balloon that's been over-inflated."

"Then it worked." Gavin looked at the timer he had superimposed on his otherwise black field of view. "Only five minutes to go. Tell me something, Sergeant."

"Something?"

"Something about home." He sighed. Softly, he murmured, "I miss Andal. Every morning when I get up, I feel like a fruit that has fallen from a tree and can never become part of it again. It slowly rots without the nurturing connection, alone and parched."

"I know what you mean, my lord," the Marine said. "My father was a vertical farmer on the plains of Skyr, and I spent all of my time before enlisting in Skaland maintaining agrarian drones and driving out stone burrowers."

"We had those on the property, too. My little sisters were always trying to shoot them down with homemade Geminis."

"Then I guess they only saw the little heads they poked out of their holes," the master sergeant opined. Despite the transducer voice in Gavin's head, he sounded amused. "Once they dig all the way out, they don't look so funny. A handful of them can even kill a cow."

"Why did you leave the farm? Skyr is beautiful, and I heard farmers were doing pretty well since the '95 farm reform."

"I needed to get off the land. Everything at home reminded me of my mother. She was a lieutenant in the Marines and was the only one of her crew to die in a reactor accident in the Ring."

"She was the last one left on board," Gavin speculated.

"Yes. Heroes don't usually live long," the Master Sergeant said bitterly. "That's why I never wanted to pursue an officer's career. Playing hero, that's not for me. I want to do something where I use both hands to get things done, if you know what I mean. No offense."

"I wanted to be a member of the Angry Aces," he said.

"The Crown Prince's personal *Stingray* squadron?"

"Yes. I never wanted to command. I preferred to prove my prowess with a flightstick and chasing skirts. My brother Artas always claimed that leading a command was too hard for a human. Duty, he said, was a mountain compared to which even death was but a feather."

"An old samurai saying from ancient Japan on Terra," the master sergeant said appreciatively.

"At the time I ridiculed him for it, thought it a luxury problem. That he would talk himself out of his duties in order to appear level-headed in front of our father." Gavin snorted at his own shallow stupidity at the time and stared into the empty space where the *Lady* had disappeared. "Today I understand what he meant."

"We'll get her, my lord."

I hope so, he thought, and his heart bled at the thought that Hellcat, of all people, was now sitting on the bridge, leaving him behind. What had to be going through her mind? How had she been able to first throw her heart at him and then steal his? Just like that?

"My lord, if you'll permit me a question?"

"Of course, sergeant."

"Shouldn't we inform the First Secretary of State that your ship has been stolen by terrorists?" the Marine asked, and it didn't really sound like a question.

"No," Gavin decided. "If we do, the *Invincible* will shoot them down."

12
JANUS

Janus stood at the command podium, staring at the processed sensor data that created a false sense of closeness between the factions involved. On the three-dimensional holo display, it looked as if Akwa Marquandt's frigate was on the other side of the debris cloud, the first pieces of which were already bouncing against her hull. The *Invincible* was staying close to the *Lady Vengeance*. In reality, the frigate was six thousand clicks away, the distance from New York to Berlin on Terra. Gavin Andal's ship only two hundred clicks, which was still far enough that no human eye - even with augments - would have detected it from at that distance.

Cosmically, it was still close, even if the mind could not comprehend the distances, and the holodisplay was good at emphasizing that fact. Still, their hands were tied. He wanted to destroy the traitor's strange ship, to blast it out of the universe once and for all, so that it could never commit another crime. The missiles had already been fired, a volley of forty that would make short work of the frigate. But the flight time of the guided missiles was eleven minutes, because they had to fly around the debris cloud, otherwise the majority of them would have been shredded by the accelerated fragments. While the warheads had advanced sensors and sophisticated guidance software, many of the shrapnel were so small that they were difficult or impossible to detect, and at the speeds the missiles were flying, any collision would be fatal.

"She's so close," he growled with clenched fists. "Damn traitor."

"Whoever flew the prospector ship is obviously not cooperating with her," Captain Gianni remarked.

The small *Thetis*-class starship was nothing more than a mangled corpse of metal, not much of which had been left by the *Triumph* frigate's melee cannons. But he knew, of course, that Mirage was still alive. She did nothing without calculating her chances and being sure they were good.

"She wants the ship," he said aloud without realizing.

"She?"

"Whoever was on that prospector ship knew about the stealth ship and is now snagging it right out from under our noses."

"Not if our missiles have anything to say about it," Gianni decided grimly. "I wish we could…"

"Ma'am, the *Lady Vengeance* is leaving her position!" someone from the bridge crew reported.

Janus and Gianni watched as the sleek Sphinx frigate with the strange helium freighter disguise accelerated over the debris cloud and toward the spike-topped alien ship.

"Shall we intercept it?" The commander gave him a questioning look, and he wrestled with himself.

"No. They will take care of what we cannot. That is how I would have done it." Janus watched as their own

The last Fleet

ship moved sideways toward the survivors, allowing the crew to pull the group of four into one of the hangars while the shuttles took care of those farther out. Two life signs had just attached themselves to the two survivors in their direction - one was sending the transponder of an Imperial Marine with an identifier from Andal, and one was that of Gavin Andal.

He was relieved that the young High Lord had come to the same thought he had now - only faster. Fear for his emperor made Janus slow and unreliable, and he was ashamed of it.

"We can't lose anyone, Captain," he said, looking at the hologram. "I'd like nothing better than to blast Marquandt out of space myself, but if the Emperor is among the survivors, we can't take any chances."

"His ship had a crew of five hundred sailors, sir," Gianni reminded him with an expression of both frustration and sadness. He had forgotten that standby crews were composed of only the most loyal and devoted servants of the throne. For them, the Emperor and his protection were probably as much the center of life as they were for himself.

"I know," he muttered. "But we must be sure."

"Yes," she agreed with him, straightening with her arms folded behind her back. "I've assigned forty Marines to this. They'll be as fast as anyone can be in the recovery effort."

"Of course." Janus did not like having to be idle while others did the work. One would have thought that after five years of politics and administration he would have gotten used to it, but it had never set in. He would always rather be on-site himself with his boots on the ground, his hand on his gun and his nose in the wind, feeling out the situation and doing his best. He realized it was because of his special past, which had taught him not to trust anyone's abilities as much as his own. But even now, his hands were tied.

"Ma'am, sir?" the young officer from Recon spoke up again. "The *Lady Vengeance* has taken a parallel course to the unidentified ship, but she is not firing."

"What?" asked Janus and Gianni simultaneously, zooming in on the holo display. The two frigates were indeed close together, less than one-hundred-twenty miles apart. Neither ship made any move to attack the other. A third signature, small and with a narrow radar cross-section, flew toward the *Lady Vengeance*.

"Is that..."

"An escape pod, yes," the commander confirmed. Silently, they watched as the Lady turned on its side and opened the hangar door from the cargo compartment. The escape pod swung around, slowed down, and seemed to hang motionless in space until it was swallowed by the yawning indentation and the gate closed again. Then the Sphinx frigate sped away with heavy thrust, accelerating steadily.

"What the hell was that? They took off."

Gianni nodded.

"Get Andal and our Marine," Janus ordered with growing frustration, watching as their swarm of missiles approached the last remaining ship on different trajectories. They were like drugged wasps pouncing on a dead fish in fast motion. *I'm going to get you, Mirage.*

If he couldn't bring the Emperor's assassin directly to justice, he would at least stop his former colleague from taking the second prize from him as well. The stealth ship was the most dangerous piece of technology in the Star Empire at that moment.

"It's about to be over," Gianni said with undisguised

The last Fleet

satisfaction in her voice as only thirty seconds were displayed until the first projectiles hit.

Over it was, because Mirage disappeared with her prey. From one moment to the next, she was simply gone.

It became deadly quiet on the bridge. No one dared to say anything. Janus breathed calmly and looked at the tactical display as if it were a mirage, because reality could not be so unfair.

"Bring in the survivors," he said hoarsely. "After that, set a course for the *Rubov*. We're going home."

"Sir?" asked Gianni.

"There's nothing more we can do here once we've collected the last survivors."

"Shouldn't we wait until the fleet ..."

"No."

"Marquandt."

"Yes." He nodded with a stony expression. "Princess Elayne needs my support now. We need to get there before anyone else."

Gianni understood.

INTERLUDE
AKWA MARQUANDT

Akwa kicked the stubborn door out of its frame as the mechanism failed. It flew off its hinges and somewhere into the cargo hold of the *Lady Vengeance*.

A childish name, in her opinion.

Climbing out of the clear opening, she eyed the three figures waiting for her on the deck. One was slightly shorter than she, with blond hair combed to one side and a rebellious undercut, her face contorted in seasoned anger, but her eyes full of sorrow. Flanking her was an even shorter, considerably older mechanic in an orange jumpsuit, carrying something as rare as a slight beer belly in front of him, eyeing her like an intractable enigma. Her only concern was the mutant on the other side, well over six feet and of the stature of a tree, with millimeter-short white hair. She had her mighty arms folded under her chest and was calmly looking Akwa up and down.

She deftly leapt to the ground in front of them. Her magnetic boots clanged on the metal. It echoed off the walls, to which cargo containers with magnetic shackles were attached. A walkway with railings led further up around.

"What an unexpected turn of events," Akwa said, focusing on the middle one of the three. "You are the Republicans who flew with young Andal."

"That's right. I'm Hellcat," the angry one replied, pointing first to the left and then to the right. "Bambam, Dodger."

Akwa pointed vaguely at her data jacks, their wound edges nearly healed. "You guys must have liked the upgrade."

Hellcat made a growling sound, and Akwa smiled.

"You didn't call us terrorists," Bambam commented, sounding amazed. Or pleased.

"One man's freedom fighters are another man's terrorists." She shrugged. "That's the way it's always been. In the eyes of most, I would be considered a terrorist, too."

"But you're going to tell us you're the other one now; a freedom fighter, am I right?" speculated Hellcat suspiciously.

"If you didn't believe that, you wouldn't have picked me up. Let me guess: Gavin Andal," she spat the words with appropriate disdain, "has turned out to be what he is after all: a naive, spoiled brat who thinks he's acting idealistically when in fact he's blindly following that regime that wants to keep us artificially small and obedient."

Hellcat and Bambam exchanged glances that they probably thought were meaningless. But Akwa had long worked with rebels like them. They were as brave as they were stupid, with bad poker faces. They heard what they wanted to hear, and it was not even a lie. The mutant would have smelled it, she was sure of it.

"What are you going to do?" asked Hellcat suspiciously.

"Eliminate the Emperor, but we've already done that."

"That's what we saw. Why?"

"Because he impedes the progress of humanity. In times of authoritarianism, progress is stifled. It is smothered, in a sense. Out of necessity. Development needs free thought, but free thought does not thrive under mental shackles and policemen who monitor every movement and every statement for hostility to the system. We want to unleash humanity and bring it to its full potential," she said. Telling these filthy rebels their noble goal made her want to wash.

"You are working with the Orb," the mutant said.

"Yes."

"Why?"

"Because they give us technologies."

"In return for what?" echoed Hellcat.

"It doesn't work that way." Akwa shook his head. "You picked me up - you have my thanks for that. But don't think I trust you guys for a minute. I don't know you, and you've just betrayed the one who got you out of Andal. A naïve womanizer, but a damn good pilot who nearly sent me to kingdom come. Why should I trust you?"

"Because you guys have the same goals we do. I've lived in the damn dirt with the boots of bloody authorities on my neck long enough to know what's important to me. I've known Andal for a few days, and hatred of the Star Empire since birth."

Ah, hence the anger burned into her face like a mosaic, Akwa thought, smelling weakness. She loathed weakness. But this woman did not lie, and she could respect that.

"I see. I take it we're headed toward my father's fleets?"

"Yes."

"Wise. Here's my offer: I need a new ship. You will stay

aboard as crew - along with crew members I choose." Akwa noticed the surprise on their faces and smiled thinly. "Naivety has never been one of my weaknesses. I realize you have arranged for a fallback." She pointed to the mechanic. "My money's on him. Maybe an explosive device somewhere in the superconductor nodes? A cacodemon in the on-board computer is rather not your style."

"Why would you trust us far enough to keep us on board?" wanted Hellcat to know.

"Trust is a feeling nurtured by time. It's going to take that. But what I need is people who have spent time with Gavin Andal."

"Why is that?" asked Bambam.

"Because we're going to track him and destroy him, and because I believe you know where he's headed."

13

GAVIN

When Gavin opened his eyes, the *Reaper* suit had already largely retreated back into the small box at his chest. In his arms he held a young woman in a technician's orange jumpsuit. Her face looked like a pastel painting of blue rivers winding through a colorless landscape. Her eyes were closed, her short hair was frozen into ice crystals, and she felt infinitely cold.

Paramedics stood around them, talking to him. But their voices were like distant calls on the surface as he drifted deep in the ocean. Only gradually did he return to the present, realizing that he was not dead but breathing on his own.

"Lord Captain," one of the medics with the insignia of a Marine sergeant got through to him. "I must politely ask you to release the Chief Petty Officer."

"Sure," he muttered dazedly, trying to disengage his arms from the unconscious woman. But they were slow to obey him. The Sergeant and his comrade helped him after he gave them a weak nod, freeing the young woman from his grasp.

"Thank you, my lord." The medics quickly placed her on a stretcher and wheeled her away. Then someone appeared in front of him, also wearing the white ship's overalls of the medical corps, but with the crossed yellow swords of a lieutenant on his epaulets. He shined a light in each eye and put a medi-cuff around his wrist.

"Do you have feeling in your fingers and toes, Lord Captain?" the doctor asked, looking at the readouts on his datapad streaming from the cuff.

"No, but my hands and feet are starting to tingle. I cannot hear very well, though," Gavin said, dazed.

"That should go away soon, the eardrums haven't burst, just a large number of vessels in the ear canal, that's why the blood is coming from your ears."

"Blood from my ears?" he asked in surprise, wanting to grab his right ear, but the doctor stopped him. "What about my companion? Sergeant..."

"He's fine. No losses, except for two of those rescued."

Gavin looked around consciously for the first time. He was sitting on the floor of a hangar large enough to make it a gymnasium. Four shuttles hung from magnetic devices on the opposite wall, and powerful gates were closed behind him, with a force field flickering in front of them. Two more shuttles with open tail ramps stood across in front of the walls. Several small groups sat on the floor, surrounded by medics, some of whom were engaged in frantic attempts at resuscitation. Everything happened in a paradoxical silence, as if in a church, where there seemed to be a silent agreement not to incur divine wrath.

But the divine wrath had long since descended upon them. On *him*. Hellcat had betrayed him. And Dodger and Bambam. His heart bled at the thought of Hellcat, for he had really imagined he felt something for her. The delicate hint of a spring breeze only, but a beginning

The last Fleet

from which a summer could develop. At least that was what he had thought. Her dagger in his back hurt in particular. Worst of all, however, was the anger at himself. How naive he had been. He had trusted a fighting dog just because it had barked at the same people, run away from the same people. Now he had been bitten for his efforts.

"Were there any other survivors?" Gavin asked hopefully.

"No," a second voice answered him, and a shadow settled over him.

Blinking, he looked up and into the face of the First Secretary of State. Janus Darishma wore hardened military armor, massive and composed of countless moving parts that made his body look like a beefy bug. His face looked older than it did in the feeds, his nut-brown hair a little thinning, the crow's feet around his kind eyes a little deeper.

"Then I failed," Gavin whispered, crestfallen. This time, no pressure spread behind his eyes, no knot formed in his chest, taking away his breath. Instead, there was only a yawning void inside him, the black hole he had feared before. He had failed to protect his family, trusted the wrong people, and had failed to protect the one person who could have held those responsible for the genocide of his homeland and his family accountable.

"No, High Lord," the First Secretary said, eyeing him sympathetically. His eyes reflected a deep hurt which Gavin found in himself. "If anyone failed, it was me."

"The stealth ship?"

"A third party stole it."

"Akwa Marquandt?"

"Your crew saved her escape pod and fled."

Gavin wanted to shout, but instead remained silent.

He merely nodded. Just another nail that fate had driven into his flesh.

"I can't believe he's dead. Just like that."

"He has an implanted tracker that no longer transmits, and nothing out there can be alive now. Also, there are no life signatures of any kind," the First Secretary explained, sounding as if he had to keep reminding himself of these facts.

"First Secretary..."

"Call me Janus, please. You and I are a dying species now, and we should not separate ourselves with formalities."

Gavin paused for a moment, surprised by the sudden informality. Then he saw the pain and anger in the man's eyes again. The same pain and anger he himself felt. Darishma, too, had been betrayed - by his own people. Darishma, too, had lost someone he cared about, and if Marquandt got away with his coup, this man would lose his family, too, just as it had happened to Gavin, he had no illusions about that. Janus knew that.

"Thank you... Janus," he said as Janus held out a hand and effortlessly pulled him to his feet. His legs felt like pudding. As he stood, he was still cold, even though the doctor had given him medication several times with the Diffundator before pulling back. "At least we saved these two."

"Yes," Janus replied seriously.

"What's happening now? Where are we?"

"Captain Gianni is loading the jump knots now. In forty minutes, Marquandt's first units will be here. Some have already jumped to Terra."

"Jumped?" asked Gavin incredulously.

"Apparently you and I have set a precedent," Janus replied somberly.

The last Fleet

"Did Marquandt...?"

"Yes. And it looks bad."

Gavin paused. "What did you mean... When you said that we were a part of a dying species?"

"We are loyalists." Janus took him by the shoulder. "Come with me. I will show you. And then I will need your help."

They left the hangar after Gavin exchanged a look with the master sergeant who was helping to care for the survivors. Down a long corridor, they came to multidirectional elevators that reminded him how big *Dominus*-class cruisers really were. Along the way, they encountered many crew members walking through the corridors with frozen faces, greeting them formally but absently. Gloomy thoughts blew around their heads like dark clouds, making their way into the ship's lifelines as doom and gloom.

Their destination was apparently not the bridge, as Gavin had expected, but a small conference room with a holoprojector built into the table where they were alone. He raised an eyebrow questioningly, but Janus did not seem to notice and turned on the projector. A three-dimensional still image of Dain Marquandt came to life, and Gavin instinctively clenched his fists at the sight of it.

Janus noticed, "Listen to it."

"Citizens of the Star Empire," the Fleet Admiral began with a serious expression and set words that seemed to express strength as much as consternation. Behind him was the Navy flag with the golden eagle over the rising sun, and next to it that of the Star Empire, with the black band of stars on a red background wrapped around a stylized terra like an orbital ring. "I regret to have to bring you somber news today. News that will change our future forever. The fires of war have been carried to our doorstep by enemies who have acted by ambush to cut off our heads." Telescopic footage played. It showed missiles fired seemingly out of nowhere at the *Majestic*. Explosions. A cut, then images of the cruiser breaking apart. It zoomed in on the escaping atmosphere from dozens of holes in the hull, the silhouettes of sailors being pulled into the vacuum, some of them shredded by much faster debris. "A few minutes ago, a cloaked Orb ship destroyed our Emperor Haeron II's ship, which had been on its way to the funeral service of Senate President Varilla Usatami. On board was his chief of staff Grand Admiral Marius Albius. There were no survivors in this cowardly attack on the heart of our star empire." With growing anger, Gavin noticed that the *Invincible*'s nuclear weapons deployment was not shown, nor was the failure of Akwa's ship's cloaking effect. It had all been cut. Dain Marquandt's features hardened, turning from a countenance of sympathy and dismay to one of determination and righteous anger. Gavin felt sick at the sight of him. "I say to you all here and now: This shameful act will not go unpunished. The Orb have terrified us for far too long, but I tell you: We are not afraid. We will not fall into terror. We will not resign ourselves. We are human beings, and humans fight. We fight for justice, we fight for retribution, and we fight for the security of our future and that of our children. Today we must be strong, citizens of the Star Empire." Marquandt paused thoughtfully. "And we must cut the rotting flesh from our wound. The stain of betrayal. The Emperor's flight path was known to only two people, one who was not aboard the *Majestic*: Grand Admiral Albius and the First Secretary of State, Janus Darishma. For a long time, the privileged and favored of the court believed they were above law and morality, but that ends today. The Emperor ordered me to Sol to ensure the protection and order of the center of humanity, and I did not even have the chance to follow his order before our enemies pounced on a moment of weakness. This ends now. Treason will be punished, those guilty will be brought to justice." Marquandt's eyes seemed to glow as he looked into the camera as if staring straight into Gavin's soul. "You cannot hide from the sword of justice. And the Orb should know this: No one transgresses against humanity. Our history was forged in the fires of battle, and they will learn very soon what it means to be our enemy. Be strong, citizens of the Star Empire, for those forces that seek to destroy us, from within and without, understand no other language. We will teach it to them."

The image froze again. Gavin was shaking with anger.

"*That* was his plan. Blame the Orb. Of course."

"Don't blame yourself," Janus said with clearly more composure than he was able to muster. "He fooled us all, and you could not have known it."

Yes, I could have, Gavin thought, thinking back to the sight of the three drones, the Orb on the *Ushuaia*. At the latest, the secret project with Yokatami on their Seed World should have opened his eyes. Even if it was already too late then.

"Did you pay attention to how he structured his speech?" asked Janus.

"He addressed the *commoners*. Not those with status and then the commoners, as usual. His words were to the *Star Empire*, not the *Imperial* Star Empire." Gavin reflected. "It will get through to them because the Emperor is dead and it is unclear what is going to happen now. But at the same time, it takes the wind out of the sail for those who would immediately call for Elayne. Which would not be much wind because the public hardly knows her except from feeds at charity events. At the same time, the mention of the Star Empire does not indicate a dreaded coup or upheaval with a new social order - something even the underprivileged might be afraid of."

"You would have made a good politician," Janus remarked, but did not smile. "This is a coup, but a creeping one. Marquandt has by far the largest fleet in the system, and the last remaining Home Fleet under Admiral Shapiro will be so angry and full of guilt that they will throw themselves blindly into the arms of whoever promises them retribution. He has made sure that his own co-conspirator Albius was aboard the *Majestic* so that Akwa can track him down and kill them both in one fell swoop. So, no accusations against Marquandt have substance either, because he can always counter that he wasn't in cahoots with the Chief of Staff, or he would not have died."

"He made himself indispensable," Gavin summarized. The emptiness inside him gave way to cold anger. "To the only strong man available right now."

"No one will think of Andal and a possible crime on Marquandt's part now. It will be all about strength and necessities."

Gavin looked up at him and turned off the image of the man around whose neck he would like to wrap his hands. "The princess. She's in danger."

"Yes." Janus nodded, and for the first time his thin mask of restraint crumbled - only for a second, but behind it he saw a crushing concern. "We have to get them out of *Rubov* before Marquandt's henchmen can. They will do it under the pretext of security, and they'll be quick. The Imperial Guard is loyal, but they will think they are doing the right thing."

"We have to warn her!"

The last Fleet

"She can hear us." Janus opened his left hand. In it was a small VR transmitter that allowed it to stream a three-dimensional image of its wearer's surroundings.

"The delay to Terra," Gavin pointed out. "It will take over half an hour to..."

"Quantcom. The signal is being sent through a Quantcom transmitter in the ship. We cannot hear them, but they can hear us."

"Why are you telling me this?" asked Gavin. It was still unusual to address the First Secretary informally, but there was nothing ordinary about their situation anymore.

"We have to save her, and I don't know how. Captain Gianni is loyal and one of the best commanders in the Navy, but she's not a pilot. I've read your files. You're a go-getter, and one of the best pilots to leave a Navy academy in the last year to boot. Actually, there were only two."

A week ago, Gavin would have had a big grin on his face at those words and basked smugly in the recognition. Now it meant nothing to him, except that he felt more useful than before.

"I'm the best there is," he said without pride. "But I don't usually fly cruisers."

"I know. But we need ideas that are not part of a Navy officer's standard repertoire, because we are running out of those. We have exactly fifteen minutes until we're ready to jump. We cannot stay here any longer than that," Janus explained, taking a step toward him. "No matter how crazy it is, if you have an idea, you have to tell me."

"Plans of the *Rubov* and the Imperial Sector," Gavin said seriously. "I need those."

He knew that few things were as secret as the blueprints of the Imperial Sector on the *Rubov* orbital ring, except perhaps the palace on Terra itself. For security reasons, the first secretary of state was probably the only one who knew them other than the Guard.

"I don't have it, but..." Janus's wrist terminal chirped. He glanced down at the holodisplay and raised an eyebrow. "But Elayne has them, and so do I now."

Gavin nodded as if this process was the most normal thing in the universe. Yet he had never heard of Quantcom units being on ships before. This new technology had not even made it to all the Frontier Worlds yet, and the barges that were available were house-sized transceivers with high power consumption.

"I'm sending the data to this holoprojector." Janus pointed to the table.

"Is that wise?"

"This ship will not serve under Marquandt, and Captain Gianni would rather blow us up than allow the traitor or any of his henchmen access. Besides, all *Dominus* cruisers are self-contained systems. No one can access our data core from the outside." Janus noticed Gavin's look. "And no one can send them out without Gianni himself authorizing it."

"But the Grand Admiral could send a signal from the *Majestic*," he said.

"Using technology we are not familiar with. Apparently, he had implanted a quantum transmitter. At least, that's what the signal strength suggests."

"I know where they got the technology and why it's unknown: because we don't have it," Gavin returned, and Janus looked at him questioningly, but seemed to have a clue. He was smart enough to put one and one together. "As soon as we rescue the Princess, I'll tell you everything I know. But right now, I need five minutes to myself to figure some things out. Alone."

"I'll wait outside the door," Janus said, nodding at him.

I just dismissed the First Secretary, Gavin thought, feeling guilty.

So his reputation had spread, and now this man expected him to perform a miracle. He turned on the holoprojector and had it display a 3-D representation of the Imperial Sector, which included a complete section of the Ring. Only now did he realize how enormous the orbital ring, which had grown larger and larger over the centuries, really was. In contrast, the Einherjar ring of Andal had been a slender band, downright fragile and tiny.

All right, what are the rules? he asked himself. *She cannot leave the sector if Darishma's fears prove true, because the Guardsmen will want to protect her and go into lockdown. Marquandt's units are already jumping to Terra and will successively take control - or be handed control. If we jump near them, they will either shoot us down or capture us. Flimsy reasons will suffice, perhaps a shot of the* Invincible *flying near the* Majestic *and doing nothing about the attackers. We have to jump, or it will take us twelve hours or more. But if we jump, we cannot disappear except with normal thrust - that will give them enough time to destroy us. So we need cover, and we need to be fast at the same time - which is impossible near Terra, in the middle of the enemy's nest, which had just recently been the bosom of safety.*

Gavin stared at the monochrome display and the marked spot where the Princess was apparently right now.

Then an idea occurred to him, and before it had fully flashed through his mind, his hands were already tingling with excitement. It was possible, but it would not please Janus or the commander of this ship.

INTERLUDE
ADMIRAL GIORGIDIS

Admiral Stavros Giorgidis stood with his arms folded behind his back on the bridge of the *Zeus*, the flagship of the Ruhr's corporate fleet. It hurt his soul to know that the pride of his fleet was clad in ugly water tanks on its hull, hastily welded on in space dock to make it look like a drift tanker. He also did not like the fact that he had to come here with mercenaries, but at least the supervisor had given him a generous budget so he could pick and choose.

They had already been in his employer's Seed System for two hours, and he had imposed a complete embargo. One hundred light and medium frigates patrolled around CX-2, plus eighty heavy and light corvettes of varying armament and equipment, and two carrier ships with hangars full of Stingrays in case anyone got any ideas.

There was nothing left of the *Demeter* but a ring of debris that spun around the Seed World and became a death trap for starships. The attackers had also left nothing of the local space defenses.

Two hours later, they received their first visit, from a

Mammoth freighter, of all things, which dropped out of subspace near the inner gas giant.

"What do we have in the vicinity?" he asked his first officer, Captain Sharee.

"Two frigates, the *Aphrodite* and the *Hellespont*. Light armament. The *Hellespont* has a detachment of HTR mercenaries on board."

Giorgidis nodded. Warfield's *High-Threat Response* teams were professional and extremely well equipped.

"Open a channel to the ships."

"It's open, Admiral," reported Lieutenant O'Leary from communications.

"Captains," he said. "I'm giving you an order to intercept the freighter. Disable its maneuvering. After that, you have clearance to board."

He did not wait for the commanders' acknowledgements and instead called up the gas giant's tactical display. The *Mammoth* freighter hung like an overweight maggot just outside the gravity funnel. Its two frigates, which had been there searching for hidden pirates, had already moved to intercept and would be in weapons range in twenty minutes.

"Admiral, are you sure we can just attack the ship?" his first officer asked. "S1-Ruhr is not a restricted area."

"Yes. There are transit licenses for Science Corps prospectors and civilian ships with a declared course. What do you think a *Mammoth* freighter is doing here? What does anyone need to send the largest cargo ship in the Star Empire here for? The Seed World is in shambles, the *Demeter* no longer exists."

"A transit," Shahee concluded.

"That's right. And a transit from here can only go to the neighboring Yokatami system," Giorgidis continued. "Reuffurth does not make sense because they could only have come from there - or from Andal, which is also currently a restricted military area enforced by units from Kerrhain."

"Smugglers."

"Possibly. Paid by Yokatami."

Shahee pursed his mouth and nodded.

Twenty minutes later, the brief, one-sided skirmish took place. The commander of the Mammoth freighter lodged a protest and sent a transponder code, but no licenses. That smugglers could get their hands on such a valuable ship but had not even raised enough money to get a fake license only confirmed Giorgidis' suspicions.

The *Aphrodite* and the *Hellespont* made short work of the unarmed giant like two hyenas pouncing on a crippled elephant. After less than two minutes, the *Hellespont* was already docked at the bow section. After a few minutes delay, they could watch on the bridge of the *Zeus* as the highly equipped mercenaries in their modified engine armor stormed the alien ship.

Giorgidis raised a brow as he watched them seem to view every movement in the corridors as hostile, shooting everything that was flesh and blood until they reached the bridge and he gave the order to stand down. But even there, the opposition was minimal.

The captain was taken away and the *Mammoth* was taken over by a lieutenant from the *Aphrodite*.

Another hour later, and he was sent the interrogation results. He could only wrinkle his nose at the methods, but the brutality of the mercenaries at least had the effect of producing results. Naruto Ikame was the name of the freighter's commander, an employee of Yokatami, as he had admitted after losing all his toenails. Interesting.

It was also interesting that he had known of the risk that units of Ruhr might be here, but had nevertheless been ordered to go. His destination was actually S2-Yokatami, and he was coming from Kerrhain with transit via Andal. So High Lady Kerrhain was also behind it or had once again put dirty money in her pocket.

The *Mammoth* had nothing loaded. The storerooms were empty, and Ikame could credibly assure that he did not know what his mission would be once he reached his destination. But he did possess information about the restricted military area in the neighboring system, which Giorgidis found useful.

"I'll talk to the supervisor," he declared after reviewing the data, turning command over to his second-in-command.

In his quarters, he established a quantcom link with the supervisor.

"Admiral. Do you have something for me?" asked Ludwig Sorg with the typical businesslike manner that expressed impatience and attentiveness at the same time.

Giorgidis summarized everything in a brief verbal report.

"I knew Sato Ran was in this. But I did not expect him to go this far."

"What should we do with the freighter?"

"As far as we are concerned, no freighter has ever appeared in our Seed System," Sorg said. "It probably jumped right into the gas giant due to a navigational error."

"I understand," Giorgidis replied. "Very unfortunate. What is to be done regarding Yokatami?"

"What your prisoner reported about the defenses can only mean that they are hiding something. I want to know what it is. What is your assessment of the military situation if you intervene?"

"We have clear superiority. With good transit preparation, we can overwhelm what Yokatami has in orbit with thirty percent casualties. Even with the death premiums to be paid accordingly, we would still be within budget," Giorgidis concluded.

"Fine, do it then. We will deny everything."

"Yokatami will know."

"But cannot prove it, the same as us. They will deny everything as well. Until then, we will return the favor and take what they hid from us," Sorg decided.

"Won't that lead to a conflict?"

"Document everything you find in S2-Yokatami. The PR department will spin it that we've had information leaked to us, while also leaking it to the other veto members. Then Sato Ran's hands will be tied. Is that all, Admiral?"

"Yes, sir."

"Good, you have your orders." Sorg disconnected, and Giorgidis returned to the bridge to join a holo-conference with the commanders of his mercenary fleet to begin battle planning.

14

GAVIN

"That's your idea?" the Commander asked, blinking as if she were trying to escape from a bad dream. Her voice was not raised, but there was something like anger in it. If he were not a member of the high nobility and she of the low, she probably would have yelled at him to see if he had lost his mind.

"It's possible," he said.

"It's suicidal," she countered.

"It's necessary," Janus objected, and they both looked to the First Secretary, who gazed inquiringly into Gavin's eyes. "You've done something similar before, am I right?"

"Yes." Gavin nodded. "With the Einherjar orbital ring back home in Andal. I needed cover, and we need it now. It can work."

"*Can*," Gianni repeated. "But it's very unlikely. The multiple magnetic fields on the *Rubov* will tear us apart."

"Not if we calculate the jump extremely well. I understand that only the very best of the very best are even allowed to apply for the Emperor's Flight Readiness. That would mean you'd have at least two of the best navigators in the Star Empire on board." Gavin paused for a moment. He pointed to the hologram in front of them. "You have exactly five minutes to get us in there perfectly, and I still need something from you personally that you may need the Princess' authorization for."

"What's that?"

"A tactical advantage if we make it out of here, but for which we need access to the mainframe of the Imperial mainframe." Gavin explained what he needed and asked her not to ask him why. After all, it was based on a tiny hope that he himself didn't believe in. But if it proved to be accurate...

"Do it, captain," Janus said. "That's an order."

Gianni made a pained expression, but nodded obediently and gave appropriate orders to their navigation officer, and had his two replacement crewmembers summoned to join in the incredibly complex calculation.

"We have been brought to within one hundred yards of the Aurora habitat by a single woman over five light years," he said in their direction. "It's doable, and if it is, these people can do it."

That Mirage was possibly a robot, operating with an outlawed powerful AI in her head, he kept to himself for now. The commander had to believe it was possible, or they would fail before they started.

"Is the Princess on her way to the rendezvous point?"

Janus looked down at his wrist terminal. After two breaths, he received a text message.

"Yes. She's worried about the Imperial Guardsmen."

"Have my master sergeant bring it up. He may have an idea on how we can deal with this problem," Gavin suggested, and Janus nodded to Gianni to give the appropriate order. "Before I head out, is there any news on Marquandt's units?"

The last Fleet

"Two fleets have already jumped into orbit around Terra. They're setting up no-fly zones and checkpoints, probably to root out alleged traitors," Janus explained.

"So they're preparing a purge of loyalists. Marquandt will put his loyalists in key positions."

"Yes. Where they are not already in place."

Gavin turned to the First Secretary. "I have to go. Tell the Princess to be at the exact location I marked in the blueprint. In exactly eight minutes."

"I already have," Janus assured him. "She will be there."

"Good." He straightened. When he had almost reached the door, he heard Janus call out again.

"Gavin?"

"Yes?" He turned around.

"Bring her back safe and sound. She is important to the Star Empire. And she is important to me."

"You can count on it. If anyone can get her out, it's me." It felt good to let his old self speak, untroubled by the sheer lunacy of his idea. The plan was so crazy that he barely felt the weight of fate, as if he had let go of everything because there was nothing left. Either he died trying to do something that would be remembered for a long time and would be a thorn in Marquandt's flesh, or he succeeded and the thorn became a dagger. Both were prospects he could live - or die - with.

As he left the bridge, his magnetic boots made clacking sounds each time they hit the metal floor. The clattering became a harsh melody on the way to the forward bays, of which there were only two. He reached the bow section via the elevators, where a female technician with the rank of chief petty officer was already waiting for him. She looked as if she had had a night of drinking - a sight he would probably have to get used to among the Emperor's loyal servants in the near future.

"Lord Captain," she greeted him, saluting briskly. He returned the gesture without pausing, and she had to hurry to stay beside him while he looked around for the two launch bays.

"Where..."

"That's what I was about to say. We don't have any access tubes." The technician gestured with an outstretched hand toward a stairway and a circular walkway above them, from which two doors led off. "Right door, sir."

"Thank you, Petty Officer." Gavin walked to the stairway and heard more footsteps behind him.

"What about your G-suit?"

"I don't have one with me."

"But..."

"I'll have to get by like this," he said without turning around, and ran across the metal walkway to the door on the right. There he turned briefly to face her. She looked startled. Below them, several other technicians were hurrying around, apparently frantically getting his *Stingray* ready for action. "Give me the most important data."

"The catapult is twenty yards long. Ejection acceleration 5g. The Flynites supply is complete. You do have the flight pattern recognition for..."

"Petty Officer," he said curtly, opening the door. "I'm the best you'll ever see flying a Stingray."

With that, he left them behind, coming into a small anteroom with the flight readiness lockers. Eight of them with names engraved on them and a hatch in the floor. It was already open, so he slid down and landed right in the pilot's seat of the tiny cockpit. Despite the insanity of what he was about to do, he felt electrified by his own arrogance, as if something of the Gavin that had died with his family and Andal shone on him. Or perhaps it was the ease of a man who knew he was going to die.

But it was all the same to him. He saw before him the complex manual controls of the fighter, felt the familiar confines of the cockpit, the cushions of memory foam beneath him that would mold their shape to his and soften the acceleration forces coming at him.

"I'm closing up. Good luck, Lord Captain," the technician called to him above his head, closing the hatch.

"Don't need it," he replied to himself as his fingers routinely ran over the manual controls to power up the fusion engine and check the major systems for proper function. It was in his hands now, his alone. No crew to make mistakes or betray him. Luck was a concept for those who doubted themselves - and he did not. For him to be back in the cockpit felt like a puzzle piece falling into place, and he accomplished something he hadn't in days: he blanked out fate, and with it, the entire universe. He answered the launch control queries from the bridge mechanically like a robot, more through years of experience than conscious thought processes. His right hand clasped the flightstick, his left rested on the neural pad for primary system control.

"Two minutes to launch clearance," Lieutenant Harper informed him from launch control. Her voice was muffled and mechanical, almost like a computer's, and made him feel increasingly calm. Every bridge officer spoke to fighter pilots this way, and for good reason. Nowhere was the mortality rate as high as among his peers.

Gavin moved his head in circles to relax his neck. After sixty seconds, the ship's jump alarm went off, a distant drone that made itself known in his cockpit as a small red light above his head. Downright unimpressive in the face of what it meant.

He began pilot breathing as his instructor had taught him. Two seconds inhale, six seconds exhale. Calm quickly settled over the rising excitement like a balm to his spirit. The lights in the launch shaft came on.

Sixty seconds.

The narrow tube with the recesses for the Stingray's stubby wings had wide grooves at the top and bottom where the electromagnetic tracks ran that would hurl him out of the *Majestic* at twenty yards with 5g. The protective gate on the other side was dark as a black hole. It would not open until after the transit.

Thirty seconds from now.

"Good luck, Gavin Andal," Janus said over the radio.

"Thanks. It will work."

"It will. See you on the other side. That's what they say among fighter pilots, right?"

Gavin laughed. "No. Only in the VR movies."

Ten seconds to transit.

His hands did not shake or become damp. But his stomach tingled.

Then the jump. A tiny moment of cold, like the distant echo of a fading memory that he could no longer tell had been pure imagination or genuine experience. The image in front of him distorted, disappeared, was there again and yet had never been gone. Everything was still and yet it had been moving all the time when the *Majestic* fell out of normal space in its subspace vacuole and crashed back into it, several hundred million miles away in the inner system. To where enemies swarmed and friends no longer knew where their loyalties lay. Right into the hornet's nest, in the cockpit of a mosquito.

The last Fleet

The gate at the end of the launch bay opened, and a jolt went through the *Stingray*. Gavin was pressed into the seat by an invisible fist as the fighter was hurled forward by the counter-rotating electromagnetic fields.

It took less than a heartbeat for him to hurtle out of the bow. In front of his cockpit window, everything was green and occasionally punctuated by light. Sounds resembling breaking bones and old leaves under boots whipped at him. He immediately went into a brutal 180-degree turn, tilting the flightstick forward at just the right angle.

The Stingray somersaulted, violently pressing Gavin into the straps and slamming him back so hard he lost his breath. Hypodermic needles pressed into his neck from the head section of his seat, automatically injecting him with Flynites in large numbers as the on-board computer suspected sustained g-loads in the critical range. With maximum reverse thrust, he aimed for the *Majestic*'s open mouth, a tiny black hole in the front of the behemoth. A trail of annihilation stretched through the three hundred yards of woodland he had pierced at treetop level like a fireball.

A proximity alarm blared, and the distance indicator on the rear sensors showed five yards separating him from the wall.

"Bloody heavens!" he growled as initial acceleration and counterthrust cancelled each other out and a wave of nausea rolled through his stomach. His body always seemed to lag several seconds behind his head in keeping up with the ever-changing physical conditions.

The Stingray slumped to the ground as his direction of flight was snatched away from him until he accelerated again, this time not even at half a percent maximum power. Under the canopy, it sped along between tree trunks, felling two young birch trees it couldn't avoid. His stubby wings cut them in half like blades.

The parkland was empty. No gardeners in the meadows, no walkers on the meticulously manicured gravel paths. Gavin zoomed over them, kicking up bits of rock, foliage and grass, leaving a trail of devastation from the force of his engine and the plasma flame that dragged it along behind him like an oversized welding torch. The damage he was causing to something as precious as the Imperial Gardens of the *Rubov* Orbital Ring hurt his soul. But he had no time for his soul. He had a princess to rescue.

Two seconds after his acceleration in the opposite direction, he had reached the *Majestic*. Only now that he saw it not in endless space, but amidst trees and bushes, did he realize the scale of the cruiser. Like a gigantic skyscraper lying on its side with a gloomy facade, it bisected the gardens. The underside lay on the ground, having dented the sinfully expensive earth by several yards, the upper sensor superstructures almost touching the roof of Duroglas through which he could see Terra's bands of clouds stretching across one of the oceans, their reflected light shining on the artificial forest.

Gavin braked and did a sideways roll with his *Stingray* that sent him overhead along the *Majestic*'s hull. Once at the topside, he chased through a four-yard gap between the ship and the glass that gave him only ten inches of clearance up and down.

He breathed a sigh of relief when he reached the other side, only to look through the glass in surprise. Behind a huge tree with bluish veins on its leaves, which had narrowly escaped a fate similar to hundreds of other trees that had now disappeared into subspace just a few yards

The last Fleet

from the cruiser, hundreds of guardsmen in titanium armor poured out of a dozen double doors.

From above, they looked like somewhat crudely painted stick figures, but he knew that impression was deceiving. Above them, on one of the many viewing balconies that had looked far larger in the blueprints, stood a lone figure in black clothing.

"You've got company," he radioed to the *Majestic*'s bridge.

"Spotted it already," Janus replied. "I guess there's not much they can do."

"I'll get the Princess, she's here." He tried hard not to let his relief show.

As he sped over the Imperial Guardsmen, he was surprised to find that they were not firing at him. A cruiser was not itching for even powerful small arms like Gauss rifles or pulse cannons, but a fighter was no more than a paper airplane with far too many weapons.

In front of the balcony, he went into a daring 90-degree turn and then braked so hard it felt like the straps would press into his flesh and leave lifelong imprints. A push of a button, and the windshield flipped open.

"NOW!" he yelled, as gravity was already sending him downward.

A shadow appeared and landed on him. His right leg felt as if someone had amputated it with a ragged axe.

No time for pain, he thought, closing the cockpit window again and going into forward thrust.

The shadow turned out to be a young woman with unruly blonde curls tamed in a braid. She wore form-fitting black body armor that accentuated her handsome curves. Her face was lightly tanned, her fine nose flanked by dimpled cheeks, and her curved mouth sat above a pert little chin.

And he looked straight into her blue eyes as he sought her gaze.

"Found what you're looking for?" she asked provocatively.

"If you are the Princess, then yes," he deflected and smiled.

The brief moment of carelessness caused them to smash through a tree and be thrown to the side. Reflexively, he grabbed his passenger and pressed her against him so that she would not bump into the instruments and hurt herself. He ignored the fact that she was the Princess and legitimate successor to the Emperor.

"Turn around," he ordered, and she fortunately obeyed immediately. "Sit between my legs and lean back."

As soon as her hair tickled his chin and she squeezed in front of him, he commanded the nanonic seat belts to expand on her. They liquefied and crawled over her body to bind them both to the seat as one. It would not be comfortable, and more extreme maneuvers were impossible this way, but it would have to work for what they were about to do.

He flew a curve around the destroyed tree to maintain speed and not crash.

"The guardsmen," he said.

"Coming with us," she replied before he could speak. "The entire legion. Janus already knows."

"Okay." He hid his surprise. Out of the corner of his eye, he saw the stick figures disappear into the *Majestic*'s flank like ants returning to their burrow in droves. He only hoped it wasn't a ruse. But that was Janus' and Gianni's problem now. He had another. "Princess, Highness, I need to know exactly where the main corridor is."

"I'll mark the spot," she returned against his chest, tapping the touch pad between the sensor control and the maintenance panel. Feeling her closeness and warmth, in a way he'd done more often in the past to impress female crewmates, felt wrong, like he was committing a crime.

The HUD in the windshield marked a section of the eastern wall that reached nearly twenty stories up to the Duroglas. He pushed the flightstick forward and banked a wide turn toward the marked section to have enough of a run-up. As soon as he dropped below the minimum speed, they would crash, since the Stingray was about as aerodynamic as a stone. A flat stone, to be sure, but still a stone.

"You did not mention in your plan what you were going to do once you crazy people jumped into the Imperial Gardens," the Princess said in a strained voice. As he navigated the end of the turn and they flew toward the gray wall of armored composite, she pulled her hands back and clutched at his knees with them.

"I was worried you were going to call me insane," he admitted bluntly.

"I still might do that. What are we doing right now?"

"Your enemies are about to find out what we're doing here. That means we cannot stay in one spot. Did you order the lockdown of the vaktrams in the central tube?"

"Yes."

"Good, then we don't have a problem. At least not yet." Gavin fired the two Hellfire missiles under the hull. They whizzed away with thick clouds of steam, shredding the marked section ahead of them. Before the fire and dust had settled, they chased through and into the main corridor in Section H, which the inhabitants called *Hellgate*, he had learned. He pulled up his nose so that they flew on a course right between the light tube at the very top and the street below, a respectful distance from the walls of buildings to the right and left.

Below them, passersby ran away in panic, jumping into building entrances or behind their vehicles. Thanks to the gridlink, traffic kept moving and didn't get into the same panic. Gavin even imagined he could hear screams and shouts, even though that was impossible with the volume of the engine and the roar of the wind.

"Are we flying through the main corridor at supersonic speeds in a spaceship right now?" the Princess asked breathlessly.

"Yes. I hope word gets out soon and these people protect themselves," he replied with concern for the passersby. Even the great concentration he had to exert to fly steadily and not collide with anything could not displace it. Although burst eardrums were among the injuries that could be easily treated, he felt like a terrorist at the thought that the civilians below them were being knocked down by the sonic booms and losing their hearing.

And it would get worse as he continued to accelerate. Drag increased with its speed, requiring more and more helium-3 pellets for the small *Raptor* engine.

The Princess gasped in fright as the facades of buildings blurred into a gray mass as they entered the double-digit supersonic range. The streets had cleared by now, and red alert sirens flared like short-lived ignitions in the cockpit window. He did not know how much sound pressure the Duroglas installed in the *Rubov* could withstand, but there would be a limit. When it was reached, they would not only create extreme dynamic pressure that would turn windows into a shower of shards that they would drag behind them like spray - but also ignite the air molecules themselves and create extreme heat.

Don't let anyone out, he urged station security. *Lock the doors.*

Gavin switched the HUD to project a simple 3-D representation of his surroundings into the Duroglass, consisting only of soothing green color. This made it look almost like a simulator game and blanked out anything that might distract him. There was only the slightly curved path ahead of him. They were now a proton in a particle accelerator ring trying to hit its associated electron.

"How can you see anything anymore?" asked the princess in a pressed voice.

"The *Rubov* is a perfect ring. I could let the control software take over by just keeping the angle," he explained. "I just can't lose concentration."

"How long will it take us once around?"

"Two hours."

"But we don't have two hours!" she said, startled. "They will catch us."

"No, they won't," he returned. It was easy for him to remain calm and composed because there was little room in his mind for anything other than maintaining his course down the main corridor. According to his calculations, the house fronts to the right and left would begin to glow after half an hour when they reached their maximum speed. So would the hull of his Stingray. Then they would see how tough the Carbin armor really was. "They can't stop us. If they shoot at us from outside, they will vent the entire main corridor. The only way to stop that is if they lower the security bulkheads and seal off the sections. Then we would crash in like a meteor, releasing kinetic energy equivalent to a nuclear bomb. Inside the ring, it would be a death sentence. The *Rubov* would tear apart. Likewise, if they prepared a gun in the main corridor and fired at us. The debris would just be a lot of smaller bombs instead of one big one."

"Why a complete perimeter?" asked the Princess.

"Three-quarters, to be exact. There's the only connection there between the main corridor and the artery."

"You mean the central corridor for the vacuums?"

"Yes. The *Invincible* just about fits in there, and thanks to your order to the vaktram systems, it has a clear path," he explained as they sped along the corridor like a force of nature.

"They're doing the same thing we're doing." She seemed to ponder. "We're going to the maintenance tunnel for the construction equipment, am I right? It goes off diagonally from the main to the central corridor, big enough for construction equipment and Stingrays. But it's only flyable in that direction of flight."

"Well, actually, it's *not flyable* at all," Gavin muttered, and she apparently noticed that he preferred not to speak in order to concentrate. Even the tiniest contact with one of the walls, the fluorescent tube above them, or the road below them, would be enough at their speed to disintegrate them into their atoms. After half an hour, he sent the first ping to the *Invincible* and received a reply shortly after. They were on a parallel course and both were still intact.

The short ping had to be enough, along with a second in half an hour, to ensure that the previously calculated velocities were maintained to the second.

After an hour, they were still alive. His right wrist ached from the forced position around the flightstick. Probably it would have been safer to let the on-board computer take over, at least it didn't get tired or lose concentration. But it was susceptible to jamming, and Gavin trusted only himself. He had to have it in his own hands.

"I'm very sorry about your father," he said ten minutes

before their entry point into the maintenance tunnel. Why he did it, he didn't know. The words just came to his lips before he had thought about it.

"Thank you," she replied in a strained voice. He noticed that her hair smelled like jasmine tea. Quietly, she said, "I still cannot believe it."

"I know." He swallowed. "I don't have anyone anymore, and it feels like I'm alone in the universe."

"I'm very sorry, too, Gavin Andal. I heard what happened to your family. To your home."

"They're all dead. Everything I ever loved. That's part of who I am now. Just a before and an after."

"I still have my sister," the princess said.

"Peraia?"

"I know she's still alive. I just feel it."

Because you fervently desire it, he thought, but said nothing.

"Hold on, Princess," he commanded, knowing the reason he had addressed her - to distract her.

First, he switched the projection of the green walls off the HUD so they could see outside again. Everything was blurry, as if they were racing through dense fog. He sent the final ping to the *Invincible* and received the response at exactly the same time. Then he cut thrust by fifty percent on the approach to the maintenance tunnel and fired the railgun mounted under the nose at the preprogrammed moment to blow open the lower gate, which was still two miles ahead of them.

The throttle turned the fog into a washed-out gray tube. The HUD showed him the tunnel for the construction equipment, along with the exact dimensions of the hole he had blasted in the gate.

"Best close your eyes," he advised his passenger, but

she answered nothing, stiffening noticeably against his chest.

When the time came, he exhaled for a long time and then tugged on the flightstick at just the right moment, as dictated by the on-board computer, to adjust her up eight degrees. The darkness surrounded them. The five-hundred-yard tunnel was flown through within a second and their destination merely a flicker of light ahead. At the next point marked in the HUD, he lowered the nose and entered a 45-degree left turn.

In one fell swoop, everything seemed to slow down. They were in the port hangar of the *Invincible*, which had flown past the exit of the maintenance tunnel at exactly the right time with the gates open. Now that they were moving at the same speed, it appeared in the illuminated hangar as if they were standing still. His engine was burning the rear wall with its plasma beam, but that was only a minimal concern. He accepted the request from the cruiser's on-board computer to take control so that throttling the speed of both starships down was simultaneous to the millisecond.

They lowered just gently to the ground and then the thrusters shut down. Extinguishing foam shot out of the ceiling and walls at them, quickly enveloping them to cool the Stingray and make the hangar passable again for the ship's technicians.

"You can open your eyes again, Princess," he said, taking his trembling right hand off the flightstick. Relieved, he exhaled.

"I did not close them," she replied, "but let's not do that again."

"Some things are better tried only once in a lifetime, so as not to tempt luck."

"I am certain you do not believe in luck."

The last Fleet

"No," he admitted.

Ten minutes later, the nanofoam enveloping them dissolved and had absorbed all the heat. Entire crews of orange-clad engineers and technicians pumped out the liquid and scurried around his Stingray. Ladders were placed against the cockpit, and Gavin opened the windshield. It crackled and creaked, finally breaking free of its mount and popping upward.

Only now did he notice the transital alarm, noticeable by yellow lights and a muffled siren yelp. The jump happened at the moment a lieutenant appeared at the end of the ladder and looked in at them. Just a brief moment of confusion, a fleeting hiccup of the universe, and it went on as if nothing had happened.

They had jumped. And they were still alive.

INTERLUDE
ADMIRAL GIORGIDIS

Giorgidis had planned the raid on Yokatami's Seed World with his commanders to look like a chaotic pirate attack. He had no illusions that Sato Ran and Yokatami's military would understand that only a similarly powerful competitor would be capable of an action like this, but he had not come to make it easy for them. Deniability for his employer was paramount.

The first fifty units jumped in seemingly erratic chaos near the only moon of the Seed World, while he and the *Zeus* and thirty other units disguised as support ships plunged out of subspace slightly outside at the L2 point. The two other battle groups of fifty ships each emerged on the opposite side of the planet and set about circling it.

The defensive systems were the last clue Giorgidis needed that something was wholly amiss here, for as it turned out, the captain of the *Mammoth* freighter had not lied when he had described to them the number and positions of the installations. He would have preferred to take the man with him, but they could not take any chances and had taken him back to his ship, where he had remained bound and gagged on the bridge with the rest of his crew. They had flown the *Mammoth* by autopilot directly into the gas giant's equator, where it had been torn apart by the powerful gales of the hydrogen-helium mixture and its remains swallowed up.

"Battle group 1 under heavy fire," he heard his first officer say, but he saw it himself on the tactical display. The first battle group, deployed as a vanguard, had jumped into the middle of the defenses focused on the orbit of the moon, which was in a tethered orbit to the Seed World and always facing the same side. Since there were no orbital installations on the other side, it had not been difficult to assume what Yokatami was trying to hide here was on the moon-facing hemisphere.

So the first fifty units had to draw fire and keep the facilities' sensors busy, while the other two battle groups could approach from the flanks and see exactly where which platforms and ships with which armaments were located. Giorgidis sacrificed his infantry so that the cavalry could advance into the weak points.

The first engagement was short and brutal. They were not called in, there was not even an attempt at a transponder intercept. The sixty ships in all - twenty of which were Imperial Navy - fought silently and at full strength. They held no reserve and struck like cornered predators. In Giorgidis' mind, this only reinforced his suspicion that something really expensive was going on here, especially since obviously high places on Terra had been greased to bring the Navy on board. Not hailing potentially hostile ships and asking them to surrender or at least leave the exclusion zone was against general fleet procedure.

The fact that they were stirring up a hornet's nest became apparent at the latest when he switched energy signatures as a filter into the tactical view. Through the virtual window at the front of the bridge he saw flashes, short-lived explosions, no more than distant flickering between the planet and its meager satellite. But on the holoscreen between them, the real extent of the battle became apparent. Directed bursts of radiation - laser, maser and X-ray beams, invisible to the human eye, overwhelming on sensors, hundreds of missiles with seemingly confused trajectories, long plasma flares where ships maneuvered and threw themselves into the fray. Explosions and escaping gases from the spaceships filled with people and potential for destruction. In between all the chaos, there were still the barely traceable railgun shells that brought death invisibly and silently. A ship that was just maneuvering or accelerating to get close to an enemy or out of the worst area could be ripped open by the tungsten bolts at any moment and shatter into countless pieces.

"What about the Quantcom barge?" he asked his first officer.

"Was on the edge of the asteroid belt. The *Delphi* destroyed it right after the jump," Shahee replied.

They had been lucky that the captain of the *Mammoth* freighter had also been the one who had brought the expensive communication equipment into the system a few years ago, since hardly any freighter in the Star Empire was big enough to load it. So communication only worked classically via courier drones or by ships jumping - which is why he had designated a half-hour window for the battle.

After fifteen minutes, their two battle groups reached their flanking positions and fired swarms of missiles, before they also added their railguns. Due to the extremely dense battlefield between the defenders and their orbital assets and the first battle group, some of their own units also went down in the hail of projectiles. However, the corresponding losses had been calculated in advance.

Everything lasted no more than twenty minutes, then there was no signature left in the orbit of the Seed World that did not belong to them. Disbanding one of the battle groups, he sent it out into the system to search for hidden assets while he himself focused on the planet.

"It's completely terraformed," Shahee remarked in amazement as she looked down over the virtual bridge window at the green world, which was covered every five seconds by a blue glow that seemed to focus on a point at the equator before spreading out again from there. It appeared to be some sort of node.

"Five years and they turn a barren rock world with minimal atmosphere into Pandora?" asked Giorgidis doubtfully.

"I don't know how that can be possible."

"It apparently is. I was there for the inauguration of Yokatami's seed ship, the Musashi, at that time. That planet was more inhospitable than our CX-2."

"Admiral," one of his bridge officers called out. "We've spotted a large structure at the equator that appears to be at the center of the light effects."

"On screen."

Giorgidis eyed the gray disk in a green jungle world with the strange blue glow that kept appearing and disappearing. A *Mammoth* freighter with its engines pointed upward was stuck right in the middle. They looked like four empty eye sockets of a giant staring directly into Zeus' telescopes. The fact that this behemoth of a spacecraft covered less than thirty percent of the megastructure's surface showed him how big it really must be.

"Electronic magnification, eightfold," he ordered,

taking a step toward the holodisplay in front of him and Shahee. In the cleared field that surrounded the circular structure like a ring, several dozen outlines lay among plowed and scorched earth. "Are those bodies?"

"Looks like it," said his first officer.

"We're going down there. Order the *Sophocles* to fill up four Skyhooks with HTR strike teams and send them down there. I want to know what's in there. O'Leary?"

"Yes, Admiral?" the communications officer replied from his console.

"Send word on all frequencies to this facility that anyone inside should come out into the open and surrender before we begin firing from orbit in ten minutes. Instruct units above the site to charge their laser weapons," Giorgidis instructed, then waited. Gradually, on the telescopic images, he saw figures come running out of the sides like tiny ants out of their burrow. There were hundreds of them, and they all seemed to be dressed in gray coveralls. They ran out onto the grassland and toward the edge of the forest, which was about a quarter-mile away. Before the first of them reached the strange forest, no new ones joined them.

"Fire control," he called out. "Orders to the *Damocles*, *Samson* and *Heracles*, open fire."

"Admiral?"

"There are no survivors on this planet. If you don't understand that, you're fired."

Giorgidis watched as the three mercenary frigates sterilized the entire ring of grass around the megastructure. The fleeing people on the ground evaporated, and the vegetation went up in flames. He glanced at the tactics screen and saw the Sophocles' four Skyhooks detach from their mothership and, with afterburners ignited, swoop down into the atmosphere to storm the structure on the ground.

"Shahee, you take over communications with these mercenaries. Have them survey and scan everything with drones. I want a complete one-to-one simulation of the inside of this facility. When they're done, I want them to blow it up. And then we're out of here."

"Roger that, Admiral."

15

JANUS

Janus knocked on the heavy composite bulkhead and waited. At some point, he knocked again until it was opened for him.

"First Secretary of State," Gavin Andal greeted him and took a step aside to let him enter.

"Janus," he reminded the young man, accepting the invitation. The COB's cabin was spacious, but not as luxurious as the Commander and First Officer's. As High Lord, it was his right to choose either cabin, but first and foremost, Gavin was an officer of the fleet and would never have exercised that right. So he had moved in here.

Janus's eyes looked tired, pale from the veil of deep melancholy.

"That was a crazy plan," Janus said, walking over to the decanting table to pour them scotch. But when he handed Gavin a glass, he declined.

"I'd rather not. If I start now, I won't stop. It's too tempting to drown all the darkness in it. I have to stay strong."

"You are," Janus assured him, raising his glass in salute

before taking a sip. "I need a drink or my head will burst into flames."

They took a seat on the small settee in the corner between the recycler and the door.

"I know what you mean."

"We're still six hours away from Dust. Gianni has assured me that we are not being followed. So the enemy doesn't know where we're headed. A small piece of news, but a good one."

"The enemy knows where I'll be headed." Gavin sighed as Janus looked at him questioningly. "Parts of my brother's fleet escaped Andal because we were able to warn them early enough via Marquandt's command code. They jumped before their system software could be overwritten. I think I know where they escaped to regroup."

"That means there's still a fleet from your sector?" asked Janus in surprise.

"I hope so."

"And you think you know where your brother sent them?"

"Yes." Gavin nodded and hesitated.

"If you don't trust me now, boy, then probably never."

"Sorry. I think they jumped to Pulau Weh."

"Pulau Weh?" Janus wondered feverishly where he had heard that name before. But he could not recall it. "What is that? A system?"

"An ocean world beyond Tartarus-Void, discovered only eight years ago by a Science Corps prospector. It is located in the 777-Goggins system. My brother and I read Doctor Heinrich's report on the Tartarus circumnavigation and were fascinated. When we were younger, we always imagined emigrating there to escape the whole court circus." Gavin bit his lower lip. "I think my brother was looking for a place I would come to, but no

The last Fleet

one else. A place far enough away from the Border Worlds and Sol that Marquandt wouldn't have on his mind."

"Marquandt probably counted on them jumping to another Border World sector or to Sol to report the betrayal," Janus opined, nodding. It made sense. "Your brother seems to me to have been farsighted, as befitted his reputation."

The pain in the young captain's gaze was answer enough.

"Tell you what," he continued, leaning forward. "We'll jump to Dust, which is on the edge of the Tartarus Void. The Emperor's brother will be able to help us hide Elayne and get her to safety. After that, I will personally make sure we continue to Pulau Weh. Right now, we have nothing, but with a fleet - your fleet - behind us, we have a chance to rally other supporters among the loyalists and prevent Marquandt from destroying the entire Star Empire."

"You believe he will start a war against the Orb."

"Yes. And it would be suicide. Admiral Taggert has destroyed a handful of their ships and lost several fleets in return."

"Maybe not."

Janus looked up and raised an eyebrow. "What do you mean?"

Gavin told him in detail about Yokatami's Seed World and what had happened there. At the mention of Mirage and what she had done, Janus flinched.

"They're sacrificing Arcturians to research Orb communications?" he asked rhetorically, dropping into the cushions as if an invisible blow had struck him.

"Yes, and I think it is dealing with technologies. They were talking about some reactor parameters."

"That would explain where they got the stealth technology."

"And the jump capabilities."

Janus rubbed his chin and stood up to pour himself another drink.

"Still, the Orb have attacked Trafalgar. Only military targets, though. Five ships."

"Only five?" asked Gavin.

"There were more after that. Many more. But they did not do anything, it wasn't until later, when Taggert arrived, that there was another battle with a small group of stealth ships, which the Admiral was able to defeat until the big brothers arrived."

"What if there are two factions?"

"One that cooperated with Marquandt and Yokatami and initiated a technology transfer and one that doesn't know about it," Janus continued the thought and sat down again. "But to what end?"

"A coup, perhaps. An inferior faction that needs humanity to break free from the superior one. We don't have the technology to defeat them, but we have the mass and experience in war. They give us what we need to defeat each other and then they take over. Marquandt gets his leap into the future, negotiating a peace treaty after showing strength and coming out victorious, even though it was all a set-up," Gavin said. "The Seed World could have been a technology demonstration by the aliens to show what they can offer. Terraforming in a few years or even months? More people than just Marquandt would walk over dead bodies for that. It would abruptly create new habitat, equalize humanity, and provide a new wave of growth."

"At the price of a dangerous war against enemies we know next to nothing about, alongside friends they know

The last Fleet

next to nothing about," Janus summarized. He felt cold at the thought that the traitor was willing to risk the future of the Empire for his 'vision'.

A knock sounded from the door. Gavin didn't even seem to have noticed, so much was his brow furrowed. Janus rose and went to the door.

It was Elayne who stood before him, blinking in surprise when she saw him.

"Oh," she said, "I'm sorry, Janus. I thought this ..."

"It is," he interrupted her gently. Her eyes were red, and she looked paler than usual. He wished he could take away some of the pain she was feeling right now. Magnus' death had broken her heart, her father's so soon after should have destroyed the last remnants of it, but she still had her chin thrust out defiantly, as she had been wont to do since childhood. It hadn't broken yet, but the cracks were beginning to show. "Come in."

Elayne hesitated, but then followed his invitation and turned toward the sitting area and Gavin, who practically jumped up from the sofa and his musings and cleared his throat.

"Princess."

"Daredevil."

The corners of his mouth twitched in a hint of what once would have been a haughty grin before this conflict and now died halfway to a smile. "I was just trying to find a solution to a problem."

"You mean I was a problem?" she asked.

"No, you didn't throw up," he countered.

"At most, I surrendered to your flying skills."

"Because you are wise and recognize competence when it presents itself to you."

"You were the only one available at the time." She casually waved it off.

"Of course, since the availability of pilots with such skills boils down to the number one, you are absolutely correct in that assessment, Princess," Gavin explained, walking over to the drinks to pour her Antibes champagne.

Elayne turned to Janus and showed the hint of a smile.

"Self-absorbed, haughty, boastful, and shameless at that," she summarized, accepting the glass. Gavin himself drank water.

"We were just planning our next steps," Janus informed her. He was not in the mood for young people's hormone-fueled wars of words while the universe burned around them.

"Without me?", Elayne wanted to know and gallantly sat down in a corner of the sofa.

"We were just updating each other to have options to present to you," Gavin helped him out and sat down again. Janus followed his lead and began to repeat what information they had gathered so far about what was really happening in the Andal system, the entanglements of Marquandt, Albius and Usatami, the secret Seed World of Yokatami, the experiments with the Orb, and Marquandt's cunning plan to get rid of her father and Albius and stick it to the Orb.

"He seems to have had a long time to plan his moves and prepare them perfectly," Elayne found.

"Yes. He's been planning for a long time, and he's got every cog perfectly aligned. We don't know how many gears are involved in the overall work or what they look like, but we have to assume that there are probably more than we would like. So the question we have to ask ourselves is, how can we act without him anticipating it?"

"He must kill me to eliminate the last witness with

credibility who can testify to his original betrayal. And he must kill you to wipe out House Hartholm-Harrow and change your father's succession," Gavin summarized. "I'm sorry, princess. I didn't mean that to be so harsh ..."

"It's harsh reality," she countered with a steely expression. "Wrapping me in pillows isn't going to help me either. So, what are we going to do about this killer achieving his goal?"

"We fly to your uncle," Janus replied, and Gavin was already expecting her to protest, which he would have welcomed in order to get to his fellow countrymen faster.

"That's probably a good idea. I have one more request: I need sensor dust in my quarters."

16

GAVIN

When they reached Dust, Gavin stood on the bridge with Janus, the Princess, and Captain Gianni, looking at the holodisplay that showed a dirty sand-colored sphere before them. Deep furrows stretched across the planet's surface, silhouetted as dark brown against the drab land masses. There were only two oceans, located at the polar caps, and they were green instead of blue. But it wasn't an inviting green; it was a dirty one, more reminiscent of a bacterial hotbed than water.

"I don't see any cities," he remarked, playing with the small signal amplifier that Bambam had given him on Yokatami's Seed World and that he had gotten back from Marshall. Not only did it make an excellent charm, but it also served as a reminder of what trust meant and how quickly it could be lost. A finger-sized memorial to him.

"And no space control," Gianni added with a wrinkled nose. It was no secret that Jurgan Hartholm-Harrow was not a popular figure among followers of the Emperor, and probably never would be.

"For my uncle, space control would be like shooting

himself in the knee," Elayne explained with not much more visible affection for the place. Or her uncle. He probably wasn't part of her favorite family, but now he was the last remaining blood relative. Gavin had avoided asking them about whether the emperor's brother might try to stake a claim to power so as not to offend the princess.

"Because of his illegal dealings?" asked Gianni, a growl rising low from her throat like distant thunder. Only when Elayne gave her a sidelong glance did she seem to realize to whom she had been speaking and bowed her head. "Please forgive me, Your Highness."

"There is nothing to forgive, Captain. You are quite right. My uncle is a scoundrel and has never made any secret of it. The reason he doesn't have space control is that he would then have to forward data to the central space flight administration on Terra - number of transits per day, per week, per month. In addition, all the data would have to be checked, security officers in the system would have to be responsible for auditing the employees, lawyers would have to check compliance with the space control laws - the list could be continued endlessly. None of the items on it would be in Jurgan's interest. He wants nothing to do with the Star Empire, and my father granted him that wish for the price of giving my uncle the least profitable and attractive planet in the Frontier as a fiefdom."

"Someone really lives there?" asked Gavin doubtfully. "It looks like a mud ball that's been in the oven too long."

"The cities are underground. It's too hot on the surface. Up to one-hundred-and-forty degrees Fahrenheit in the vast deserts. No one survives long without special clothing." Janus reached out a hand and placed his index finger on one of the brown longitudinal grooves that

The last Fleet

looked as if the planet had been scratched by a wildcat. The directed photons of the hologram flickered around the finger as if taking offense at the interruption. "There is always shadow in these canyons because they are so deep. It's only about eighty-five degrees in them."

"But that's not where the cities are."

"Yes, their entrances. The cities themselves are deep underneath. No one knows exactly how deep or how big they are, Jurgan made sure of that," Janus continued. "But the IIA estimates that Dust generates an annual GDP equivalent to that of a mid-tier Frontier World, which is pretty amazing considering there's not even space control or police units to protect commerce."

"That's because the only people who trade here are the ones who don't need protection," Elayne interjected.

"Mercenaries," Gavin said. "I've heard of that."

"But not of the true proportions. Many corporations make it public that they train their ground troops in desert combat on Dust, but many more do it in secret, not wanting to risk negative PR," Janus replied in their place. "It's quite possible that Dust has a population in the tens of millions. The IIA only knows of a few thousand."

"Because my uncle has spies eliminated."

"Yes. Dust is not a preferred area of operation for IIA agents."

"What's that there?" asked Gavin, pointing to a field of lightning and what looked like large forest fires, except there were no plants visible from orbit for miles on Dust. Since the planet was slightly larger than Terra, the area affected was roughly the dimensions of Australia.

"War," Janus said. "The corporations are not just testing their weapons here, Captain. They could do that on every other Frontier World that's sparsely populated and wants to get rid of a few mountains and forests. On

Dust, there are no rules for them, no regulation of their activities. Jurgan establishes an area, issues deployment licenses for princely pay, and then whatever happens there happens."

"But that one looks like a large-scale war," Gianni opined, putting Gavin's own disbelief into words. "Are you saying that..."

"Yes." The First Secretary nodded. "The mercenary corporations are fighting there according to their own pre-determined rules with everything they have. It's not about the most secret weapons or strategies, it's about training soldiers. They are supposed to gain combat experience in order to be powerful and experienced in case of doubt. There are few opportunities to do that in the Star Empire."

"That means men and women die down there?" the Commander wanted to know.

"Yes. Thousands every year. Even the corporate guardsmen of the Big Five were trained here. Red Samurai, Rhine Guard, Alpha Legion - they all went through the hell of sand and blood to become the best," Janus confirmed, and though his expression remained unmoved, Gavin sensed that what was happening there disgusted the man.

"They're capitalists," Elayne cut in again. "Every Guardsman is an expensive investment when they get their augments. They're supplied with Deltaware. A single samurai, guard, or legionnaire costs at least half a million crowns by the time he earns his badge. The CFOs only spend that much on those who got out of there alive and know what they're getting into."

"Barbaric," Gavin muttered.

"My uncle," she corrected him, and unlike Janus, she made no effort to hide her disapproval.

"Atmosphere entry in thirty seconds," reported a female soldier from the bridge crew located somewhere behind the holo-image.

Dust by now nearly filled the entire image, as if the telescope's lens had turned brown.

"We're not going down in shuttles?" asked Gavin in wonder.

"No. There's no space control and no ground station for us to check in with, so we're going right up to the door. After all, there's no law against it because there are no laws at all," Janus replied.

"And what if he has us shot down?"

"He doesn't have the means to do that."

"Besides, my uncle is notoriously nosy," Elayne opined. "If anything unforeseen happens, he will want all the information there is to gather. He won't be satisfied before that. A *Dominus*-class ship will make him think that..." She faltered for a moment. "That my father is coming - or me."

"He does not know about the assassination yet," Janus added. "We came here on a direct route. And even if he didn't, Dust would have heard about it last, I'm sure. We are using that to our advantage now."

The *Invincible* began to shake and vibrate. The ceiling panels above them, behind which the electronics wiring ran, made noises like nails in a tin can. Gavin let himself be shaken, shifting his weight so he wouldn't lose his footing. The Princess didn't seem to notice the hand he offered her. So he too stared at the live image of the bow telescopes, which after a few seconds were free of the fire of ignited air molecules and continued to show the desolate landscape of Dust. There were no clouds at all, just endless dunescapes with a dark brown line at the end of the horizon, just below the terminator line. The further they sank, the more texture the desert gained. Waves of sand, sometimes higher, sometimes lower, sometimes curved, as if decorated by an invisible surf, stretched from one pole to the other, disappearing into the heat streaks. The apparitions were as dense as transparent curtains.

After five minutes, the *Invincible* slowed sharply and lowered in a long right turn toward the foremost canyon that split the landscape in half. Only now did Gavin notice that the rim of the canyon rose several hundred feet above the dunes and was flat at the top. At one point he thought he spotted an object hidden under a giant camouflage net, but they were already turning into the final approach and he lost sight of it.

Gianni had the *Invincible* land directly on the canyon crest, which obviously looked artificially flattened at close range. This is also how he learned that the cruiser had crude landing struts that could be deployed for emergencies. Any *Dominus* ship had to be able to go months without supplies and evacuate the Emperor to anywhere in the Star Empire - including the surfaces of planets.

As soon as they landed, the bridge grew quieter. Janus pointed to him and Elayne. "You should now dress appropriately for your encounter with the Emperor's brother."

Gavin nodded and left the bridge.

Fifteen minutes later, they were standing in the port hangar in hardened military armor, along with Elayne's bodyguard of ten Imperial Guardsmen in Titan armor and Master Sergeant Gunter Marshall as Gavin's bodyguard. They looked even more formidable and massive and had their helmets closed. Elayne, Janus, and he wore simple breathing masks. Dust possessed a basically breathable atmosphere, but the oxygen level was five percent too low and the CO2 level five percent too high. The First Secretary had explained to him that it would feel like breathing into a bag, against an invisible resistance, and that after fifteen minutes they could experience shortness of breath and headaches. So now they breathed into simple plastic forms that they had fastened behind their heads with rubber bands.

"Only ten?" asked Janus of the princess, looking at the bodyguard. "Surely you don't trust your uncle, do you?"

"No. But I don't want to make him nervous."

Ahead of them the gate of the hangar opened which had been completely cleared except for the magnetically attached shuttles on the walls.

Before the size of the gate, he felt tiny, like a character in a set that was far too large. With the first light that shone on them, so did the heat. It hit him like a blow. Dry and scratchy from the sand it brought with it. Sweat immediately broke out on Gavin's forehead. His armor began to cool him down with its built-in cooling system, automatically opening its pores.

Elayne, standing half a step in front of him and Janus, with the guardsmen in five rows of two behind them, waited patiently until the huge hangar doors had moved completely aside before starting. Since they had not taken the time to create a ramp, nearly fifteen yards separated them from the rugged rocky floor of the canyon rim. So they jumped off the edge and let their boots break their fall by means of short bursts from the thrusters in their heels. Normally intended for use in a vacuum, this feature proved decidedly useful in Dust's gravity as well. At 1.1g, it was a bit more than he was used to from Andal, which was noticeable from the moment they landed with a subtle feeling of heaviness, an unaccustomed pressure on the soles of his feet. He felt reminded of his basic training in the Navy and the forced marches during which they had had to lug several dozen pounds of baggage as recruits. The feeling had been quite similar, if a bit stronger.

The Princess faltered slightly as she landed, obviously inexperienced with the military armor she was wearing. Gavin caught her, grabbing her left arm. Janus did the same on the other side. Then they quickly withdrew their hands. He was already expecting her to complain and inform him that she was doing very well on her own, but instead she thanked him.

"The stairs are somewhere to our left," Janus said. His hair was already sticking to his forehead in a sweaty mess, just like Gavin's own curls. The heat was unbearable, as if they were standing in a furnace. The skin of his face felt like it was covered in invisible lava. A glance across the canyon showed him the endless desert and streaks of heat that stretched like a curtain into the slightly reddish sky.

Elayne led them ten yards to the left, where the sensors had spotted the stairs carved into the rock. It was several yards wide, the steps long and covered with sand drifts. As they descended, he could see properly into the gorge for the first time. It was several hundred yards deep and shaped like a V. After about fifty yards, everything was in shadow, and individual creepers in the rock waved their ugly leaves in the light wind that felt like circulating air in an oven.

The steps led them rapidly downward, and with each yard the temperature dropped at least a little. But it wasn't until they entered the shadows that a real jump took place, and his skin finally stopped feeling like magma. There was still no movement, no signs of civilization or even a city. If their situation wasn't so serious, he would have believed that the Princess and the First Secretary of State were joking with him. This place looked as uninhabited as it was inhospitable. A dusty sphere in a system with no major asteroid belts or gas giants, far from major trade routes, and hostile to life because of its heat and lack of fertile soil.

The closer they got to the valley, which turned out to be a ten-yard-wide gully between the canyon's rising slopes, the more pleasant the air became. Had Gavin not known better, he would have instinctively removed his mask in anticipation of fresh breath. The rock here was washed out, perhaps it had once been a riverbed, but water here was no more than a distant dream.

Once they reached the bottom, they waited. Gunter sent up a palm-sized drone, which took off whirring to survey the canyon and scan it across the electromagnetic spectrum.

"Faint energy signatures," Gunter said, pointing downward. "Sporadic in the canyon walls, but mostly in the ground."

"Uncle!" yelled Elayne suddenly, and her voice echoed loudly through the base of the canyon. It continued as an eerie echo, repeated many times, echoing back to them. "I know it has been a long time. But I hope you still recognize your niece when she knocks on your door."

There was no reply as the echo drifted away. Only a minimal wind rustled the knotty creepers that formed small nests in the rock of the steep slopes.

"What are we going to do if he will not let us in?" asked Gavin quietly.

"He'll let us in," Elayne answered aloud, pausing for a moment. "Because my father died."

The Princess uttered the painful words with a self-control that impressed him. The Emperor's death had been just twenty hours ago, and even though she had had reddened eyes every time she had come out of her quarters, she did not let on in company. But perhaps it was the anger and the will to survive that had also helped Gavin to temporarily put aside the pain.

Silence reigned for another minute until a gentle vibration went through the floor. Gavin first thought it was a slight earthquake, but then a passage opened in the rock diagonally in front of them. What had just looked like rock pulled aside like a piece of cloth, and behind it a massive steel door retracted into the ground. A hydraulic hiss filled the canyon, then a single figure emerged. The figure wore a dark coat with a high collar and heavy boots. Around his belly the garment stretched. His face was roundish with drooping cheeks and fleshy chin. The eyes watery and small like a pig's, the hair gray and brittle, but full. This man had to be around seventy years old - without rejuvenating treatments. Gavin could not remember the last time he had seen someone who hadn't had a cell rejuvenation.

"Ah, my dear niece," Jurgan Hartholm-Harrow greeted Elayne, approaching her without a breathing mask. His smile was broad, his teeth yellow.

"Uncle," she replied.

"I would hug you, but then I would probably break my bones." The Emperor's younger brother made a sad face and tapped the chest section of her hardened military armor with his knuckle. "I don't know whether to take it as a slap in the face that you show up here like you're going to storm my house, or as a sign of respect."

"Sorry, Uncle," she replied politely. "But circumstances have forced my hand. I am the last remaining heir to the throne, and Terra is besieged by traitors who could be anywhere."

Jurgan eyed her thoughtfully. It was hard for Gavin to

imagine that the man who came from the Imperial House should be the brother of such a lordly person as Haeron II. He seemed to him more like an old butcher of Grassov, part of the lower class in the Frontier Worlds where rejuvinating treatments were only the promise of distant advancement. Old, but spry and steeled by decades of hard work, even if the skin was already beginning to sag.

Her host's smile did not disappear, but it changed, as if he had received some information he could not quite place.

"This isn't a cheap joke, is it?" he asked after a while, with only the light breeze blowing around them.

"No." Elayne sounded a touch angry now. "I don't joke about such things, and neither should you. He was your brother, Uncle."

"He stopped being my brother when he disowned me."

"He disowned you because you were..."

"... an embarrassment to him?" asked Jurgan provocatively, his small eyes flashing with combativeness.

"Yes," she returned.

The Emperor's brother opened his mouth to retort something. His lower lip twitched briefly, and he looked like he was about to answer something angry, until he finally grinned.

"Honesty," he said, laughing barkingly. "If that isn't something new at court." He gave a laconic curtsy and pointed to the door. "Come on in before you fog up in your damn armor. Your chained dogs stay outside, though."

"Not a chance. My life is in danger."

"Then take two with you, and those two spitfires." He pointed at Janus and Gavin. "That's all, this isn't a negotiation. I don't let fanatical dogs in my house."

17

GAVIN

Jurgan Hartholm-Harrow led them through narrow corridors and large caverns. All the walls were gray and cold like granite. It smelled of moisture and solvents, probably because of the ventilation system. Apparently, no attention was paid to appearances during the construction of the underground facilities. The rock lay bare, and under the low ceilings ran bundles of cables roughly tied together and sewage pipes as thick as arms, which rushed noisily. They had left their breathing masks in the entrance area, where there was a whole wardrobe of similar models.

Remarkably, they encountered no passersby, only occasional workers in simple coveralls who seemed to pay no attention to either Jurgan or them. At one point they passed a group of workers who had pulled a plain steel panel from the rock wall of a large cavern with machinery stored in it and were tending to some amazingly complex electronics behind it. Gavin was surprised to see the familiar superconductor cables and state-of-the-art nanite interfaces. His family's estate in Skaland had had a similar system: a nanite-based automated repair system. The myriad small robots could thus spread throughout the house, responding to fires and other damage, or using their sensor functions to report problems that otherwise would not have been noticed until it was too late.

Gavin felt confirmed in his impression after his conversations with Janus and Elayne that their uncle had put up a meaningless facade here, behind which there was clearly more than he wanted to show. This man was not a ruler in the usual sense, but rather something like the Broker, only more rough and more grounded in reality. The image of a cockroach came to his mind, small and unimpressive, but impossible to kill. Jurgan himself would probably even like this metaphor.

In a long, much wider corridor, they passed windows that were electronically blackened. Whatever was behind them, they were obviously not supposed to see. Cargo carts drove past them, piloted by robots that had been banned since the circuit genocide. Gavin shuddered at the sight of them. While they did not look like people, they were humanoid with arms and legs, the mimic disks in front of their heads gray and featureless, as if they were ghosts.

He should not have been surprised to encounter illegal technology down here, and yet it frightened him. What else was Jurgan hiding in his personal shadow realm on the edge of human-populated territory? A powerful AI? Antimatter weapons? Mutants?

He noticed that Elayne's hands kept stroking the walls, as if the touches were evoking memories in her. It was probably not the first time she had been here. Which surprised him, considering how much her father and his brother had supposedly despised each other.

After the relatively busy shaft, they turned through a

The last Fleet

simple door into a large hall with a ceiling two stories high and the rock hewn smoothly. A horseshoe-shaped banquet arrangement of tables and chairs was in the center, surrounded by holoprojectors on the unadorned walls.

Jurgan walked to the head end and motioned for them to sit. Had they not been wearing armor that provided thermoregulation, they would surely have frozen here.

They sat down around the short end of the horseshoe and the simple composite chairs creaked under their weight. Gunter and the other guardsman stopped a few feet away behind them, unarmed except for their implant weapons.

Employees in simple white pants and jackets came in, bringing plates of food, carafes of water, and glasses.

"I'm sorry it's so simple," Jurgan explained, looking at the protein packs and water. "But life on Dust is not about luxury. More like deprivation and simplicity. Your father made sure of that."

"Or you made sure father made sure of that," Elayne replied, grabbing one of the plastic bags of cheap soy protein.

Jurgan eyed them and slurped listlessly at his own packet before tossing it on the table in front of him and appraising them one by one.

"I've got my niece sitting here, along with my brother's top bureaucrat fart and old Cornelius' snooty son," he summarized.

"Careful," Gavin growled at the mention of his father.

"Don't piss your pants, kid. I liked Cornelius, he had a sense of humor and wasn't as pseudo-reverent as all the other spasmodics on the Council of Nobility. From what I've heard about you, you're an arrogant little shit. Janus here is stiffer than a morning glory after an overdose of

Assai, and my niece hates me like the plague," Jurgan summarized. "The first word she could speak was *asshole*, and it was directed at me. She wasn't even a year old then."

"And who do you think taught me that word?" retorted Elayne.

"My family's education has always been close to my heart."

"We are not here for fun," Janus interjected. "So before we get lost in niceties, perhaps we can get to the point?"

"Gladly. Why are you here? And why is there an Imperial cruiser on my doorstep with enough weapons on board to vitrify this turd of a planet?"

"Dain Marquandt has been plotting against the Emperor. With the help of Chief of Staff Albius and the Senate President. The Paris riots were just a pretext to prepare the ground, force Haeron II to take unpopular measures, and fake the death of Usatami so your brother could be assassinated on the way to the funeral service and blame it on the Orb," Janus explained, raising an eyebrow. "You don't seem surprised."

"I always told the old fucker this would happen eventually." Jurgan shook his head so that his sagging cheeks fluttered. "All those lickspittles and power-hungry assholes that every autocracy produces. Eventually they'll do to you what you did to your predecessor. Augustus came to power then because he couped against McMaster's son. Now, a few decades later, the same shit is happening. Who's surprised by that shit anymore. I just wish he would have listened."

"You are deflecting, Uncle," Elayne cut in again, leaning forward. Her armored forearms scraped across the aluminum tabletop as she did so. "That is not the only reason you weren't surprised. The mention of the Orb, at the latest, should have."

"The Seed Traverse," Gavin agreed, not taking his eyes off Jurgan, who eyed him dismissively. "You knew about it."

"Boy, Dust may be a turd, but it's one that provides food for plenty of vermin. I take care of the vermin of the Star Empire, the lepers and the undesirables, the losers of the supposed prosperity for all. How good do you think I'd be at it if I didn't know what was going on in the black market and how to provide discretion?"

"You sold equipment to Yokatami," Janus speculated.

"No. They did that themselves. I have no idea what they did, but I knew it was going to be weird. I sent construction crews to drill holes and build underground facilities. No one is as good at that as my people," Jurgan said with a shrug. "If you've built a planet from the ground up, you know how to do it. Sure, other worlds do too, but none of them shut the fuck up like we do. We don't give a damn who does what where. It's called privacy."

"*Don't give a damn*," Gavin repeated, growling. "I was there, on S2-Yokatami."

"Goru," Jurgan corrected him impassively, but he paid no attention to the old man, continuing to stare into his watery piggy eyes.

"That's where abductees from Arcturus were sacrificed like lambs on the slaughter to communicate with an Orb."

"I know," Elayne's uncle said simply.

"Spies," Janus surmised.

"I'm not as well connected as the Broker, but I like to know what I'm getting into beforehand. Just serves my safety." Their host looked to the two Marines. "Which is very important to me. I'm an old man."

Janus seemed to deliberately ignore the implication. "What exactly did your spies know?"

Jurgan hesitated until he met Elayne's gaze.

"It's over anyway," Gavin said. "The Orb has disappeared, and the abductees have risen and massacred the entire staff."

This time the old man seemed surprised.

"You didn't know that."

"You can't know everything." His counterpart shrugged again. "But thanks for the update."

"You didn't answer Janus' question," Elayne reminded her uncle.

"It's not like you offered me anything. You come in here and ask me questions, but you didn't even bring gifts. Instead, you park your behemoth in my backyard. How rude. Who comes to visit family with a fucking axe on their shoulder, hey?" Jurgan's bushy eyebrows drew together. "So, what do you have to offer me?"

"Is it not enough that we are family?" the Princess asked.

"The family that banished me here, you mean?"

"That was my father."

"And you are his daughter."

"And your niece."

"Ah. How many times did you visit me? Once, and that was about Peraia." Jurgan leaned forward. "Don't pretend we are *family*."

"If we're not family, maybe we're business partners," Janus suggested, trying to forestall an argument. "What do you want?"

"No, no, that's not the question. You've come to me. Of all the places you could have escaped to, this is the last one that makes sense. In the Border Worlds, they would have welcomed you with open arms after what happened in Andal. Word of Marquandt's actions got around there, and the motherfuckers have always been as obedient as harbor bitches with their panties down."

"The word you are looking for is *loyal*."

"Pah." Jurgan spat out. "Damn pets. What about the Wall Sectors? A lot of them don't like Marquandt and resent him for abandoning his post for a political maneuver and having Trafalgar on his conscience."

"They hate the Orb too much."

"Or the Corporate Protectorate. The Star Empire has no power there."

"All thoughts Marquandt will have, too," Janus declared impatiently.

"Ah. But of course." Jurgan snorted contemptuously. "Staying one step ahead of the enemy, eh? If Marquandt really had so long to prepare his grand plan, and even managed to keep his conspiratorial meetings with the Orb secret - what makes you think he didn't predict this move from you as well?"

"Can't you just answer our question?" asked Elayne, annoyed. "My father is dead - your *brother*! If you know what was happening on Yokatami's Seed World, then you have to tell us."

"Technology transfers." Jurgan spread his fleshy hands in front of his chest and leaned back. "They've been formulating questions in response to pressing problems in the research fields from the Science Corps - for several years. Ironic that it's only now that it's come to our attention that Arcturians have disappeared. No one else cares about the poor sods. Since communication with the damned aliens is difficult because they don't make normal sounds like we do, it was a tough job. They could pull one sentence an hour out of a hundred brains until the juice ran out of their noses and they were only good for recyclers."

Gavin winced inwardly at the cold way the Emperor's brother spoke about the abductees. He didn't seem to notice, however, and continued unapologetically.

"They've improved the jump drives and taken care of cloaking devices. A few other minor things, but that's about it in general."

"What about the drones?" asked Gavin. "I saw them in Andal."

"I know," Jurgan replied candidly, to his surprise. "Little round crap things that can attract the Never. Transmitters of some sort we don't know about. At least the signals they emit are indecipherable to us. Can only be activated by Orb that are nearby, though, I think."

"You *knew* about this?" Gavin clenched his hands into fists.

"Easy, kid. I knew about the technology, not that Marquandt had it."

"But then how did you even know about it?" wondered Elayne.

"The Orb gave Marquandt and Yokatami some things in exchange for stuff from us," Jurgan replied.

"From us?"

"Yes. Us humans."

"What kind of things? Slaves? Weapons? Access codes to our defense systems?" asked Janus.

"Cardamom."

"Cardamom?" Elayne shook her head, uncomprehending. "What is it?"

"A spice," Janus explained without taking his eyes off Jurgan. "That's a bad joke, right?"

"Nah." Their host spread his hands like a magician reluctantly relinquishing his crystal ball. "The damn aliens are totally into it, apparently. Don't ask me why. But now I want to know something from you: Why in the devil's name did you come here? You know very well that Marquandt will be looking everywhere."

Elayne hesitated, Gavin only came here to get to Pulau Weh, so it was Janus who finally forced himself to answer, "If anyone can make someone disappear, it's you."

Gavin was puzzled by the usually direct Secretary of State's vague implication. What did he mean by that? They weren't going to disappear, they were going to fly on to Pulau Weh and enlist Jurgan and his mercenaries as allies.

"You want me to make Elayne disappear and protect her from Marquandt."

"Peraia," Elayne said.

"Ah. Now we get to the heart of the matter." Her uncle looked amused. "You think I helped her then."

"Who else could have done it? She did not have the contacts to have *Persephone* assembled in secret and cover her tracks."

"You underestimate your sister."

"I don't underestimate *you*," she returned.

"Clever girl. You can tell we come from the same stable." Jurgan laughed. It sounded like the bleating of a goat. "If not from a barn, you would have been considerably more clever."

"You forget yourself, Governor," Janus growled angrily, though his expression remained a mask of control.

"Nope, I'm just not interested in gibberish."

"Your brother was murdered."

"And I told him long ago. For me, he died when he banished me here over two decades ago because I was an *embarrassment* at court, like a cursed leper."

"You broke the law and set up a prostitution ring in the *Rubov*!" objected Janus.

"For high society. And business was booming. Half the snozies from the noble council fucked their brains out there."

"Uncle!" interjected Elayne.

"Don't pretend you're the immaculate Mother Mary, Elayne. You're in your mid-twenties, and hopefully you've spotted the boy on the boat a long time ago."

"You do not speak to the Princess like that!" Janus snapped at him.

"She's a grown woman, no matter what you've dreamed up in all this empire fantasy. So I'm going to treat her like a grown woman, too." Jurgan waved a hand in front of his face, seemingly bored, as if he were trying to drive away a pesky fly.

"It's all right, Janus," Elayne said calmly. "A bully like him can't impress me with his disrespectful manner."

"At that, I've gone to such lengths. But you still haven't said what you actually want from me. Or did you only come here because you wanted to accuse me of being to blame for your big sister's death?"

"First of all, she's not dead. Two, I'm not accusing you, I know it. Third, I need a ship and the information where Peraia was going," the Princess enumerated.

"And you think I know that?"

"Yes. You never do anything without something in return, and I think you wanted to know from her what she knew before you gave her what you wanted."

"And why should I tell you if I did?" asked her uncle, amused.

"I have already told you: because you're asking for quid pro quos."

"What could the most wanted, most powerless person in the Star Kingdom have to offer me?"

"Your niece's affection and gratitude, of course," she replied laconically.

Jurgan laughed cacklingly and leaned back even further, appraising her wait-and-see. "I'm more of a pragmatist."

"I have to find her, Uncle. If there's even the slightest chance she's alive, I have to find her."

"She's dead. No one stays missing for twenty years and then turns up."

"We need a ship. *Thetis*-class or comparable," Janus interjected. "With fake transponder codes to get us through the Wall Worlds."

Elayne gave him a surprised sideways glance. Apparently she hadn't expected him to support her plan. Which meant he was out of the loop and the two of them had come here for different reasons. Gavin didn't know, in any case. If it had been up to him, their path would have taken them straight through the Tartarus Void to Pulau Weh.

"And why do you think I have this?" asked Jurgan.

"Actually, you want to know why we think you're giving it to us," speculated Elayne.

"After all, you have nothing to offer me in return. Under other circumstances, I would have asked for a few administrative favors. These are really important things for me. But like this..."

Janus stood up so abruptly that Gavin winced in shock.

"Oh, Janus," Jurgan chortled, "don't get upset."

"What is it?" asked Elayne, confused.

"A trap!"

Behind them, Gunter and the Imperial Guardsman

stirred and suddenly stood protectively at their backs, arms outstretched with their implant weapons.

Everything happened very fast all at once. Metallic scraping could be heard. The wall panels of the cavern turned into doors from which gunmen poured. Men and women in body armor with Gauss rifles, shock launchers, submachine guns and laser weapons. They flooded the room from all directions. Gunter and the guardsman tried to protect Gavin, Elayne and Janus with their bodies, but they were surrounded within seconds. There were so many that it was not worth counting. Ice spread through Gavin's veins.

"How could you?" the Princess asked, revealing an amazing composure for having a hundred muzzles pointed at her.

"You said it yourself." Jurgan sighed. "Marquandt had a long time to plan, and apparently he was one step ahead of you again."

"You're betraying your own family."

"Oh, no. You don't put your *family* on the sidelines only to have them back in your arms when you need them." The governor of Dust did not even sound angry.

"What did he offer you?" asked Janus.

"That which you cannot."

"The Sector Governance. Priority codes for your smuggler ships. Things Marquandt can't give you until he's emperor."

"Oh, you can do that by decree. You should know," Jurgan countered.

"My men," Elayne said, and her uncle pretended to think.

"Ah, I remember. The Imperial Guardsmen who accompanied you to intimidate me." Jurgan gave a wave, and a holodisplay appeared behind him out of nowhere. It

The last Fleet

showed eight burly men lying lifeless in the large cavern where they had left them to wait for them. Their powered armor was nowhere to be seen, they were wearing only their formal clothing, and each of them had had their throats cut like cattle on the slaughter block.

"You damned murderer!" escaped Elayne in a quivering voice.

"Traitor," growled Janus. "You lay in bed with the murderer of your brother and nephew. You are a disgrace."

"I am disappointed in you," Jurgan said, shaking his head. He eyed the First Secretary of State like a master would his dog that needed to be put down. "You think I'm doing this for short-term profit? I guess your knowledge of human nature isn't as good as it's made out to be. I was one of the first people Marquandt contacted many years ago. He knew exactly that he would need me and my network."

"And mercenaries."

"And mercenaries. And construction engineers for secret underground facilities. When you have a monopoly and can keep your mouth shut to boot, you're a popular port of call for pretty much everyone."

"Why?" asked Elayne quietly. The many guns pointed at her seemed to make the room smaller and the air thinner.

"Because he's right," Jurgan answered seriously. "The *Star Empire* is a bureaucratic turd that's the enrichment of a few wankers who've seen too many costume movies and want to live off Antibes champagne while an entire generation toils as slaves in the Navy or the shipyards' production hells."

"Quite the do-gooder, aren't you?" she returned wryly.

"We're a species bogged down in too many civil wars and upheavals. There are bans on everything, but no progress anymore because everything is geared toward maintaining power and imaginary enemies. The fucking Orb care about us as much as we care about ants or dirt," the governor of Dust continued unapologetically. "Marquandt has managed to do what no one else has, let alone attempted: talk to them and give them something they need in return for technological breakthroughs. All this while my brocade-cloaked brother has been enthroned on Terra, preoccupied with how to deal with the growing support for Republican elements in his star empire so that no one saws at his throne. Marquandt has a perspective to offer. It requires sacrifice, but so does any upheaval. How many people do you think died when the McMaster dynasty was overthrown in the middle of the last century? Millions and millions, most of them civilians. Marquandt wiped out ten fleets with tens of thousands of sailors, and that many more Arcturians to usher in a new future. Arcturians who had no perspective, whose life consisted only of stealing and being stolen from. Twenty percent of them kill themselves before the age of thirty. So why not contribute to international understanding."

"Keep telling yourself that as long as you have to," Elayne sneered.

"Oh, I don't care what they do in Sol, as long as they leave me alone here. I like life as a cockroach in the shadows. I'll keep on living even if the whole spiral arm goes to hell. But the disgusting double standards of you privileged people is just disgusting. Marquandt's coup is smart, targeted and relatively bloodless. Something our forefathers could not pull off."

"What's to stop us from blowing your faces off now?" interjected Gunter. The master sergeant had his right hand outstretched and was aiming his palm at Jurgan. The latter calmly folded his hands in front of his fat belly.

The last Fleet

"My niece's life, of course. I have no interest in killing her. Part of the deal is that she stays safe. With me."

"In exile," Elayne said. "Do you really think I would do that? You murdered my men. Betrayed us."

"Yes, you will, because if you don't, I'll have your friends here killed, too." Jurgan stood up and smoothed his clothes. The little pig eyes eyed them in turn. "I'll give you a little time in the cell until you decide how it's going to go. In two hours you will be obedient and submit to your fate. You have come here to keep you safe. That's exactly what I'm offering you. In two hours, I'll start killing one of you an hour at a time. And I'll start with young Gavin. So, think it over, my dear *niece*."

18

GAVIN

The cell was five by five yards and set into the floor, the walls ground so smooth that it was impossible to climb up. A simpler kind of prison was hardly possible and yet it was extremely effective, managing without doors and security mechanisms. Apt for their *host*, he thought. Stingy, efficient, and unimpressive. Gunter and the guardsman sat stripped of their armor, leaning side by side against the wall. Their expressions were motionless, but he knew they were seething inside, despairing at their helplessness. They would rather have died in a hail of bullets in the cavern than rot in a cell.

Elayne had not spoken a word since they had been brought in with bags over their heads. Janus, too, seemed to be preoccupied with his own dark thoughts. Gavin had tried several times to contact the ship by transducer, but he could not get a connection. Apparently, all signals were blocked, or they were far too deep beneath the surface, surrounded by hundreds of yards of rock.

For some time, the ground had been vibrating on and off, and minor tremors could be felt. Apparently, Dust was extremely seismically active, which was another explanation for why they only built underground.

"He'll come for me first," Gavin said at one point. "Marquandt has to get rid of me to maintain his narrative."

"Elayne will be the only one to get out of here alive," Janus agreed with him. "He may be a mean son of a bitch, selfish and vindictive, but he cares about her."

"I don't care," the Princess said. "We're all getting out of here."

She raised her gaze, and her big green eyes searched his. Even now in this cell, she was beautiful, almost kitschy princess-like, as if she had stepped out of a medieval fable. Her golden curls looked like they had been freshly blow-dried, and even though they were in an ugly, dark environment, she radiated grace and an angelic glow. Only the slightly swollen skin around her reddened eyes betrayed that she was in pain on the inside.

"If you give me a Stingray, I might be able to do something," he grumbled. "But I'm afraid we're not going to get out of here."

"Yes, we will," she insisted. "Have faith, young captain."

Gavin raised an eyebrow. She was nearly ten years younger than he and yet managed to sound majestic and old. But she was naive behind all that obsessive optimism. Even four smooth walls and a damp floor couldn't bring her back to reality.

"This is my fault, Elayne," Janus said after a moment of lingering silence. "We shouldn't have come here, and I should have known."

"No one could have known how my uncle would react," she countered. "Neither you nor I even saw him more than once, and what we knew about him was extremely scant intelligence."

"He was a risk we shouldn't have taken."

"Yes, but for a different reason. We should have gone to Gavin Andal's missing fleet immediately." Elayne fixed Janus with her gaze.

"I didn't want to put you at any more risk," Janus replied.

"I know you didn't. It's not your fault. I myself wanted to come here to find a way to follow Peraia. I knew Jurgan was helping her then." She turned to Gavin. "I'm very sorry we didn't reunite you with your people first."

"A fleet is what we need now," Janus agreed with her.

"And we will have it."

"Elayne," Janus said patiently. "We are in the middle of an underground city where pirates, smugglers, murderers, thieves, and pimps are in charge, all of whom your uncle has rallied around him over two decades and made his chain dogs. You'll have to come to terms with the fact that ..."

"That you will be taken out one by one and killed while I rot on a leash necklace?" she asked.

"No, that you *survive,* and eventually find a way. The two hours will soon be up, and then..."

"Nobody dies. We all survive."

Janus sighed and was about to retort something when the rattle of automatic weapons was heard above them. It continued as a deafening echo in their square cell, hurting their ears. Gunter and the guardsman had already jumped to their feet, their hands cuffed in front of their bodies and fitted with eye blockers. Yet they still looked like predators, ready to bite at any moment.

A scream rang out, the smacking sound of bursting flesh. Then a shadow came over them, and Gavin was able to pull the Princess aside just enough to keep her from being struck down by it. There was an ugly clap, and between them lay a shattered figure in tattered body armor. Half the face had been blown off.

Gavin looked up at the same time as the others at six figures in whirring Titan Motorized Armor with the Imperial sigil on their chests and red glowing visor eyes.

"Highness," boomed the electronic voice from one down to them.

"That took a long time," Elayne remarked, stepping back against the wall. Gavin and Janus quickly did likewise, and a moment later one of the behemoths landed springily between them, causing the ground to tremble. He waited for an approving nod from the Princess and then effortlessly lifted her up so that another guardsman could pull her out of her hole. They repeated the process until they were all standing in the cell wing, a shallow, wide cavern with dozens, if not hundreds, of holes in the floor. Bodies lay everywhere, with not much left to identify them as human. The six guardsmen near them were joined by two at one of the doors waiting for them there, aiming into the corridor beyond.

"How?" asked Janus as they hurried toward the exit.

"We have the entire First Legion of the Imperial Guard on board," Elayne said. "After I came here once as a teenager to spite my father, I swore I would never come here again alone. I told Colonel Bazagan to storm if I didn't report back after an hour. My uncle may be well-connected and a smuggler king, but against a thousand of the Star Empire's finest warriors in the latest powered armor, even he has no chance."

"But how did they find us?" wanted Gavin to know.

"Sensor dust." She held out a hand to him, it was admittedly a little gray. He remembered her asking about sensor dust when she'd been in his cabin. Then of how she had painted over the walls when she arrived. "I've never trusted my uncle before, but I need him to find my sister. Colonel?"

One of the guardsmen, apparently Bazagan, turned his helmet in her direction. His armor had no discernible insignia. Gavin knew this was intentional, and the ranks were only visible as virtual symbols to guardsmen logged into the closed Battlenet.

"Yes, Your Majesty?"

"Give me a brief report," he said.

"We blew up the entire flank of the canyon with the *Invincible*'s railguns and flew in with our Titans. Your uncle was prepared, but not for this. We lost four legionnaires. We wiped out the security forces in the caverns and tunnels. However, the governor apparently escaped into the city."

"There's a city?" asked Gavin.

"You will see, my lord."

Bazagan led them through a long tunnel and up a ramp. Bodies with firearms lay everywhere on the floor, which was covered in blood and bodily fluids. Elayne looked as pale next to him as Gavin felt, but kept his eyes straight ahead and his chin tucked forward. Only Janus did not give the impression of feeling queasy.

So it went for a quarter of an hour, working their way through a trail of devastation and death, back the way the guardsmen had come. All remained silent, except for once when a side door opened and a figure came running through with eyes wide. One of the Princess's bodyguards merely reached out in a flash with his armored hand and nailed the unfortunate man's head to the wall like a jackhammer, where it burst and left a large stain.

At some point they reached a long shaft with markings on the floor, one wall of which was lined with guardsmen standing shoulder to shoulder. Standing eight feet tall in Titan armor, their helmets almost touched the ceiling. There were bodies here as well, close to a hundred. There was no one standing against the open wall, which was strangely dark and not made of rock. But there was a single double door.

"Here?" asked Elayne at the foot of the shaft.

Bazagan nodded. A colossus next to a child.

"My uncle?"

"Yes. He escaped into the city. We sent several drones in, it's big and has several entrances and exits leading out of the cave," the Colonel explained. "He has a half-hour head start."

"Do you have any ideas?"

"These guardsmen here still have enough power on their boots to fly to the exits and occupy them. That should make them fast enough. The rest will have to scour the city. But that's going to be bloody. We need a scalpel, but have only a broadsword, if you understand, Your Majesty."

"I understand," Elayne said gravely. "Show me."

Bazagan gave a wave to his lined-up soldiers and they extended their massive Gauss rifles. There was a loud thunder as they fired simultaneously at the opposite wall, which unceremoniously disintegrated in a shower of shards that flew off in the opposite direction.

Gavin followed Elayne and Janus to the destroyed window front and looked down in disbelief at a gigantic cavern where a sea of houses and industrial plants stretched out. He saw apartment blocks that reached almost to the ceiling, an artificial sun hanging from the rock in the middle, giving dim light, warehouses on the edges, small winding streets where tiny looking figures ran around from up here, trying to get to safety. There must have been tens of thousands living and working there, if not hundreds of thousands.

"Do it, Colonel. Bring my uncle to me alive, do what it takes," the Princess ordered decisively as her gaze roamed over the surreal scenery.

"Elayne," Janus spoke up. "There are a lot of innocents down there. Once the Legion is unleashed..."

"There are no innocents on Dust, Janus," she interrupted him. "My uncle trusts only those as devious as he. Everything he makes money from is illegal, and that includes this place. Murderers, cutthroats, smugglers, mercenaries. He won't escape us because we show leniency for criminals."

"She's right," Gavin agreed grimly. "I've seen what they've had a hand in on the Seed World. Mercy is something no one here deserves."

"You have your orders," Elayne turned to the Colonel, who took a stance in his armor and gave a wave to the lined-up guardsmen. At that, they ran forward and plunged into the depths. Shortly after, they were followed by two rows of other legionnaires who came running out of the end of the shaft and rushed toward the stairs that led down behind the door. Those who had jumped activated the jets in their boots and flew off like stone gargoyles toward the exits of the gigantic cavern, sealing it off.

Silently, Gavin stood beside Elayne and Janus, who looked down on the secret city from above, protected by two dozen guardsmen under Bazagan's command who stayed behind with them. It was not long before the first shots rang out. They echoed up to them like the thunder of a summer storm. The intervals became shorter and the muzzle flashes more numerous in the canyons of houses.

Soon the screams grew louder, blending into a cacophony of terror. Gavin noticed at one point that the residents were either running toward the exits or seemed to be barricading themselves inside the buildings, which was the wiser option. While he could see too little detail to say with certainty, it looked like many of the people down there were armed, and the guardsmen of the First Legion were not exactly squeamish. They mowed down everything in their path, including those streaming for the exits, so that a backward movement soon formed and they were pulverized between the straggling units.

It was carnage, the fall of a city where fires were already breaking out here and there and houses were collapsing.

Gavin didn't know how long they stood there with petrified expressions, searching for a spark of compassion within him but unable to find it. He saw only the need to put a stop to evil. Again and again, he reminded himself that these people were over corpses themselves and had had no trouble cutting the throats of eight of the Princess's guardsmen just to scare them. The Princess's broadsword might be stained with blood, but this place had been built and bought with blood.

After what felt like an eternity, the noise died down and Bazagan approached the princess.

"Your Majesty? Jurgan Hartholm-Harrow has just been located by my men."

"Good, withdraw from the city and take him to the *Invincible*," she ordered.

"What about the Legion?" the Colonel asked.

"Secure the city and facilities. Send out drones to map everything and find out who's in charge and at the key counters."

"Of course, Your Majesty."

. . .

An hour later, Gavin knocked on the Princess' cabin door on the *Invincible*. She had retired to change, but had not appeared in the brig's interrogation rooms as agreed.

It took a while for her to open. When she stood before him, she was still wearing the form-fitting body armor, which was so thin that it showed more of her curves than it hid. Shame rose hot in his cheeks, but she didn't seem to notice. Her eyes were red and watery and the traces of fresh tears shone on her cheeks.

"I'm sorry, Princess, I'll come back later." He was already about to retreat when she shook her head.

"I was just crying. It's not a contagious disease," she countered, defiantly wiping her cheeks dry.

Gavin did not know how to respond. Without knowing why, he envied her at that moment.

"Weakness is only weakness when it makes you weak." She motioned for him to enter. Hesitantly, he accepted the invitation. He felt like he should not even be here. Despite all the circumstances, she was still the Emperor's daughter, a figure from the feeds who had always had something unattainable for him, just like her father. Too big to be real, too important to be bothered with.

"Weakness," Elayne continued, "comes from not allowing your feelings - or allowing them in the wrong place."

He quickly realized that she was talking to him as much as she was talking to herself. Still, she knew what she was talking about. Perhaps she had learned this wisdom from someone and only recently truly understood it, but apparently she had chosen to act on it, for which he had respect.

"When my family was taken by the Never..." Gavin

faltered briefly, taking the time for three long breaths. "It was as if in a movie. Driven by what was happening, my own survival instincts that drove everything else out. But there was this pain spreading in my chest that I misinterpreted at first as emptiness. When the dying and running for my life stopped momentarily, I had a panic attack because it all came to the surface at once."

She listened patiently and nodded weakly when he finished. At that moment, they connected something deeper than merely two people being together, giving each other comfort through their mutual presence: an understanding that only those who had lost everything could have, as she had.

"The universe feels so empty all at once," she murmured.

"And I've had butterflies in my stomach ever since," he replied. "Evil butterflies with dark wings."

"Yes. That is a good description."

"I don't know if it's going to get better, everything is still so fresh. But I know we cannot let Marquandt get away with this. That keeps me going, and even though I'd prefer not to wake up when I go to bed, knowing that this pig is still out there, and has done the same thing to thousands and thousands of other families makes me get up and get dressed. Someone has to stop him."

"We will," she assured him. He felt the impulse to embrace her, to share her burden through closeness, but held back. She was the Princess.

The moment had passed when she finally stirred. "Wait here, I'll be right back."

She disappeared into the bathroom and returned a short time later wearing white pants and a white jacket made of modern polymer fabric trimmed with gold trim.

The fabric was tight against her body, but was high-waisted and exuded significant elegance.

"So," she said, her face serious and her eyes mirrors of determination. She had put her mask back on. "Let's go put my uncle through the wringer."

"I'm looking forward to it," he replied, not bothering to conceal his satisfaction.

They left the cabin and walked down the side corridor in the bow section, where the hum of the reactors was quietest, to the central corridor and elevators. There they met Janus, who had apparently been waiting for them.

"Elayne, Gavin," he greeted them. As they were in the cabin on their way to the port brig, he cleared his throat. "Is there a strategy yet?"

Elayne turned her head toward him. "Are you angry because I didn't tell you about my plan with the Guard beforehand?"

"I merely hope you did not do it because you do not trust me."

"Janus." Now she turned to face him fully and placed a gentle hand on his forearm. "I think we are long past that. At the latest, when I risked everything during your rescue mission in the Imperial Gardens, I would have bailed if I had not blindly trusted you. You are probably the only person I currently trust one hundred percent."

Gavin felt a brief twinge of hurt and knew it was childish.

"Then you could have told me," Janus insisted.

"I did not see any advantage in it. Besides, you would not have been sure we could fully trust Colonel Bazagan and the Legion, am I right?"

"Yes."

"Now you know."

"But you were not certain."

"Now I am, in any case," she returned, turning back to the cabin door as the elevator informed them with an ascending triad that they had reached the destination deck.

"You have more in common with your big sister than you think." Janus sighed in surrender.

Outside the brig, two guardsmen in uniform stood guard and at attention as they approached. As per protocol, their eyes followed the Princess as she entered.

Jurgan Hartholm-Harrow was housed in the rearmost of the five small cells, which turned out to be surprisingly luxurious with a bed, a seat, a separate toilet unit, and a display film on the wall that could be controlled by gestures. The Governor of Dust still wore his coat, even if it now bore the scars of his arrest by the guardsmen: scuffed patches, dirt and holes in the sleeves. He had also suffered two lacerations to his face, and a nanonic bandage hid his entire left ear.

"Ah, my sly niece," he greeted Elayne, grinning through yellow teeth. He studiously ignored Janus and Gavin.

"Why does that sound like a compliment coming from you?"

"It certainly is. You double-crossed me."

"Yes, because you are easy to see through in your vicious selfishness." Elayne thanked a soldier who brought chairs for the three of them.

Gavin sat down and eyed the old man with growing disgust. He stood behind the wall of Duroglass like a relic of a bygone era when there had been no rejuvinating treatments and people had looked ugly and unkempt. Everything about him looked repulsive and probably that was exactly his strategy.

The last Fleet

"I wouldn't have thought you capable of such a move, kid."

"Don't call me that."

"Oh, don't be so snippy or I'll lose all my freshly won respect for you. If I'd liked your mother more, I could almost have taken you for my own cuckold child." Jurgan laughed, and the speakers distorted the repulsive sound into something sinister.

"If you put her name in your mouth again, there's no deal."

Deal? Gavin thought, looking to Elayne, who ignored him as much as Janus on the other side.

"Ah. And here I was thinking you were *really* like me, telling me you'd let my wrinkled old ass be hauled to the bow before you took off," Jurgan said, acting disappointed.

"Admittedly, a tempting notion." Elayne waved it off. "But I have something better in mind for you. You keep control of Dust. You tell Marquandt you've held up your end of the deal, and fabricate a sensor recording showing you executing Gavin Andal and Janus Darishma."

"And what makes you think I'm capable of something like that?"

She merely tilted her head and his yellow smile returned. But it was as joyless as it was noncommittal.

"When you've done that, you'll turn over to us all the hidden ships parked on Dust." As he was about to retort something, she raised a hand and silenced him. "Before you try to convince us that you do not have any, and that your customers do not have anything parked here, I want to cut that off now: You give us the access code to the mainframe of your little kingdom of shadows, and my data analysts will do a little inventory."

"I don't like that."

"I could not care less."

"And what should be in it for me? My customers don't like me stealing their equipment," Jurgan said, crossing his arms in front of his chest as if resting them on the bulge of his stomach.

"I was worried about that, of course, because I know you don't like to go out of negotiations empty-handed." Elayne stood up, and Gavin followed her lead. He felt like an extra, but for a change it did not bother him in the least, because he would have ripped her obnoxious uncle's head off in anger instead of acting so detached. Something in this man caused sheer anger bubble up inside him. "You will get a powerful new bodyguard from me, so that something like the invasion of your little town down there will never happen to you again. Since you should hardly have any soldiers left, I'll use it to patch up the most serious bleeding wound. That is what family is for, is it not?"

"But who...?"

"The First Legion of the Imperial Guard," she interrupted him, giving him an angelic smile. "Colonel Bazagan knows his way around now, and the *Invincible* is way too cramped for a thousand elite Marines. He is sure they can guarantee your protection, and he will not leave your side to make sure you sleep soundly."

Jurgan bared his teeth and opened his mouth like a choking fish. Before a sound could cross his lips, his jaws clenched again and began to grind.

"Ah, one more request," Elayne added as she turned to leave, pausing once more. Her smile had vanished and given way to calculating seriousness. "You're going to write down for me everything you know about Peraia and what happened when she came to you back then." She pointed to the display slide. "One hour, then Bazagan will come for you. Whether you will then return together to your second life, down in your cave, or you will have a VIP seat on the bow when we take off, is your decision."

When they were back in the corridor, Janus stopped the Princess.

"I don't know whether to be proud of you or afraid of you," he said. Judging from the warmth in his voice, he had long since made up his mind. "When did you grow up so fast?"

"I spent half my time eavesdropping on Father's negotiations, the other in disguise in the dark corners of *Rubov*, following my sister's trail in the underworld," she explained. "I know how criminals like my uncle talk, what they want and how to get it. And I know how the cold calculation of the high nobility works. The scheming maneuvers of the Admiralty in the mess halls and offices, during squash ball and the holiday parties. Anyone who can listen soon realizes that they are all not as clever as they think. In the end, it's just a game of greed and fear, with threats and offers swinging back and forth between them - and my uncle has plenty of both."

19

JANUS

"Zenith," the Voice said. Janus sat in his quarters on the *Invincible* and turned off the flight data display. They were about to jump into the Tartarus Void, the great void in the cosmic south of the Star Empire.

"I should have known the Network had Quantcom barges hidden in the Dust system," he replied. "If not here, then where?"

"Dust is a widely under-appreciated place," he said.

"Which makes it valuable."

"I take it you're angry."

"And what on earth makes you think that? Angry that you had the opportunity to stop Akwa Marquandt but did not take it? That you deceived and used young Gavin Andal? That Mirage, through your instructions, made sure that no one could prove Marquandt's treachery?" Janus recounted and went to the kitchen unit to pour himself a glass of scotch. The lights were already dimmed because he really wanted to sleep. He felt that his mind could not keep up with what was happening, and his emotions even less so. Besides, he was worried about his family, even though he had sent a message to his homeland right after the attack on the Emperor to take them away.

"You know it was necessary. The stealth ship is too important to risk it falling back into the hands of Marquandt," the Voice said in its typically cool androgynous way. "We need to find out what technologies are powering it and make sure there are countermeasures in place."

"For the Network."

"For the Network means for humanity. You know that, Zenith."

"I used to *believe* that," he corrected.

"We allowed you to go."

"Freedom to choose should be a basic human right."

"It is. And you freely chose to be an agent of the Network, including all the knowledge and secrets that entails," the Voice stated.

"I know you only let me go because I would still be useful in my new position even as a retired member." Janus snorted and drained the glass of amber liquid that settled like a soft glow on his throat and esophagus. He bared his teeth.

"Yes. And it paid off. For you, too. We helped you when you needed us."

"Because it fit into your plans."

"Aren't mutually beneficial agreements the epitome of an efficient transaction?" the Voice asked. "I feel such a starting position is honest and reliable; after all, there's no imbalance or problem after the fact when you know no one will want to call in a favor later."

Janus wanted to disagree, but knew he would merely

sound like a rebellious child going through puberty. The logic made sense to him, or he would not have worked for them for several decades. They knew that, just as they knew almost everything. Arguing made no sense and it would only cause them to hold him in lower esteem due to irrational emotionalism.

"Why did you call me?" he asked instead.

"I told Mirage to evacuate your family." The voice paused for a moment. "But I am not aware of their current location."

A smile stole onto Janus' face. "I'm still in shape, apparently. Even without the gifts of the Network."

"Looks like it. Despite your obvious limitations, you still have your training. The offer remains: Mirage will evacuate your family. For that, all you have to do is tell me the transponder code of their ship."

Janus considered it. He trusted Mirage for two reasons: She was predictable in her absolute loyalty to the Network and the Voice, and she had built exactly one relationship in her life: with him. His wife and children would never be as safe anywhere as they were with her. But there was always a price, even if it was only that she would have his loved ones in her pocket as collateral.

"What is the price?"

"Your family in our care guarantees me that you will remain operational and that there is a chance you will rejoin us," the Voice explained.

"I have said already that it is not going to happen," he growled.

"That was before your new master died. Things have changed."

"And that is your fault, too."

"No."

"Omission is also a type of offense."

"I need not remind you that we are under no moral obligation to any government," the Voice explained. "Marquandt's plan would have worked anyway, according to our calculations. In addition, rulers come and go, but the course for humanity must always be adjusted no matter who is holding the scepter. The recovery and evaluation of the stealth ship had to be the top priority. I'm sure you are aware of that fact."

Janus did not answer immediately, and the Voice fell silent. The window for their communications would close in fifteen minutes when they jumped out of the Star Empire's territory into the Void. So, sleeping on it for a night was not an option, which put him at a disadvantage, and he knew it.

"Mirage takes in my family, and the Network keeps them safe," he finally said. "I will stay with Gavin Andal and help him through the political shoals of what's to come once he is reunited with his fleet. We will stay in touch, and I will pass on to you what I know, on one condition: you will not interfere in his or my efforts to bring Marquandt to justice."

"The Network has no interest in supporting or even condoning Dain Marquandt. His course is daring and dangerous to the continued existence of humanity and the Network. We will not stand in the way of Gavin Andal, even though we have no data that there is even a fleet left," the Voice said, and Janus' heart sank a little. "We would agree, with one change to the deal."

"Ah, here it comes after all, the prize."

"You will accompany Princess Elayne in search of her sister, Peraia Hartholm-Harrow."

He did not make the mistake of wasting time

wondering how the Voice knew about this. They had likely been monitoring the Princess's walks in disguise from the beginning, putting the pieces of the puzzle together even faster than Elayne had.

"So she is right. Peraia could still be alive," he mused aloud.

"We have come to believe that Peraia Hartholm-Harrow has obtained the information about the Orb that Dain Marquandt, Marius Albius, and Varilla Usatami also seem to have obtained. Tracing her path further seems reasonable. The Princess has proven to be resourceful and smart for her age. But she will need support in the form of experience and rationality because she is acting on emotional grounds."

"How is this different from me as your agent?"

"It is an offer. Is this arrangement acceptable to you?" the Voice asked.

Janus thought about it, but knew he had already made up his mind. Gavin Andal was a good young man, as far as he could tell so far. Too young to be a leader in a civil war, but with the charisma to fill his role if he had enough capable advisors around him, like the experienced Emilia Gianni. Elayne, on the other hand, was inexperienced and overzealous, despite her cleverness and shrewdness. It was just as the Voice had said. Moreover, he felt an almost paternal obligation to her, and the fact that the Network did not dismiss her search for Peraia as a figment of her imagination could only mean that she had indeed been on the trail of something important.

"I agree. We will jump to Pulau Weh with Gavin Andal and search for survivors of his brother's fleets. If he is reunited with them, or they do not exist, I will go with the Princess to search for Peraia. Mirage will take care of my family, and the Network will guarantee their safety," he summarized. "And it will not interfere in any coming conflict to the detriment of Gavin Andal and Imperial loyalists."

"The Network agrees."

"Good, I want to talk to Mirage."

"That is acceptable." The Voice disconnected the call. Five minutes later, another call came in, a few minutes before the jump countdown expired.

"Mirage," he greeted her.

"Zenith."

"I could have killed you for what you did."

"I was just following orders."

"Don't dump the blame on others. You make your own choices," he admonished her.

"There is no blame to offload. The Network knows. The Network is wise. The Network is the future," she calmly countered. "I did what was necessary."

"Protect my family, Mirage," Janus implored her. "Marquandt's henchmen will already be on their way to take them hostage so they can lure me out of the shadows and execute me."

"The order has already been received. You can count on it. Nothing will happen to them."

"The stealth ship. I know you will not tell me where it is or what you plan to do with it. But tell me this: what is it? Is it alien?"

"No. It is a *Triumph* frigate that has been given upgrades whose technological origin is alien. That's especially true of the magnetic coils, the jump engines, and the cloaking field," Mirage explained with surprising candor. "Built by humans, however, in my initial estimation."

"A technology transfer, not a component trade."

"Yes."

"Thank you."

"Take care, Zenith."

She knew he had to fly into Orb territory. Of course.

"I will. Take care of my family. And one more thing, I have a name and I need to know what it means, Shirin Farad."

20

GAVIN

The trip through the Tartarus Void felt strange. Twenty hours of jumping every forty-five minutes to spare the jump nodes after flying to Dust with the shortest loading intervals. Whenever he looked out the porthole of his cabin, the web of stars seemed to glow fainter and farther away than it should.

Worse than this disconcerting impression or the constant jumping, which he imagined disturbed his sleep because of the brief sense of disassociation the transit brought, was the silence.

The Imperial Guard was no longer aboard and so it was relatively empty - matching the vast void through which they jumped. The Emperor's *Dominus* cruisers consisted of full crews, but not the usual three-shift system seen on other Navy ships. Since the *Invincible* had apparently departed spontaneously, the standby crew currently on duty was aboard at the time of departure. For longer trips by the deceased Emperor, the two replacement shifts would have been called in, but by all appearances there had been no time for that. So only thirty percent of the beds were occupied, and many areas that were not essential during the voyage were unoccupied because the respective crew members had to sleep.

Gavin took advantage of this emptiness to jog the hundreds of feet of corridors and clear his head. He dreaded the silence of his cabin, where only horrible images and jumbled feelings ran through his head and he longed for sleep, which he could not find between jumps. So he had resorted to draining his body so that it would sleep on its own, because there was no other way.

After two hours, his simple ship's overalls were drenched with sweat, and his breathing was labored. The muscles in his legs burned like fire, but his mind had calmed. The whirlwind of grief and anger had subsided. The knowledge that his family would be gone forever, that Hellcat, Bambam, and Dodger had betrayed him, that the Emperor was dead, the only person who could have righted the wrongs. All of this was reduced to a painful story at the edge of his mind as his body was busy processing the extreme exertion and directing its energy to the strained muscles.

On the way back to his cabin, he paid a visit to the Master Sergeant. The Marine occupied a quad cabin that he had to himself, and apparently was not sleeping either, as he opened the door within seconds. He, too, was covered in sweat, and his artificial muscles, with their finger-thick tubes running under his synth skin like snakes, were taut.

"Lord Captain." He looked surprised and glanced over his shoulder.

"Sergeant." Gavin waved it off. "I didn't intend to come in. But I wanted to speak with you for a moment."

"Of course, my lord."

"I want to apologize to you, Marshal."

The last Fleet

"Apologize?" Now the Marine looked confused.

"I've treated you like a machine since we escaped from Andal. First I ordered you to find the Orb's body, an impossible task I should never have given you."

The sergeant listened silently.

"A leader who gives impossible orders is not a good leader, and desperation after all that has happened to our homeland has made me not a good one," Gavin continued, thinking of the three rebels he had considered his crew while he had sent the loyal former Ice Legion soldier away. Looking back, it was shameful. "I lost sight of what loyalty really means, and that it only ever works two ways."

"I'm a simple master sergeant, my lord."

"No, you're a loyal soldier and a human being. You had family on Andal, too. You had comrades and friends there who are all dead now," Gavin objected, and the Marine's expression remained stoic. Perhaps it was also due to the chrome eyes, which were always expressionless and showed no emotion whatsoever. "I should have treated you like a human being and not used you like a machine."

He was already expecting the Master Sergeant to continue to insist on their difference in rank in the Navy, but instead the significantly larger man surprised him with a nod.

"Thank you, my lord. It's very kind of you to say so." Marshall paused. "I think it was good that I had a job to do. I try to avoid thinking about what happened back home. There is only pain and death in those thoughts. If it also suits your purpose, I would like to continue to push that part aside until we stand over the body of Dain Marquandt. The cleanup will begin after the earthquake, not during it."

"I see what you mean." Gavin nodded. "That's exactly what I intend to do. You and I are the last inhabitants of Andal, Sergeant. And it will be us who put an end to the traitor."

He nodded to the Marine and returned to his quarters. There he took off his magnetic boots and showered before going to bed and quickly falling into a long, dreamless sleep.

Their imminent arrival at Pulau Weh was announced with an unpleasantly shrill alarm that hit Gavin like a sledgehammer. He bolted up from his bunk and was thrown back by the straps that pinned him to the mattress in zero gravity.

"T minus thirty minutes to final transit," Gianni's voice blared through his cabin's speakers.

Doesn't the woman ever sleep? he thought sleepily, rubbing his face. His eyes felt swollen and his legs like concrete. But his head was clear of the fog of nightmares that usually accompanied him into the wee hours of the morning like the necrotic tissue of an infected wound.

He got up, washed and put on his formal uniform. The black, ultra-dense polymer fabric with smart pores looked like it had been freshly starched and was always wrinkle-free. The gold epaulettes shone on his shoulder and the four yellow crossed swords of a captain stood out pleasantly. Actually, he had wanted to put on his black coveralls as usual in normal shipboard life, but the prospect of reuniting with other survivors of Andal, especially Navy allies, awakened a certain pride in him. What he had said to the Master Sergeant the night before was true, after all: as of now, they were the only survivors of their home planet, but there was a slim chance that there were actually more of them who wore the same insignia on their chests as he did on his parade uniform: the Norse rune of peace of Andal on the white rising sun of the Border Worlds.

When he stepped out of his cabin with immaculate hair and a perfectly fitting uniform, Marshall was there waiting for him. He, too, wore the formal uniform of the Marines, more precisely that of the Ice Legion, his father's former bodyguard, in dark blue with black stripes along the sleeves and pants. A black cord hung from his right shoulder to the penultimate lapel button. Emblazoned on his chest was a slew of medals and badges that distinguished him as a veteran of multiple ground, vacuum and shipboard missions, in addition to combat injuries, special bravery, Special Forces brevets and, of course, Andal's lapel pin, which Gavin also wore.

Their eyes met and they smiled understandingly.

"You look good, Sergeant."

"As do you, Lord Captain," Marshall replied.

"I didn't know you were wearing a formal uniform under your armor when we evacuated you from the Einherjar," Gavin said, gesturing forward toward the elevators. Together, they made their way down.

"I've been running the 3-D printers in the workshops hot all night. Some of the techs from the night shift went all out to get everything right. Luckily, they had most of the templates stored in the computers. Fleet database, I think."

"Ah. Very good. Next to all your decorations, I feel quite naked," Gavin remarked, pointing to the Marine's richly adorned chest.

"I'm a non-commissioned officer, my lord. I earn my money by doing honest work," the sergeant joked without making a face, and Gavin had to laugh. He had not even remembered how that felt.

"My father would have agreed with you for sure."

"You wouldn't?"

"Of course not." He shook his head and pressed the panel on the left elevator car before looking up at the Sergeant. "I am a pilot. Always pushing."

To punctuate his words, he pretended to grasp an imaginary flightstick and press the fire button with his thumb.

"Bridge," he said as they stepped into the elevator.

"Mess hall," Marshall said.

"Countermand."

The Sergeant looked at him uncomprehendingly.

"You're coming with me to the bridge," Gavin decided.

"My lord, I don't think that..."

"Today, you are coming with me." With that, the Sergeant was apparently content, even though he gave the impression of being uncomfortable in his own skin. The elevator brought them in close proximity to the bridge, outside of which two Imperial Guardsmen stood guard, among the last ten who had remained on board to provide protection for the Princess.

"Good morning," he greeted them, and they saluted tightly.

On the bridge, Captain Gianni, Janus, and Elayne were already waiting for him in front of the three half-circles of bridge crew that spread out before them, standing in the center of the commander's podium. The virtual bridge window encompassed almost the entire left half of the circular room, as if they were in the panoramic lookout of a space station. The twenty officers and NCOs at the consoles half sat and half reclined in their gimbaled seats, working at virtual keyboards and displays. Unlike older ships, there were no holodisplays in front of them and the commander could monitor their activities through her own screen, which, however, appeared to be offline.

"Captain," Gianni greeted him as he entered.

"Captain," he replied. "Princess, First Secretary."

"Gavin," they both said simultaneously.

"Sergeant," the Commander also turned to Marshall, who seemed only momentarily distressed, as if he did not belong here. The look on Gianni's face seemed to express just that.

"Captain. Princess. First Secretary of State."

"I am glad you are both here," Elayne said before silence could fall. "I see you have dressed up for the occasion."

There was no mockery in her voice, more something like appreciation and compassion. Gavin thought she was indeed like the princesses in the fables and stories. Perhaps even better.

"Thank you, Your Majesty." He bowed slightly, and Marshall followed his example a little awkwardly. With clacking magnetic boots, they obeyed her beckoning and joined them on the platform, where there wasn't much room left.

"Captain," Gianni turned to him. "I wish to inform you that we have intercepted the signatures of a Never Swarm."

"What?" he snapped. "When?"

"Six hours ago."

"Why didn't you wake me?"

"Her Majesty thought it would be better if you were alert and rested when we arrive at Pulau Weh," the

Commander explained, making no secret of the fact that she had disagreed with the decision.

"A single swarm heading in the opposite direction," Janus jumped in explanatorily. "Four light years away, so no danger to us - or Pulau Weh."

Gavin felt a chill run down his spine. Just the thought of cosmic horror made him want to cower. Still, he didn't let it show and nodded.

"The Never is something Marquandt has to deal with now," Janus reminded him. "We have another target. You have another target. Whatever the Never is, or whatever it is up to, the Science Corps has not figured it out in over a century, so we certainly will now. What we do know is that it is not a threat to us and we have a mission."

The First Undersecretary eyed him inquiringly and seemed relieved when Gavin nodded silently.

"Transit in thirty seconds," the navigator reported.

He felt his palms grow damp and he tensed involuntarily. Pulau Weh, the nostalgic dream destination of he and his brother, a joke between them that had stemmed from the not-at-all-joking desire to escape and rest, to spend time together away from obligations. Now it was only a jump away, beyond the other end of the Star Empire he had never really believed he would ever see. Instead of a vacation destination, it had become his last hope, a slim chance for redress and justice, because whatever was happening to the Star Empire right now, without rule and law, strength always prevailed. That was the way humanity was knit. If anything, the remnants of his brother's fleet were the only strength he had left.

"Nervous?" asked Elayne, placing a hand on his arm sympathetically.

"Yeah," he admitted quietly. "I remember like it was only yesterday that we were in the battle for Andal. I could recite every sentence I exchanged with my brother when we last spoke. How I warned him and urged him to act. He had to trust me, me of all people, and despite the immense pressure and the possibility that he was forfeiting his career. He hardly hesitated and just did it."

"I looked at your brother's record. He seemed to have been a good man."

"He was my role model. Even though I never wanted to show it and went to great lengths to do exactly the opposite of what he would do." Gavin shook his head.

"Maybe he is watching us today," she replied seriously.

"I don't even know if he really sent his ships here. It's just a guess."

"One that you have bet a lot on," she stated. "Do not doubt it. The first instinct is always the right one, if you ask me."

Gavin looked at her and nodded gratefully. In that moment, she looked like the young woman she still was, carefree and maybe even a little naive, but in an encouraging, easy way.

"Jump!"

A blink later, they dropped out of subspace in Pulau Weh.

INTERLUDE
AKWA MARQUANDT

Following the *Invincible* was easy. Akwa's father had already anticipated that Dust would be a likely target for the Princess if she were able to escape. Not that he had counted on the crazy rescue maneuver that Gavin Andal and Janus Darishma had pulled off in the *Rubov* - but even he could not know everything, after all. The *Lady Vengeance* was still disguised as a pellet freighter with ugly superstructure on its hull, and so Akwa had simply had to do two things: send both their fleets to Pulau Weh and fly the *Lady Vengeance* to Dust. Since interstellar commerce was not interrupted and even Dust was approached several times a day, they did not even attract much attention. One freighter among many, equipped with the latest transponder codes.

Her father had squirmed at first when she had asked him for the two fleets, after all her plan to destroy Gavin Andal was based on the word of a terrorist and traitor, but he had understood one thing: If the surviving Border World ships did indeed still form a cohesive fleet and had not scattered, they had to be found and destroyed. And 777-Goggins was a system neither he nor she had ever heard of, to the extent that it was not on their radar - a fact that had made her father take notice. After all, his previous attempts to find the ships had met with no success, and he did not like being outmaneuvered.

As expected, the *Invincible* had landed on Dust. What exactly the Princess had done there, she did not know until she had talked to Jurgan Hartholm-Harrow on her secure channel. By then, the cruiser had already jumped out of the system.

"The princess is with me, as agreed," he had said, sending her a video recording with a grin through sickening teeth.

"You are not to execute her," Akwa had snarled, wishing she could have flown to the planet in person to kill him.

"Don't worry, Captain, I had young Andal make a recording beforehand. If his bumpkins are really still alive, they'll hear from him, and you can blow them away like sand."

"You would know about that."

"Of course." Jurgan laughed spitefully. "The princess is young and naive. She really thinks there's a chance to avenge her father."

Akwa had wasted no further time and had sprinted after the *Invincible* toward the Tartarus Void. Her crew of ten loyal and overly eager crewmen, who had already operated with her in Kerrhain while negotiating with the Broker, kept the three rebels at bay, still performing their normal duties but locked out of key systems.

"Lady Captain," their first officer, Quill Andrews, spoke up as they were just inside the center of the Tartarus

The last Fleet

Void, waiting for their jump engines to recharge. "According to the interferometers, the *Invincible* is three quarters of an hour ahead of us," he said.

"They're conserving their engines." Akwa waved off.

"Yes. The signature intensity indicates that we always miss them by a very narrow margin."

"Let's keep it that way."

"There's something else," Andrews said.

"What?"

"Never activity."

"Here?" She frowned in surprise and let him throw the relevant sensor data on the main display. "The spikes are not large, and the imaging does not give much."

"The on-board computer is ninety-two percent certain that it is the signature of a swarm," the lieutenant replied.

"What direction is it headed?"

"Too early to tell. We'd have to stay here longer and analyze the data for that. At least an hour, and then the images are several months old, because of the distance."

Akwa leaned forward and looked at the star map. The Never was right on the edge of the great void. Either it was heading in their direction or in the opposite direction. But once it appeared, it didn't just sweep back and forth. It had a destination, which could only mean that her father had activated one of the emitters. But for what location? Was he really already forced to wipe out a recalcitrant colony? She did not like the thought, though she had understood with Andal why it had been necessary for the greater good of a better future. With any luck, this mission would be the last until all the powers-that-be understood that there was only one goal: the common future. Then they would be without this tool, which she had never felt comfortable with anyway. It was like having a rabid dog with them that did not walk on a leash, but would pounce on others if they marked their opponents with a piece of meat.

"Doesn't look like it will interfere with our targeted jump points," Akwa stated after looking at the star charts. "Even with our slightly extended jump node recharge times."

"No, but I wanted to inform you, Lady Captain."

"Carry on."

Many jumps later - she had lost count - they were ahead of the final jump to Pulau Weh. She had Hellcat, whose name she found ridiculous, summoned to the bridge, as she did regularly to make the woman feel needed and useful. That was not true, but it could change at any time. Unlike herself, the rebel knew Gavin Andal at least a little. And she should also understand that Akwa would promote her out of the airlock with her friends if Pulau Weh turned out to be a bust. She had no patience with false informants.

"Captain," Hellcat said in a neutral voice.

"Hi. We're almost there. I wanted you to witness this from up here so we can react quickly if a situation arises."

The rebel nodded and took a seat in one of the empty seats.

"You look tense."

"I'm angry," Hellcat growled, and her eyes betrayed that she wasn't lying. They were like crackling fires.

"I heard young Andal was a real heartbreaker at the Academy, but he seems to have done something to you."

"No, he didn't. He just turned out to be another blue-blood with a golden spoon up his ass, for whom we were just staffage to help his shitty emperor." Hellcat literally spat out the words, dripping with contempt.

Akwa thought back to the moment when the bomb

The last Fleet

her father had planted on the end cap of the Aurora habitat had exploded and, at the same time, all the doors inside had opened via an infiltrated computer virus. The look on the young woman's face as she watched the entire Senate and most of the full Noble Assembly being sucked into a vacuum one by one. Helpless little figures who died within minutes, drifting like tiny pawns toward Saturn. A cloud of corrupt bastards that the Star Empire had been rid of in under an hour, thanks to her father. The contention in Hellcat's eyes had been something Akwa had felt in herself as well: a disbelief that it had really worked, and that such a powerful goal that had seemed unattainable only a short time ago had finally been achieved. The rebel had wept with joy. A silly weakness, but she was also a guttersnipe, after all, probably a former trash kid who had joined the Republican underground out of lack of alternatives and sheer desperation. Nonetheless, for years she must have imagined this moment when the promises of her leaders would come true. And Akwa had shown it to her, signaling that she was true to her word. Now it was time for it to work the other way around, and for that she had ordered Hellcat to the bridge. She needed to understand, to see the ties to her past torn before Akwa recruited her for her spy network. They needed more eyes and ears on the underground, her father had made that clear to her. And who was better suited than the children of the revolution, who had been the ones to make victory possible?

"Well, whatever we find in Pulau Weh," she said, "Gavin Andal will be there, and it will be his end."

Attentively, she kept her eyes on the young woman's expression, saw the pulsing anger and an inkblot of hurt in her eyes. Of course. An offended sense of honor? A rejected love? There was a reason Akwa stayed away from such things. They clouded the view of the true nature of the universe, which consisted merely of action and reaction and did not bother about sensitivities. Trifles. Of course, she had not told Hellcat about Andal's execution. Why should she. She had to make sure she could trust her, and what better way to seal the death of her former captain - and presumably lover - herself?

"I don't know what you want from me, Captain," the Rebel said. "But I do know that you don't give a shit about the Republican cause."

Akwa was surprised by the sudden openness. In a positive way. "Ah, a few direct words."

"If your father's intrigues lead to the chains of the Emperor and the nobility being broken, then that suits our cause. Until both arms are free, we will help you do so. It is as simple as that."

"You know why I brought you along, I suppose?"

"We are supposed to bite the hand that fed us to prove to you that we accept the new master that holds the leash." Hellcat glared challengingly at her. "That's exactly what you mean, am I right?"

"Something like that."

"We don't accept a leash, and Gavin Andal was never our master," the Rebel clarified. "Besides, I don't like this shit, but I know there's not going to be a deal between us if we don't play ball."

"Good point."

"When this is over, we're going to take the *Lady* and leave. What happens after that, we'll settle via a secure communications link using a virtual mailbox."

"Sounds acceptable," Akwa decided. She had imagined it to be something like that. However, the frank words surprised her in a positive way. She hated verbiage and play-acting. She turned to her first officer, "Lieutenant, what about our fleets?"

"They should have arrived at Oort's Cloud from 777-Goggins about six hours ago."

"Good, let's see if Gavin Andal's voice can wake dead spirits. We'll jump as soon as we can."

21
GAVIN

The 777-Goggins system was special for several reasons: Since its discovery in 2393 by the prospector Yuri Halenko, no one had come here. No ship of the Star Empire had paid a second visit to the system, which had a number of causes. There was only the central star of spectral class F4, relatively similar to the Sun, a rather thin asteroid belt, and Pulau Weh, the only planet in the system except for an ice giant forty astronomical units out. So the sole resources were in the asteroid belt, but it was neither particularly dense nor particularly productive. In addition, there was the distance: jumps through the Tartarus void always carried the risk of being stranded if the jump engines malfunctioned. There were neither combarks nor quantcom systems. Anyone who could not jump was lost here in a forty-light-year diameter void. In addition, Yuri Halenko's circumnavigation of the void was only a few years ago and had barely made a ripple. His brother Artas had only come across the relevant report at all because he had met Halenko at a reception on Andal, where the prospector had been appointed the new head of a Science Corps research station.

Although circumnavigating the Tartarus void was a major achievement and required considerable risk-taking, both Halenko and his discoveries ultimately remained mere gray notes in the Corps' files. No habitable planets, no major resource accumulations, no particularly productive gas giants that would have justified such long, risky missions for helium-3 ventures. Gavin recalled that Halenko had reported sightings of the Never in his reports, but they had been dismissed in the assessment as an attempt to lend attention to his several-month mission. The calls of a man who wanted to be seen.

Well, it had worked for Artas and Gavin. The footage of Pulau Weh, the only planet that turned out to be basically habitable and on which the prospector and his team had set foot. It was oceanic and covered only by a few smaller islands that dotted the bright blue of the world like freckles. Still, the idea of spending a few weeks on one of these islands in absolute peace and seclusion awakened an indescribable longing in him. It would be an untouched world, warm and probably full of aquatic life that had not yet been explored. Everything he would do would be on his island for the first time, and the problems and conflicts of the Star Empire would be but the distant chatter of short-lived beings.

Their exit point was at the L2 of Pulau Weh's only moon, a rocky body shaped like a potato, fifty miles across on its long axis. Navigation missed the point by only a few thousand clicks, proving once again that only the Navy's best worked in the Emperor's readiness.

Through the virtual bridge window, he gazed at the beautiful blue sphere that filled most of it. The flock of spotless white fluffy clouds that moved eastward in the equatorial region, over Gavin's Islands. Being so close to the place he knew only from his thoughts and a few animation images from the Halenko report felt strange.

"Sensor array deployed, beginning close-range scan," the recon reported.

"I can now imagine why you wanted to come here with your brother, Gavin Andal," Elayne remarked without taking her eyes off the window. "What a beautiful, pristine planet."

"It's a long way from anywhere," he replied.

"Put the Hermes out," Gianni ordered in a loud voice. "I want a survey of the system from here to the asteroid belt as soon as possible."

"Your Majesty, Lord Captains, my lord," Marshall hesitantly spoke up, and all eyes turned to him.

"Yes, Sergeant?" asked Gavin, seeing that Gianni had something disapproving on his lips.

"I was just wondering one thing, sir: if Never really has been sighted in the void, we have no way of detecting it if it comes here. There are no deep space listening stations of any kind, and it moves almost at the speed of light, as far as I know. You have experienced it yourselves. It's just as fast as radar and lidar signals."

"The Sergeant is right," Janus agreed with him. "But I see no reason why we should be threatened by Never here. Not with a ship."

Gavin knew that the theories that the Never came from the Tartarus Void had several reasons: first, there were stars and planets missing there, suggesting that it might have engulfed them all, like Turan-II or Andal. In addition, there was largely discarded circumstantial evidence, such as Halenko's alleged attempt to gain attention or the fact that New Berlin was not far from the void. Turan-II, on the other hand, had been in an entirely different corner of the Star Realm. He shuddered at the thought that Never might be in close proximity, with no way for them to detect it early. Or even notice it at all.

"I suggest we deal with our primary objective first," Gianni suggested, giving the Sergeant a reproving look. "The finding of the Border World fleet."

No one objected. It took several hours and a circumnavigation of Pulau Weh before they could be sure that no other ships or celestial bodies larger than a human fist were near the planet or its moon. This fact was sobering and felt to Gavin like a punch in the gut. If they weren't here, they had to be in the asteroid belt, which made sense in principle, since water and oxygen could be found there in the form of ice, easily mined in a vacuum away from gravity wells and split by electrolysis. But scouring an asteroid belt was not an option, as it would take weeks. With the advanced Hermes drones that were currently scanning the system, maybe a week, but even that was still far too long. Hellcat, Bambam and Dodger knew exactly where he would be headed, and if they were going to betray him with one thing, why not with that?

Just the thought that they could betray him like that stabbed him straight in the heart. Could they suddenly hate him so much because of the Aurora thing that they brought Akwa Marquandt here to kill him and nip a possible civil war in the bud? That wouldn't even be in their best interest. Unless Marquandt had promised them something that coincided with their rebel goals. If the fleet admiral had proven one thing, it was that he was a master of deception - so why wouldn't it work with three angry terrorists?

"What if they're not here?" asked Gianni the question he had been dreading.

"They are here," he answered firmly. *They have to be here*. "They could be hiding in the asteroid belt."

"It's not very dense," the commander pointed out. "Not a good place to hide."

"It is, but if they put it on passive systems only, they'd save a lot of energy, which probably makes sense to them after the long trip here, coming out of the middle of a battle."

"Which would mean," Janus interjected into his musings, "that they would not be able to detect us either. They would only pick up radar signals with passive systems, but wouldn't know who they were coming from."

"Or radio waves," Gavin and Gianni countered simultaneously.

Five minutes later, he rubbed his fingers together and tightened when the commander signaled that they were on broadband transmission. What he was saying now would reach the asteroid belt from their position in a little over twenty minutes.

"This is Gavin Andal, High Lord of House Andal, Lord Captain of the Imperial Fleet and the Order of the Border Worlds. Comrades, brothers and sisters of the Karpshyn Sector, if you can hear me: I bring you bad news. The Never has devoured Andal, which was home to many of you, after the betrayal of Dain Marquandt. My brother Artas died in an effort to help you retreat, and now I ask you to come forth and join me. Marquandt did not stop after our people and murdered the Emperor as well. Our right to justice must be fought for, and it will be. I am aboard the *Invincible*, a *Dominus*-class cruiser.

Beside me are the heir to the throne, Elayne Hartholm-Harrow, and the First Secretary of State, Janus Darishma. They await you, as do I. Come forth, step out of the shadows, and prepare yourselves." Gavin paused, building the retarding moment. "Our revenge begins today."

He nodded and the broadcast ended. After a few seconds, it began again in the form of a recording. In a continuous loop, they were now sending out the radio waves, which were spreading in all directions at the speed of light.

"Now it's time to wait," Gianni said. "I truly hope you are right, and they really are out there."

Because otherwise we have no strategy whatsoever for what to do next, he added in his mind, because that was what she actually wanted to say, and what everyone was thinking.

"More ships would be a start," he voiced the problem, not wanting to waste time ignoring the elephant in the room until it was too late. Besides, it was hard to stand waiting silently for his radio message to reach the asteroid belt and for a reply to come back. "But they will not be enough to change anything in Sol."

"No, they will not," Janus agreed with him. "But they would be a sign. Every avalanche begins with a single piece of snow that breaks loose and grows and grows until it can't be stopped."

"You mean allies," Gianni speculated.

"Yes. With military behind us - especially well-trained crews from the Border World fleets and modern ships - they will not dismiss our cause as the righteous yet naïve anger of losers who are fighting for what's right but have nothing on their side but their wounded pride and anger in their stomachs. The Border Worlds will join us if you call to arms, Gavin. They have all lost sons and daughters to Marquandt's treachery. Your word carries more weight there than that of any high official or admiral from the Core Worlds. Ruhr Heavy Industries may also be interested in avenging Yokatami and Marquandt alike for the loss of their Seed World. Their project in the Seed Traverse was among the largest investments they have made in the last thirty years. We have Jurgan in our pocket anyway, and with him his network of spies, dirty laundry, and contacts all over the shadows of the Star Empire. He will be able to help us track down possible enemies of Marquandt and loyalists who don't agree with the new circumstances and are asking questions."

"Also, it should be possible to get some of the Wall Worlds on our side," Gianni added. "The idea of a war with the Orb is far from popular there. The Core Worlds have always been shielded from this threat, and some inhabitants there don't even believe in the existence of the aliens. But the Wall Worlds know exactly what kind of danger they pose. We may be able to take advantage of that."

"That is all well and good," Elayne interjected. "But these considerations will only get us anywhere if Gavin's brother's ships are really here. It's a long way to get here, and a lot can happen. Besides, they do not even know what fate befell Andal. If they were really here and held out, doing nothing and waiting should have driven them insane."

"My brother will have instructed them," Gavin said firmly.

"What makes you so sure of that?"

"He believed in me. I know it."

. . .

Gavin waited on the bridge for an hour. No one from the others left the command platform in the middle either. No one sat down. They just looked motionless through the window into the endless star field. Silently, since there was nothing more to say. It was only a matter of waiting, for they had no way of forcing what they were waiting for with ever-increasing tension.

They got no answer, until a shrill alarm suddenly howled.

"CONTACT!" shouted someone from reconnaissance.

"Combat readiness!" ordered Gianni, tapping her wrist terminal. Four jump seats folded out of the floor behind the two commander's chairs, to which she directed Gavin, Janus, Elayne, and Marshall with a curt gesture. She herself and her first officer, a four-shouldered commander with piercing blue eyes and a red-brush cut, buckled in after they were seated.

"Specify, lieutenant," he ordered gruffly.

"Receiving transit waves in close proximity. Several dozen contacts and counting."

"Signatures?" demanded Gianni to know.

"Navy signatures, ma'am, but no active transponders."

Akwa, Gavin thought in horror. Hellcat really led them here. We're too late.

"Activate all weapons systems, magnetize hull. Power up jammers and put Stingrays on standby," the commander ordered, and Gavin envied her calm. He could hardly form a clear thought in the knowledge that he had let them all fall into a death trap.

"We're being hailed, ma'am," the lieutenant reported from communications. The tactics screen in front of the command pod filled rapidly with bad news as the sensors updated the display with fresh data. The *Invincible* was a lone green triangle surrounded by countless red dots marked 'Unknown' by the on-board computer.

"Put it through."

"This is Rear Admiral Bjorn Svarthammer of the *Thor*," a piercing voice announced, and Gavin had already jumped up out of his seat before it had spoken. "Identify yourself."

Gianni turned to him and nodded.

"Bjorn, it's Gavin," he gasped, excitement spreading through him like effervescence coursing through his blood, making every vessel tingle. Then it occurred to him that the officer must expect this to be a trick. A trick he was betting his entire fleet on. A man he had been on a first-name basis with for years - for good reason.

A fleet. He glanced at the tactical screen, that was well over a hundred signatures surrounding them.

"I remember only once in my life being so happy to see you," he said. "And that was at Artas' farewell party from the Academy."

"The Pope," came the reply a moment later. "Bloody heavens, boy. I'm glad to hear it's really you. We were beginning to think we'd have to fly to Sol with colors flying to claim our right."

"We will, Bjorn. But we'll have to take a few detours." Gavin wiped a few tears of relief from the corner of his eye and laughed as all his tension was released at once.

"Ma'am," the lieutenant from Recon called out again. "One of the Hermes drones reports the presence of a Never Swarm that has appeared beyond the Ice Giant."

"Appeared?" asked Gianni tensely. "What do you mean?"

"It looks like it jumped out of subspace. The gravity wave pattern is reminiscent of transit waves."

"How long until they get here?"

"Two hours."

"Damn. We are going to have to jump. Vice Admiral," Gianni addressed Bjorn, who was still on the line. "I suggest we get the hell out of this system."

"No objections from me, Captain."

INTERLUDE
AKWA MARQUANDT

"Perhaps it was your father?" suggested Andrews, as they stared at the sensor screen's warnings, scurrying for attention, of the approaching Never swarm. Their two fleets had jumped out of Oort's Cloud into the shadow of the unnamed ice giant, which was far from the system's central star. The Never was still fifty light minutes away, and their jump nodes were fully charged. They had already detected the *Invincible*'s *Hermes* drone ten minutes ago. Now it was time to make a decision.

"Maybe. He could have placed a transmitter on the *Invincible*." She considered. "Or had it brought here first."

"Why wouldn't he have informed you?"

"In this age of espionage, anyone could be a spy."

"What about the drone? We have to shoot it down before it spies our positions."

"We need to be sure it relays the presence of the Never," she decided, "Prepare the maser."

"Andal's fleet should ramp up their jump nodes," Hellcat surmised.

"Yes. They are now reunited with him." Soon she

would have to give up the lie that Andal was still alive. But not yet. "That means there's no reason to stay here anymore anyway. The Never's presence will only startle them more quickly. That means that if they have been informed now, they will get the message in about forty-five minutes. Andrews, set an appropriate timer and pass it on to our battle group."

"But we're outnumbered two to one," Rebel agreed. "Why don't we jump now and take them out immediately?"

"Why would I give up a tactical advantage for no reason?" asked Akwa. "If we jump now, they'll be ready to fight. If we jump only when they have their jump nodes up and their weapons systems down accordingly, we will catch them with their pants down. We jump right in between them and pick them apart like a pit bull picks apart a couple of kittens. Fewer casualties and no chance of escape. I'm not going to give up a trump card just because I get impatient in the last few feet."

Hellcat didn't answer, so she obviously understood.

"Andrews, shoot down the *Hermes*. By the time the Borderworlders have determined that it's no longer transmitting, they will be well on their way to jumping. We are jumping in forty-five minutes, that's an order."

22

GAVIN

Gavin could not avoid staring at the image of the Never swarm flying toward the inner system, roughly to Pulau Weh. It could not be a coincidence that it appeared right now and here. The computer calculated its trajectory and speed based on the initial data the Hermes had sent over a five-minute period. A realistic simulation, and yet he could not wrap his head around the fact that coincidence would deal them such a nasty blow now.

"How long until we can jump?" asked Janus tensely.

"Still twenty-five minutes," Gianni replied.

"Abort," Gavin snapped.

"Excuse me?"

"Abort jump preparations."

"No," decided the Commander. "Have you gone insane? This system is lost and with it everything that remains in it."

"Yes. But I think I know why it's here, and we have to fight," he affirmed. His heart was pounding in his chest like a steam hammer. The roulette in his head had stopped spinning, and the knowledge that he had made up his mind calmed his mind, but electrified his body in an almost uncomfortable way. "You'll have to trust me."

"I'm sorry, Captain, but this is my command, and I'm not willing to put Her Majesty and this crew at risk because of your trauma. That one," Gianni pointed with an outstretched arm at the tactical number and the black shadow approaching from the outer system, "cannot be defeated. You should know that better than anyone."

Gavin knew where a fight could not be won. The Commander was the mistress on her ship and could not be outvoted. So he turned to the only person who could.

"Your Majesty," he said, looking Elayne in the eye so she could see he had not lost his mind. "When you look at me, I hope you see the same determination in my eyes that you saw in the *Rubov*. The plan sounded crazy, but it worked. That is exactly what we need right now."

"And what is the plan?"

"If I explain it, Captain Gianni will shoot me, and besides, we don't have time. It will only work if we act now."

The Princess looked him in the eye, and Gavin just vibrated with impatience. Finally, she nodded and turned to Gianni: "I'm putting Captain Gavin Andal in temporary command of this fleet. Put it in the logs and send it to the other ships."

Gianni's mouth narrowed, but she tightened and nodded.

"Order the fleet," Gavin said immediately. "Abort jump preparations, full power toward the moon. We need to push as deep into its gravity field as we can. We'll try to go around it."

"Why..."

The last Fleet

"No time," he interrupted the Commander more harshly than intended, and she finally relayed the order over a fleet-wide channel. Shortly after, he had to sit down again, this time next to Gianni, as their first officer made room for him. The *Invincible* accelerated and gradually increased to 8g. No further, since the emergency seats did not have flynites and neither the Princess nor Janus were used to higher forces. Even their genetically enhanced bodies ran the risk of stroke at higher levels.

As they sped toward the moon, with the close-flying fleet following them like steel shrapnel to a magnet, Gavin stared at the tactics screen. If he was wrong now, he had put it all on the line, all on one card, one flash of inspiration. But it felt like the last piece of the puzzle had fallen into place, completing something that had not made sense before.

They were just reaching the moon's gravity field for their fly-by maneuver when he gave the next order: "Have the two carriers ready their Stingrays. All pilots to their cockpits immediately. Weapons up, full combat readiness!"

Gianni wanted to protest again; the Never was still far away, after all. As he shook his head wearily, she relayed the appropriate orders over transducers.

"Your Majesty. What you downloaded for me from the fleet headquarters mainframe: we're going to need it now," he said. At the same time, the battle alert on the bridge began to howl.

"Contact!" he heard from Recon the message he had been waiting for.

Gianni bared her teeth. Gavin was sure she would have stared at him questioningly if she had still been able to turn her head under the brutal acceleration forces.

Communication now played out only over the internal transducer network directly in their heads.

"Identify."

"Akwa Marquandt," Gavin growled.

"Nearly four hundred transit signatures, Captain," replied the lieutenant from reconnaissance.

The enemy ships formed a dense sphere around the position where they themselves had been sitting in space between Pulau Weh and its moon just ten minutes ago, waiting for their jump thrusters. They would not have survived even five minutes with their weapons systems deactivated and their thrusters shut down.

The on-board computer marked the ships according to their Navy codes. They were the third and fourth fleets of Wall Sector Delta. Modern, heavily armed and manned by well-trained crews. His own fleet was not even half as large as the two enemy fleets, but at least on a technically almost equal level. The only question was how much ammunition Svarthammer had left; after all, his brother Artas' units had jumped out of the middle of a strafing-intensive engagement.

"We're cutting back on acceleration," he decided after looking at the tactics screen.

"An explanation would be helpful right now," Gianni replied, and he could understand her anger. So he took a minute to explain to her exactly what he was up to.

"This is complete insanity," escaped the commander a moment later.

"It is business as usual for him," Janus interjected. The First Undersecretary, usually always surrounded by an aura of superiority, sat in his seat like a passenger feeling nauseous, pale and restless, well out of his comfort zone.

"The way I see it, Captain Andal just saved us from being shot to pieces," Rear Admiral Svarthammer of the

Thor joined the conversation. "The plan is crazy. But crazy is what we need right now."

"Sergeant," Gavin turned to Marshall. "You don't have to go along with this. I understand if you..."

"No, my lord. I'm all in."

23

GAVIN

Gavin ran alongside the Sergeant down the corridor to the elevators. Each step was exhausting as they still accelerated at 2g, doubling their body weight. Arriving at the launch bays, they split up. Marshall went to the airlock, where his Titan Motorized Armor was already waiting for him as ordered. Two technicians had unfolded it, so all the Marine had to do was step inside after removing his parade uniform.

"Last chance to say no," Gavin opined.

"No way I'm missing this one," the Sergeant countered, and for the first time he saw the usually haggard man grin.

"Good luck to us both." Gavin ran up the stairs, slipped into a g-suit in the locker room, accepted the helmet from a technician, then wormed his way into the Stingray through the top hatch. It was like repeating the Princess rescue mission, except now he had a few minutes rather than a few seconds.

In the pilot's seat, the straps flowed around him and hardened to match his body shape as he booted up all the systems, did a quick launch check, and then leaned his head against the headrest as instructed so as not to endanger his neck during the catapult launch.

"Sergeant?"

"I'm ready."

"Bridge?"

"Clearance granted. Good luck, Captain," Gianni herself answered.

"Thank you, Captain. See you on the other side."

"I thought they only said that in VR movies?" interjected Janus with feigned indignation.

"Not today. Rear Admiral?"

"The *Jotunheim* has been cleared. The Stingrays programmed," Svarthammer reported. "Good luck, Gavin."

"To all of us." He pressed the launch button and was pushed violently into the seat as the magnetic slide momentarily accelerated his Stingray to 8g and fired like a projectile - not from the bow this time - from the *Invincible*'s flank. As he had last time, Gavin went into a one-hundred-eighty-degree spin around the transverse axis and accelerated back toward the cruiser, which lay before him like a huge colossus of dull metal. To his right, the moon was emblazoned in front of the much larger Pulau Weh, which filled half the field of view like an angry blue face staring back at him over its satellite.

The airlock was a hundred yards ahead when he gave the order to Marshall and abruptly slowed the Stingray. As the hatch opened to reveal the clunky Titan armor flying toward him with its hands and feet extended in front of it, he jerked the top of his fighter up ninety degrees so that its underside faced forward. The on-board computer warned him of a dangerous approach with a red triangle, which he ignored. Shortly thereafter, a loud clonk! went through

The last Fleet

the cabin, and the total mass of his Stingray increased by half a ton, according to his readout.

"Hold on tight," he radioed to the Sergeant, who was now clinging to the underside like a tick with magnetized gloves and boots. "That was the easy part."

He turned the Stingray again, this time around a diagonal axis until the fleet came into view. They were now crowded behind the moon in the blind spot of Akwa Marquandt's fleet chasing them. The window was only a few minutes, so he had to hurry. The hundred and forty Border World ships under Bjorn Svarhammer's command glittered against the darkness of space like metal shavings in the pale light of the moon, which was illuminated by the central star. A particularly large one of these slivers was closest to them at the head of the fleet and was just turning with engines blazing.

Gavin accelerated toward it at 5g, which they had been told was the maximum of what the magnets of the Titan armor could withstand. Thirty seconds later, he chased past the mile-long carrier ship with *Jotunheim* written on its flank. It looked like a cylinder, except that its hull was hexagonal, the sides peppered with hundreds of holes - ejection chutes for Stingrays, five hundred of which it carried in its hull. The hangars were on the top and bottom, but they were still sealed.

He matched his speed to that of the carrier and sped with it through the formation of the fleet - his fleet - already veering off toward the outer system and its single ice giant far out, which the Never should have passed by now to pounce on.

The launch bay marked for him was in the starboard center area, one of many that could be identified only by the fact that the two position lights on the outside were flashing white. He turned the Stingray around and shut down the main engine to let the on-board computer do the parking. It fired small bursts from the maneuvering thrusters, dozens per second, pushing it backward into the bay. It was precision work by millimeters, but eventually he was enveloped by the dark walls. Marshall had climbed to the nose and was stuck directly in front of his cockpit window in front of the circular cutout that was getting smaller and smaller in front of them, shrinking the universe. Two minutes later, they had reached the end of the slide. The Sergeant slid over him onto the Duroglas and gave him a curt wave.

Gavin returned it, and then plugged into the *Jotunheim*'s internal network as an observer, flying guideless past its sister ships in the direction from which they had come. Plugged into the sensors, it felt as if he were the ship, as if he could feel the cold of the vacuum, and also the sense of loneliness as they left the last of their people's units behind and headed back toward Pulau Weh alone.

The *Jotunheim* continued to accelerate, tracing a tight arc along the ugly little moon as the first enemies came into view. They formed a spear formation and sped toward them with glaring exhaust flares. Gavin felt like a sprinter running straight toward a stampede of four hundred angry bulls. They were still separated by fifty thousand clicks.

Behind them, at the edge of the ecliptic, their allies sped away toward the Never, away from their pursuers. They did what Gavin's thoughts were trying to hammer into him louder with each passing second: Run!

"Has the shelling started yet?" asked Marshall.

"No," Gavin replied, looking at the melting distance to the enemy's first forward units. The *Jotunheim*'s sensors searched and searched. When they finally found what he needed, the firing started. At the same moment that Akwa

Marquandt broke formation, the forward ships fired their first salvos of missiles, eighty in all. The second salvo brought the same amount again shortly after. Tiny projectiles with glowing plasma flares and insane acceleration levels headed toward them like gnats toward light.

Carrier ships had no launch bays for guided weapons, no railguns or gauss cannons, but plenty of short-range defenses like gatlings and lasers. Normally protected deep within a fleet formation, it needed only defense against penetrating missiles and no offensive activity at all. They had to eject and land fighters to repair them and throw them back into the fight. Now the *Jotunheim* had to do everything at once. Through the sensors, Gavin watched as it threw tens of thousands of projectiles at the attacking swarms of missiles, and invisible laser beams licked at the tiny warheads. Many of them exploded or disintegrated into pieces of debris, but it was far from enough. The impacts of the surviving twenty missiles from the first salvo struck along the entire upper half of the bow, making Gavin tremble even far back in the hull still in his pilot's seat. The second salvo chased twice that number again into the carrier, shattering the entire forward third and with it much of the fighters in their launch bays.

Gavin was glad they were at least unmanned.

With reactors and drive nacelles in the rear, the *Jotunheim* flew on like a half-mangled zombie in a hail of shotgun blasts.

Or like a meteor being melted away by atmospheric fire - and we're sitting in the middle of it, he thought with growing nervousness.

The *Lady Vengeance* had not been hard to spot, since he knew the exact signature profile and had preset the *Jotunheim*'s sensors accordingly. The problem was rather that Akwa Marquandt - if she was still on board at all -

apparently did not display any egocentricity and did not fly at the head of her huge fleet unit as hoped. Instead, she was directly in the middle of the formation, protected by dozens of ships.

The carrier had just dived into the enemy lines like a fireball, with bystanders jumping for cover as railgun fire began. A hail straight from hell. Thousands of projectiles literally shredded the *Jotunheim*, and within seconds. So he loaded a secondary command into the on-board computer to get one last burst of acceleration out as the entire system failed.

"What the bloody hell?" he muttered in confusion as he realized what had just happened. The *Lady Vengeance* had deployed the damned jammer prototype the Broker had told him about. The carrier's electronic countermeasures had instantly buckled like a paper wall before a tsunami. "DAMN IT!"

The first tungsten bolts shot just past his Stingray - and Marshall - punching holes in the catapult tube, through which fire leaked, instantly suffocating in the vacuum.

"Getting a little uncomfortable here..." The sergeant broke off, and Gavin was beginning to fear he'd fallen victim to a railgun projectile when he himself was flung to the side and his straps struggled to catch him. The carrier had apparently been hit by a larger warhead, causing it to change direction. It turned thirty degrees, and what was left of its mangled body dissolved in a cloud of debris. Shortly before that, all the remaining Stingrays ignited their engines and shot out of the launch tubes as programmed, except that the timing was far too late.

By the time Gavin pushed the flightstick forward and hurtled into space on an explosion that nearly engulfed him, there were only eighty fighters left on autopilot out of a total of five hundred trying to escape the debris. Ten did not make it because they collided with smoldering debris and crashed shortly after takeoff. Eight more fell victim to stray tungsten bolts. The sixty-two remaining swung around to their intended destination: the *Lady Vengeance*.

They formed a wide formation so that the enemy would not know too quickly what they were targeting. The defensive fire was massive, but not as dense as it could have been, as they enjoyed some protection from the cloud of debris, some of which consisted of hull segments the size of houses, which were as fast as they were. On top of that was the high inherent speed of Marquandt's ships, so that only thirty seconds separated them from the nearest units. They were already dodging or using all their short-range defenses to intercept debris large enough to be considered a kinetic threat for a collision.

Still, his fighters were dropping like flies. There were only thirty left flying with him, and more were disappearing from his tactical display every second. But he could already see the *Lady* ahead of him. She raced upward in a wide arc to avoid the debris as the remaining Stingrays closed in tighter and shot toward her like an arrow.

In the last two clicks, they lost another twenty. Gavin was hit three times, losing both main engines, the drive pod, life support, and the nose. Miraculously, the cockpit unit was still there and Marshall's shadow overhead.

He wanted to call the Sergeant and ask if he was still alive, but he didn't have time. Four more surviving Stingrays, looking no better than his, shot a hair's breadth past the Lady and were blown to bits by her melee cannons. Gavin brought them into a violent spin and then braked via the maneuvering thrusters so that they bumped lightly against the frigate's underside. At the last moment, he magnetized the landing nozzles, which normally connected to the electromagnetic carriage of the ejection chutes after a combat landing or attached to the deck of the hangars to avoid flying through the area due to incipient acceleration or changes in direction. Accordingly, they were powerful, even if they only had power for an hour at most, since the reactor had sprung a leak.

"Marshall, if you're still alive, now's the time."

A groan answered him on the radio.

"I... I've..."

Gavin's mouth twisted. They couldn't have failed. Not so close to the finish line. Or had he been wrong after all? His heart went cold. With his trembling right hand, which he reluctantly pulled from the useless flightstick, he fumbled for the signal booster in the lapel pocket of his G-suit.

"I... threw up all over myself." The shadow over the cockpit window moved hesitantly, then a little faster. "Give me... a moment. The auto-injector... will take care of it in a minute."

Gavin knew all was not well with the Sergeant, as he seemed to have forgotten even the polite form of address. Looking past the chunky silhouette of bulky armor, he saw the many ships of Marquandt's fleet chasing his own, and he felt like a chick in the middle of a pack of wolves. He sealed his helmet and made sure the internal life support was working.

"Marshall?"

"I'm here, my lord." The sergeant climbed down over the cockpit window, which was up for him, and out of his field of vision. "Something's happening here."

24

GUNTER

Gunter watched dazedly as the airlock door slid open before him. A bright white cutout on the dark hull of the *Lady Vengeance*, promising like the gateway to the kingdom of heaven in the midst of endless darkness.

In the lighted square stood a single figure, broad-shouldered and tall, motionless and waiting. He did not expect a helping hand; he was a Marine.

So he struggled onward on all fours. Crawled across the hull like an insect in the frost, slow and choppy, but not yet dead. His auto-injector had injected him with a cocktail of drugs - including a large amount of benzodiazepines to help him decompress and dispel the panic he had inevitably felt during the flight. Keeping his eyes open had probably been a mistake. That he was still alive was a miracle. He had shit and pissed himself for the first time since Hell Week at Andal's North Pole, during his Special Forces training.

But that did not matter now. His circulation was just stabilizing again, and his brain was like a ghost returning to the body after it had slipped away too quickly. All that was left was the airlock and the unarmed figure. The many exhaust flares around them, where spaceships chased his allies like greedy hyenas. The twinkling of the stars, the ugly gray moon and a blue glow behind him.

Arriving at the airlock, he climbed in and paused when he saw an outstretched arm. It was Dodger, the damned mutant, standing in front of him. She had a rifle strapped to her and only a breath pack in front of her face. Ice had formed on her skin.

A real tough bitch, I know, he thought, and took her arm. She pulled him in. Not that he needed her help, but gestures were sometimes more important.

She called him on their last frequency together, when they had been on the *Lady* together.

"Where is it?" he asked.

"Hidden in the mess hall," the mutant replied.

"Go there. With the others. Lock yourselves in."

"There are a dozen Marquandt crewmen. No easy guys. I can..."

"No." He closed the airlock door and waited for the atmosphere to return. Then he opened his helmet and a great gush of vomit slapped the floor. It stank like hell. Dodger merely raised a brow, but seemed neither disgusted nor amused. "Did you..." He started.

"They don't know. Bambam bypassed the airlock signal relay. Sphinx has them believing they've been hit by a piece of debris."

"Sphinx still in control?" he asked.

"Nope, was forced with new command codes. But that wasn't a lie about the piece of debris. It's a wonder you guys are still alive."

"I'm going out there now. Wait two minutes, then you call the others and you run to the mess hall and lock your-

The last Fleet

selves in there. Got it?" Gunter was beginning to fear that their mutual dislike might tempt her to show pride at the wrong moment, but she nodded calmly and rubbed the ice crystals off her arms.

Gunter commanded his helmet to lock again and peered through his visor's electronic vision enhancers. He stood in front of the inner airlock door with one hand on the control panel. Then he instructed his auto-injector to inject the entire supply of Neuroburn.

The effect set in immediately after the aggressive substance flooded his bloodstream like lava. He growled involuntarily as his muscles began to burn and he felt as if they would burst with power and speed. Energy coursed through every fiber of his body, accompanied by an almost irrepressible urge to move.

The door opens as if of its own accord. First he stomped to the left. The ship must have almost reached its maximum speed, because the acceleration forces were no more than just over 1g.

No matter.

He headed to the engine room, opened the bulkhead. Three figures. One of them was Bambam. He turned to the other two, who startled and stared at him with widened eyes. He smashed the chest of the first one with a motor-assisted punch, and hammered his elbow against the temple of the second one as she tried to run past him. No one leaves the party early. Her head burst like an over-ripe watermelon. They were numbingly slow.

"Mess hall," he growled over the loudspeaker to Bambam. "Now."

Without waiting for a response, he turned and walked forward in the corridor. Eighty yards. A figure at the end. She saw him, but it didn't matter. A few projectiles hit the hardened Carbin of his Titan armor and ricocheted uselessly. Gunter activated the jets on his boots and surged forward, braking just before his target and making two bloody halves of a ship's engineer.

Arriving in the mess hall, there were four people. One of them was Hellcat. She was lying on the floor, a bullet wound in her shoulder. One of the three Marines holding her down with his feet had some kind of belt buckle in his hand, glowing a bluish color. He had seen it before. The paneling of the table was open, and behind it was the eerie spherical Orb drone. It also glowed an ominous blue.

Hellcat's eyes grew wide. The Marines, who wore simple coveralls, turned to face him. They knew what they were in for. Before their own reflex boosters kicked in, Gunter grabbed the first one's head and slammed it onto the edge of the table with whirring servos. Then he grabbed the second one's face before he could escape, and fired the smartgun. The projectile whizzed through the face in his palm, and red rain poured onto the deck. The third tried to squeeze his pistol between the shoulder and chest segments of Gunter's armor, but he was excruciatingly slow.

Gunter got a grip on his hand and crushed it. The Marine had no chance to scream as Hellcat shot him in the neck. He went limp and clattered to the ground.

"Dodger and Bambam are on their way," he said. "Stay here until it's over."

He did not wait for an answer. He had to keep going, his energy drove him forward. Six killed, six remaining.

He found them on the bridge. With his engine armor on, he just barely fit through the narrow tube leading down. All five seats were occupied, Akwa Marquandt stood in the middle, looking startled. She had probably thought the safety hatch could withstand him. His servo motors thought otherwise. He hit her in the face with the flat of his hand and she fainted.

The other five panicked, unbuckled their seat belts and attempted to escape. Irrational. Gunter needed only five blows, brutal but precise.

25

GAVIN

Gavin came in through the airlock and let Dodger help him. Their eyes met, and he nodded. She nodded, too.

Then they ran to the mess hall, where Bambam was busy doctoring Hellcat. She was lying on the floor in the midst of a horrific bloodbath and several corpses. Gavin wanted to go to her, but he could not waste any more time.

"You devils," he merely said as they looked at him. He took off his helmet and tossed it away. "Will she..."

"It's not so bad," Hellcat gasped. There was so much in her eyes that she seemed to want to say. But they both knew now was not the time.

"Dodger. Take that thing," he pointed to the mess hall table and the eerie Orb drone, "to the Stingray."

"This must be close by, I think." Hellcat fumbled for the belt brooch she had taken from the Orb in the underground facility on Yokatami's Seed World. It glowed with the same blue pulse as the drone.

"I'll take care of it," Dodger said. "Can you get us out of here?"

"Maybe." Gavin turned and ran to the bridge, where even worse carnage awaited him. Five bodies lay on the floor, some mutilated beyond recognition. The raw brutality with which they had died made him feel sick. The Sergeant had taken off his armor and was crouching, trembling all over, next to Akwa Marquandt, whom he was in the process of putting a small bandage on.

"Is she..."

"No." Marshall shook his head. "Just put her to sleep. She'll wake up in a minute, though."

"What about you?" Gavin pointed.

"The Neuroburn is wearing off. Got a headache, but it'll be fine." The Sergeant cuffed the woman's hands behind her back and removed her magnetic boots before tying her feet to the grate of the gimbal on one of the seats.

Gavin headed for his pilot seat and loaded the imperial priority code that Janus had given him into the system.

"Hello, Sphinx."

"Hello, Gavin."

"I'm back in charge." He took a quick survey first: His fleet was already drifting with the *Invincible* at maximum speed and had cut its thrusters. They continued to head straight for the Never, a dirty brown nebula that was growing larger on the sensors. Akwa Marquandt's pursuers were also close to reaching maximum speed, and possessed a slight speed advantage because they had not had to change direction while flying around the moon. In a few minutes, they would be in range of the long-range torpedoes.

"Sphinx, can you change my voice to Akwa Marquandt's?" he asked, although he already knew the

The last Fleet

answer. Such a thing was not only illegal, but it was also programmed into every shipboard computer by hard code as a prohibition. But he possessed Janus' code.

First he sent a message that they had been hit by debris but had the situation under control and the ship was operational.

Next, he patched into the fleet's command radio. The admirals and captains involved were discussing the possible strategy of their enemies and why they were flying toward the Never. It was apparently agreed that there was no chance for them and it would be a short battle.

Good thing.

"I'm sending one last shot," he said in Akwa's voice. "Either they surrender now and hand over their ships to us, or we launch the first volleys of torpedoes."

Without waiting for responses, he opened a scrambled channel to the *Invincible*.

"Gavin?" the Princess replied excitedly. "Is that you?"

"Yes. We've taken control. Was a piece of cake," he lied. His knees were still shaking, and he wanted to vomit, probably due to the smell of blood and bodily fluids wafting around him. "Send me the code now."

"Andal," he heard a voice behind him that sounded like sandpaper on a rough stone floor.

"Marquandt," he replied, turning to face Akwa Marquandt. Though she appeared dazed, her eyes flashed with anger. He had her in checkmate.

"My commanders will crush your little rebel fleet without me,"

"They probably would if they could," he countered, not without a hint of spite in his voice. "You were there when your father betrayed us and sacrificed an entire people to Never, am I right?"

"It had to be done, I'm not going to apologize for it. Sometimes hard sacrifices have to be made."

"Good, then I'm sure you'll be able to appreciate that I feel the same way." Gavin continued to look her in the eye. "Dodger?"

"The drone is attached to the cockpit. So is the glowing thing," the mutant replied with the familiar echo of a helmet.

"There's a yellow button on the controls with a safety cover on it that has two parallel lines on it. You can use that to override the magnetization of the landing struts."

"Roger that. Coming back now."

"You know, Captain," Gavin said to Akwa Marquandt, "on your torture planet we found one of those drones you brought to Andal. And you took it over with this ship. That one," he pointed to the approaching Never Swarm, "is only here because of you."

She turned pale as she began to understand.

"My fleet will..."

"Jump?" he interrupted her, "Sphinx? Did you receive Her Majesty's code?"

"Yes, Gavin."

"Give the order to jump. That gives us thirty minutes until it's time. Send the code to all shipboard computers in Akwa Marquandt's fleet in twenty-eight minutes."

"No!" snapped the traitor's daughter.

"Our ships will jump shortly, when their jump nodes are fully charged. The *Lady* will follow them. Your coup against the Emperor may have succeeded, your father may have already overridden all Navy codes, but you left immediately in your desire to destroy us. It will take a while for the latest firmware updates to arrive out here."

"That will do you no good. Even this mass murder of our compatriots."

"Mass murder? Your people are not compatriots. They are murderers and traitors." Gavin turned to Gunter. "Sergeant? Take them to the brig."

A few minutes later, he watched on his tactical display as his fleet gradually disappeared from the screen as they jumped out of the system. Marquandt's fleet was waiting for their own jump nodes to fully charge. Just before it was time, Sphinx sent the priority code to shut down all jump engines, which wrote itself directly into the base code of the on-board computers, dooming them to die in 777-Goggins, as the Never drew ever closer.

"Sphinx, we are jumping to the following coordinates."

EPILOGUE
GAVIN

"When did you know?" asked Hellcat quietly. There was no longer any of her usual angry demeanor. They were alone in the *Invincible*'s sickbay. While she had not wanted to leave the *Lady*, the cruiser's medical facilities were so far superior to those of her ship that there had been no alternative.

"I had a suspicion when we picked up Never activities in the Tartarus Void." Gavin held her hand. She looked so fragile under the nanonic bandages on her chest.

"But the code... the jump engines..."

"That had nothing to do with it. I knew Akwa would try to destroy our fleet without giving it time to leave Pulau Weh."

"So you knew we would lead them here."

"Yes. At first I thought it was because you had betrayed me," he admitted reluctantly. "But then when the Never showed up, I knew you were thinking the same thing I was thinking: the transmitter drone."

"I don't know whether to be hurt or mad as hell that

you thought we betrayed you that way," she countered, brows drawn together.

"But you considered it when Aurora was within your grasp."

"Of course, and if you don't understand that, then you're..."

"I understand," he assured her. He had thought about it long enough. It must have been the same for her as it was for him with a knife to Admiral Marquandt's throat, only then she told him he couldn't use the knife. "Was that your plan from the beginning?"

"Yep. My plan was actually to lure the Never to Sol," she replied, to his horror. "But then I realized I was going to become what I've been fighting all my life. In a perfect future, no one has the power to put so many lives at risk." She hesitated and looked him in the eye again. "Are we okay?"

"Yes." He nodded and leaned over her. "I thought..."

"I know. But it didn't work out that way," she whispered. "We gambled high, but it worked out."

Gavin tried not to think about what would have become if even one detail had not worked out. How much they'd both put on the line with each other, with each other. He pressed a kiss to her full lips. They were soft as silk, and their warmth radiated all the way to his heart.

"Let's never do this kind of thing again."

EPILOGUE
JANUS

Janus stood with Elayne in front of the ramp of the shuttle that would take them to the corvette *Storre* - their shuttle to Dust.

Gavin Andal approached them through one of the side doors, dressed in his black uniform. His eyes appeared alert, but at the same time expressed infinite exhaustion and the depth of someone who had seen too much in too short a time.

"Sorry I'm late," he said over the din of the busy engineering crews working in the *Invincible*'s large hangar bay. "The fleet organization is a little more complex than the cockpit of a Stingray, after all."

"I guess you'll have to get used to that," Elayne commented. She wore an expensive nanosilk one-piece suit with the Imperial crest spanning her chest. She had her golden hair tied back artfully. "An admiral has different responsibilities than a swashbuckling pilot," she said.

"I am not an admiral."

The Princess furrowed her brow and looked over at

Janus. He had to smile and pulled the small box from his jacket. With a quick motion, he turned it over and opened it. Elayne took out the two pins with the yellow eagle and stepped towards Gavin, whose eyes grew bigger.

"A captain, I have been told," she began, removing the four crossed yellow swords on his epaulets, "cannot command a fleet. A rear admiral, however, can." When she had placed the new insignia, she nodded with satisfaction. "My last official act as head of the Star Empire for the time being."

"Your Majesty, I don't know..."

"What you should say? Just tell me you're going to win. Tell me that you will drive Dain Marquandt out of Sol and loosen his grip on humanity. In your hands lies what is probably the last fleet."

"I will." Gavin promised earnestly, bowing low. Elayne smiled, and Janus knew how much effort it caused her from all her emotional pain. That she had so much control over herself, which he admired, and it gave him hope for the future. She patted his arm, nodded, and then retreated into the shuttle.

"You are an amazing young man, Gavin Andal," he said. "I wish you every success."

"Are you sure you don't want to stay? You'd be a great help."

"Oh." Janus waved it off and smiled. "I would just keep you from doing crazy things, but they seem to be what you do best."

Gavin's lips split into a grin.

"I left a quantcom address on your private com in your new cabin. If you ever lose your wat, use it." Janus stepped closer to him. "You will get help there, but it always comes with a price, remember that."

Gavin blinked in confusion, but Janus merely

The last Fleet

squeezed his arms and then left him. Inside the shuttle, he closed the ramp, which pulled shut with a long drawn out sigh, and then took a seat next to Elayne. He gave the pilots a wave and shortly after they lifted off toward the *Storre*.

"You've become an amazing young woman, Elayne," he said, giving her a fatherly hug. She fell gratefully against his shoulder and relaxed a little.

"Thank you for coming with me."

"If there is a chance to find Peraia and avert a war with the Orb, we must take it."

"We will, Janus. We will. I know she's not dead." She paused. "What about Shirin Farad?"

"I asked my sources," he replied, thinking of Mirage. "She's an old acquaintance."

AFTERWORD

Dear Reader,

Next we continue with Brandon Q. Morris' volume of the Last Fleet: Dark Field. It will be about the missing Peraia Hartholm-Harrow. As always, if you support the series and want more, feel free to review on Amazon and let me know if you liked it.

If you would like to contact me directly, feel free to do so at joshua@joshuatcalvert.com - I still answer every email. As always, I would love a review for this book on Amazon.

If you subscribe to my newsletter, I'll regularly chat a bit about myself, writing, and the great themes of science fiction. Plus, as a thank you, you'll receive my e-book,

Afterword

Rift: The Passage, exclusively and for free: www.joshuatcalvert.com

Best wishes, Joshua T. Cavlert

Printed in Great Britain
by Amazon